Also from J. Conrad Guest:
*Backstop: A Love Story in Nine Innings*

Watch for new titles from J. Conrad Guest and
Blue Shift Books
at www.secondwindpublishing.com

# One Hot January

By

J. Conrad Guest

Blue Shift Books
Published by Second Wind Publishing, LLC.
Kernersville

Blue Shift Books
Second Wind Publishing, LLC
931-B South Main Street, Box 145
Kernersville, NC 27284



First Blue Shift Books edition published December 2010.
Blue Shift Books, Running Angel, and all production design are trademarks of Second Wind Publishing, used under license.

For information regarding bulk purchases of this book, digital purchase and special discounts, please contact the publisher at www.secondwindpublishing.com

Cover design by Stacy Castanedo

Manufactured in the United States of America

ISBN 978-1-935171-45-4

*To Mom, and Dad, too. Perhaps you've been peeking. If so, maybe you've smiled or laughed, or shed a spirit tear. Perhaps you've even learned something of your son. If so, then I'm pleased: the journey was worth it.*

*Apologies to Johnny Mercer for juggling the copyright date of* Blues in the Night (My Mama Done Tol' Me) *and for attributing your great lyric to a fictional character.*

*The mind of man is capable of anything—because everything is in it, all the past as well as all the future.*

*—Joseph Conrad*

# Prologue

*October 21, 2082*

*My name is Joe January. I was a private investigator from the South Bronx, circa 1940. Was once described as an indignant Humphrey Bogart. Who am I to argue? The difference between Bogie and me is that I was the real McCoy. Where he took the scripts that Hollywood wrote for him, I took on the tough cases nobody else would. Unlike Bogie's, my bumps and bruises were the real deal, not makeup. Although in retrospect I can see that this could be construed as a Hollywood type script Bogie might've been interested in bringing to the screen were he alive today.*

*In truth, I'm no Joseph Conrad, but I wrote every word on these pages. This is my story; but make no mistake, it's anything but make believe. Not being a scientist, I can't tell you the how behind what happened, only that it did happen. I know, it reads like science fiction, spanning two centuries and dealing with time travel and alternate realities, while the denouement is less than satisfactory. But such is life: a happily ever after, while often promised, is never a given.*

*I've been accused of arrogance in my self-depiction, creating a sort of comic book superhero of myself. But in truth, in youth we often view ourselves as invincible. It isn't until later that we realize how fragile life is; furthermore, that we see the repercussions of our actions. Yet given the chance to live life over again, avoiding the mistakes made during the first go-around, well, I found I couldn't turn my back.*

*As a youth, someone told me that man spends far too much time thinking and worrying about the future, and that he also spends too much time in the past, dwelling on mistakes and regretting missed opportunities. Yet in order to move into the future a man must spend a certain amount of time in the present looking at his past. I wish I'd done that more often. Now, at my age, with so little future to which to look forward, I have little else but the past and all my regrets to mull over—the missed opportunities and how, through my own foolishness, I lost the two women who meant the most to me; the first not once, but twice.*

*December 6, 1941*

The man jerked and twitched—an epileptic in seizure. His right foot stomped in rhythmic time; shoulders bunched as fingers flew in a frenzied attack on black and white ivory. Sweat poured from beneath the stocking that was a cap and ran in torrents down his face. A brief respite from his self-perpetuated paroxysm, and he mopped from his face what moisture he could with the stained handkerchief that lay beside him, before giving way to another fit of spasms.

Whether the demented cacophony that spewed from the piano he assailed with a vengeance was a result of the convulsions he initiated or the notes themselves responsible for the musician's spastic throes, I only wondered. For all the split notes, all the crazy chromatic chord changes, for all the irregular intervals and rhythms that made his music unique, Thelonious Sphere Monk, the expectant father of modern jazz, would be scorned by critics, his music laughed at, misunderstood and unappreciated by the uninitiated for years. Until his death in 1982, when with the advent of the compact disk much of his music would be reissued and embraced by a new generation, proving that all great artists enjoy their greatest success posthumously.

I sat and watched, amused, as Monk now stood and danced in a tiny circle, lost in a world of eccentricity as profound as his music, his arms swinging in time as tenor saxman Don Byas blew notes that rivaled Monk's own in their dissonance …

"I just *love* Monk, don't you?" the young woman across the table from me said.

I'd agreed to meet the woman here, at Minton's Playhouse in Harlem, to discuss locating her missing father.

I don't normally take on missing persons, but if the voice on the other end of the phone looked as good as it sounded and she was willing to meet my price, I was willing to make an exception. I'd been right about the voice. Its owner was Melissa MacIntyre, who didn't look at all Scotch but to me looked sweet enough to taste. Her auburn hair, cut in a neat pageboy, framed features more childlike in their innocence than matured glamour. Thin lips painted a deep shade of red parted to reveal straight white teeth as she waited for my approval of her musical taste.

"That's not music," her brother said.

I had taken an immediate dislike of Melissa's older sibling. Like his nose his arrogance preceded him. He was overbearing, opinionated, self-righteous and, where his sister was concerned, authoritative. All of this I had deduced through observation; his snide comment merely lent weight to my summation.

"It has no style," he continued, although neither Melissa nor I had prompted him for edification. "There's no cadence and it lacks intellect."

"*I* think it's angular," Melissa said.

I smiled. The purity of Melissa's rejoinder, the result of youthful exuberance, sounded as if she were repeating something she had read in conjunction with Monk. Whether critical acclaim or disparaging condemnation didn't matter. Apparently her brother had gotten far too used to having his own way. She would use whatever weapons at her disposal to counter his offensive.

"Why must you always be so rigid and traditional, Benjamin Junior?"

"En garde," Benjamin said. Then, with a conspiratorial wink at me, he added, "The avant-garde in defense of the accused."

Monk was now back at the piano, pounding at the keys with a savage wrath to prove to all those present in the tiny club that the instrument he played was indeed a percussive one.

In truth, I didn't care for Monk or his music, and for all

the same reasons Benjamin Junior had just smartly ticked off. But I didn't like Benjamin Junior.

"Oh, I don't know, Ben," I said. "Maybe Melissa is right. Maybe you should loosen up."

Melissa was smiling triumphantly. Her newly formed alliance outnumbered the opposition two to one; while Benjamin's eyes threw daggers at me from across the table.

"Don't call me that!" he snapped. "My name is Benjamin."

"Oh, Benjamin, why must you always be so pretentious?"

"I didn't say I agreed with her taste," I said. Melissa looked crestfallen—her champion was about to betray her. "I just think she has a right to like what she likes." Melissa brightened. In the span of a heartbeat I had gone from traitor to hero again. I thought that this was perhaps the first time in her life anyone had supported her right to her own opinion. That it had come in outright defiance of her brother only made it that much more gratifying.

"She doesn't know—"

"Not with you force-feeding her your opinions she doesn't."

"You must not want this job," Benjamin said, red with repressed anger.

"I have yet to decide that," I said. "Nor do I need it," I added, countering his inference regarding the scruples of private investigators.

"I'm not sure I want to hire you."

"And I'm emphatic about not wanting to work for you."

"Mr. January …"

Melissa's expression was a compromise between amusement—that I would have the audacity to face down her insolent brother—and dismay. Obviously taken in by my willingness to speak out on her behalf, I surmised she would've hired me then and there but for her brother. I guessed that Melissa was just learning to flex her independence, but had not yet gotten to the point where she could stand in outright insubordination of her brother's authority.

From her conflict I immediately recognized my danger. I'm a sucker for a woman in distress.

"Come along, Melissa," her brother said. "I'll not tolerate someone working for me who exhibits a lack of respect for me."

"You don't *hire* respect," I said.

"What's that supposed to mean?"

"It means first and foremost that I work for myself. Should I choose to help you find your father and you agree to pay my fee, plus expenses, then we have a business arrangement. But we do it *my* way. After all, that's what you're paying for, my expertise. I don't want any interference from you. I'm taking all the risks; that's also part of what you're paying for. But I don't need someone increasing those risks." Sensing Benjamin's unspoken skepticism, I added, "And if you don't think you're getting your money's worth you can sever our agreement."

"That's not good enough."

"Benjamin!"

"I'm sorry, but that's the way it's done in this business. However, if you believe you might find a better deal elsewhere, I suggest you shop around."

A poor response, I knew, since I also knew what game Benjamin Junior was playing. By stating my terms, I'd let slip my desire to take the job, and Benjamin Junior had picked up on that. He would now use that knowledge to try to take back control of the center of the negotiation table—revenge for having been shown up in front of his sister. In his dementia, might and right were confluent. Such convoluted rationale justified any plot against both his sister and me.

*The world is full of assholes*, I thought.

I've always loved that word, asshole, for the amusing visual that accompanies it. But I wasn't amused, not this time. Not with Benjamin *Junior* sitting there, his lips parting like a pink sphincter to reveal the putrid knowledge that he knew he had me off balance and on the ropes. I hate being on the ropes, like a boxer with his face beaten to a pulp, unable to cover up.

Suddenly I no longer wanted the job. I had more than enough work to keep me busy. I'd been a fool to allow myself to be taken in by the sound of a pretty voice on the phone. No, I certainly didn't need this job—not at this cost. I drew in a breath, prepared to withdraw my proposal, but was stopped short by Melissa's trepidation.

My own credo had always been that right is might, as penned by August and Julius Hare over a century before—the original translucence of their transcript lost through transposition—ever was and ever would be wrong. Hence my preoccupied obsession with the oppressed. My experience often showed the righteous underdog to be a casualty of the corruption might frequently engenders.

As I looked across the table at the waning hope on Melissa's face, fearful that the might I attempted to wield on behalf of the righteous would one day come up short, I felt my own hope for the future waver. The world was a gloomy place because of people like Benjamin Junior. Dismal as it was, it was no match for my own dark mood, which was threatening to grow darker by the moment.

"Ben," I began, and then quickly amended it to Benjamin. "You and I have gotten off to a shaky start here." God, how I hated having to suck hind teat. "To tell you the truth, since it was Melissa I spoke with on the phone, and since she didn't mention a brother, I'm a little taken aback by your appearance here. I assumed I would be meeting with her alone."

"So *that's* what this is about."

I only stared as Benjamin's eyes glowered with malice.

"Benjamin—"

"You think that because you get a call from a woman who arranges to meet you in this … this *dive* … you think that gives you the *right* … the *free reign* to … to …"

"Benjamin, it's not like that, not like that at all. You know I wouldn't—"

"Shut-up, Melissa, this doesn't concern you!"

"I think it does," I said.

"This is my *sister* here, not some hussy you can pick up and take home to *use* and de*grade* for the price of a few drinks." Benjamin's face was turning a dangerous shade of purple.

"I had no intention of using and degrading her."

"But you intended to take her home?"

"Benjamin, how could you think such a thing?"

None of it mattered any longer—not the job, not the girl. Pretty as she was and as taken as I was by her youthfulness, she was far too skinny for my taste.

"The thought crossed my mind," I said. My vulgarity was intended to brutalize. It did.

*"Bastard!"* Benjamin roared, drawing the notice of a few more of our fellow jazz aficionados. Standing, his tipped chair resting against the railing behind him, such was his tirade he was completely unaware, or perhaps he simply chose to ignore the fact, that he was upstaging the featured artist at Minton's.

"She's my *sister!*" he shouted, leaning forward, hands flat on the table. He towered menacingly over me, but I betrayed no sense of being menaced. "My … my …"

Suddenly aware of the startled glances of those around us, Benjamin quickly, awkwardly, regained a caricature of composure, and finished quietly, "Come along, Melissa, we have nothing further to discuss with the likes of him."

Trotting after her brother, Melissa mouthed the words *I'll be in touch,* and then she, too, was gone. Leaving me to ponder the peculiarity of what I'd just witnessed.

A woman of her word, Melissa did indeed get in touch with me. But her contact wouldn't come for five-and-a-half years.

# Part One

# Chapter One

*May 1947*

I read the carefully hand-lettered words on the tile in front of me:

PILOTS WITH SHORT EXHAUST STACKS AND LOW MANIFOLD PRESSURE PLEASE TAXI CLOSE

Grinning, I looked to my left to observe my good friend and, unknown to me, future business associate, Lance Cantrell. Lance's head was tilted back and his eyes were closed; my grin broadened.

*From which of the aforementioned maladies do you suffer, Lance?* I wondered and then grunted my amusement of the notion that he might just endure both.

"What?" Lance asked, his eyes fluttering open.

"Nothing." I knew the innocence of my reply would serve to provoke.

"I know that laugh, Joe. That was *not* a *nothing* laugh."

"Forget it." I zipped my trousers and stepped over to the washbasin.

"It's not good to laugh a nothing laugh while standing next to someone in the men's room. It can give a guy a complex."

"You, a complex? You're a war hero. War heroes don't have complexes."

"War heroes *especially* have complexes," Lance said, joining me at the sink. "Especially when they come home to find their best girl is now someone else's best girl."

"Women are fickle like that," I said, shutting off the water.

*"I* would have waited for *her."*

"You don't know that. And you don't know what it's like to have to wait."

"I waited."

"What, for the bullet that never came?" I asked, drying my hands.

"That's right."

"That's different, Lance."

"How is it any different?"

I looked squarely at Lance, a decorated bomber pilot whom I hadn't seen for nearly six years. Short but powerfully built, Lance had been a high school football star and heartthrob. The wavy blond hair of his youth was now cropped to regulation length beneath his Air Force cap, and behind the blue eyes that had, six years ago, betrayed youthful cockiness there now resided an especial worldliness tinged with a healthy dose of weariness. No doubt the war had left its indelible mark on Lance. In ways that I—because I'd turned thirty a year before the country entered the war, along with a high draw in the lottery, and therefore missed serving a tour of duty—could only speculate. But there was something else in his demeanor as well. It took me a moment to recognize it for what it was: resentment.

"How is it any different?" Lance demanded a second time, daring me to put what he was feeling into perspective for him.

"You were waiting for something that wouldn't have made any difference to you, because had it come you wouldn't have known. On the other hand, she would've had to live with the result for the rest of her life."

"So she found comfort elsewhere."

I could only shrug, and I immediately regretted the nonchalance of my gesture.

"She must not have loved you," I said.

"That's supposed to make me feel better?"

"You want me to sugar-coat it for you?" I didn't understand Lance's angst over a creature that could be found in any bar and had for the price of a couple drinks.

"I *want* the last six years of my life back!"

There was nothing I could say to appease Lance's pain.

"It's not fair," he whispered because it wasn't, and

because it wasn't there was nothing else he could say. The statement sounded like a plea: a child bemoaning the iniquity of having been cheated at a game of checkers by an older sibling.

"Who says it's supposed to be?" I said.

"You wouldn't understand."

"I guess not." I was glad that I didn't. "Look, Lance, very little of anything that happens to us in life—good, bad or indifferent—has anything to do with fairness."

"She couldn't wait six years?"

Lance's eyes lay bare a pain upon which I could only wonder.

*Six years,* I reflected.

Six years ago tears might've helped to ease Lance's grief. Apparently the war had robbed him of that release.

*No matter*, I reasoned. *He'll get over her.*

I'd never met a woman worth bleeding over. Just the same, I figured I'd do well to introduce Lance to one or two of the women I'd helped through their own grief, the result of the male mass exodus the war had propagated.

"Maybe she didn't want to wait," I said.

Glancing at the mirror's image of myself, I gave a casual tug on the leading edge of the fedora that sat atop my head and said, "Come on, Lance." Then, putting my arm around my pal's shoulders, I added, "Let's get your bags and get you home. You'll feel better once you get out of uniform."

Lance said nothing as he allowed me to steer him out of the men's room and toward baggage claim.

Some dim part of me understood why, with the war nearly over, Lance's girl, Becky, had stopped her correspondence with the man who was in his own way fighting for truth, justice and the American way. To the masses heroes are loved and worshipped. Made into larger-than-life icons, it is perhaps just that status that condemns them to exile from the lives of those closest to them. Unreal and unrecognizable, they become undesirable to those who prefer an affinity with something more attainable.

That Lance could still harbor the ache of his broken heart so long after the fact I couldn't begin to perceive; to me women were akin to a tunnel train: another would be along in a few minutes. Patience inevitably paid off. You just needed to keep your eye on your destination.

I couldn't understand Lance's reluctance to let go of the anguish that had become his copilot these last two years. Still, he was my pal, and it pained me to see him so despondent. It wasn't right. So it was no surprise when I took it upon myself to make right in Lance's life what Becky had managed to leave in such a state of disarray.

Lindy, my gal Friday and sometime lover, had a friend. Blond and buxom had been Lindy's description of Ginger—the woman I hoped would realign Lance's priorities. Certainly from Lindy's physical biography of her, Ginger should've very easily straightened out that part of his anatomy that, once straightened, would've helped him forget that Becky had ever existed.

To my relief, Lance did indeed find a new focus for his life. But it didn't come as a result of Ginger's ministrations. For all of my intuition, for all my good intentions and well-laid plans, I couldn't have foreseen what Lindy's unsolicited involvement would precipitate. For by simply taking initiative, Lindy set into motion a series of events that would forever alter my future as well as her own and the lives of countless others who hadn't yet been born.

I pushed the gearshift into first and let out the clutch; the Ford lurched into motion and Lance and I pulled away from the curb and into traffic.

"When are you going to sell this dinosaur and start supporting the post-war economy?"

I looked sidewise at Lance. I'd been right. A change of clothes *had* changed his disposition—as if by removing the uniform for the last time a letting go had taken place. We were heading on West 11$^{th}$ Street toward Sixth Avenue, and from there to Harlem, where, unbeknownst to Lance, we would rendezvous with Lindy, Ginger, and my own unsuspected destiny.

"This car's got a lot of miles left in her," I said. "Besides, my buying a new one isn't going to influence the economy one way or another."

"That's not the point."

"Then why did you make it?" I knew full well why Lance had said what he'd said: to goad me into a heated debate. Our arguments, some of them of Homeric proportions, had marked our friendship for fifteen years.

"It's 1947, Joe. The war is over. The times, they are a changin'."

"Not always for the better," I said. The brick that was the road we rode over jostled us.

Undaunted, Lance charged ahead. "Technology is exploding—they can split the atom! You're too shortsighted. You've got to keep up with the times."

"Why?"

"Competition, Joe. This country is leading the world into a new era. You don't want to be left behind."

"I hardly think—"

"The new cars coming off the assembly lines in Detroit have automatic transmissions! No clutch, Joe. Just think, no more clashing gears!"

"I haven't clashed gears since I learned to drive."

"That's not the point."

"You keep saying that," I said. Lance always did have trouble expressing his views succinctly.

"The point is, society demands that technology provide an easier, simpler life."

"Through complexity?"

"What's so complex? Change is good, it's progressive."

"I'm not arguing that it isn't, Lance. But I question the validity of change for the sake of change."

Lance ignored me: "If we don't support change, this country will fall to the back of the pack."

"Who told you that?" I asked. Lance had a habit of accepting other people's principles at face value, unwilling to look at how those principles might affect him personally.

"Everybody says so."

"I don't. Does that make me a nobody?"

Lance only sighed; I went on:

"You've been in the service taking orders too long."

"If it weren't for men like me following orders, the war would still be going."

"I won't argue that point," I said. Anger had prompted my unwarranted attack. "But anytime anybody tells me something is good for me, I question their motive. And you should, too. It could save you a lot of grief."

"Ah, you don't trust anyone."

The traffic light at the intersection of Sixth Avenue and Fourteenth Street changed from green to yellow, then red. I shifted down into second gear and stepped on the brake pedal; the brakes groaned their protest.

"No, I don't," I said. The car came to a halt. Lance and I rocked forward once, and then we, too, came to a halt. The Ford's idle was rough.

"Not even the government?"

*"Especially* the government. They gave us income tax, Lance. You think that's good?" I punctuated the words *income tax* by pushing the shift lever into first.

"You can't have government for free."

"It was good enough for our founding fathers."

"It was different back then."

"Was it?" I looked at Lance, the piercing blue that challenged me a contrast to my own green gaze. "Listen, Lance, from what I've seen of government workings, it's pretty obvious that if pro is the opposite of con, Congress is the opposite of progress."

"But the government works for us," Lance said, a schoolboy wanting to believe the representation of the people by the people in Washington held his best interest above their own.

"In theory, yes."

"We elect them, don't we?"

"And the bureaucratic special interest groups pay them off. Trust me on this, Lance. Our government representatives worked better—were more effective—when they conducted their business in Washington three months out of the year, and then went home to rub elbows with we the people they were elected to represent. Being in Washington year round has left them out of touch with the real world."

The traffic light had changed to green, so spoke the impatience of the horn behind us. I slipped the clutch and the engine sputtered, nearly stalling, but I managed to feed it enough gas and feathered the clutch to save myself from humiliation.

"The world has gotten too big, governing is a full-time job." Again the schoolboy, this time attempting to sound knowledgeable.

"Too big? Maybe I'm splitting my own atoms, but it's the same size it's always been." I shifted into second gear—Lance's cue to take up his side of the argument.

"You know what I mean."

"I think what you mean is that all that change you speak of with such fondness is making the world a little smaller and a lot more competitive. As a result, it's become a much more complex place. You've been out of the country the last few years—the last two as part of MacArthur's entourage to the Emperor of Japan—and a little out of touch with the real world yourself. You influenced me to buy this car before you left on your tour of duty. 'It'll make your life easier,' you said. 'No more having to take the tunnel train.' I admit it's convenient, but a car costs money to operate and maintain. More money than it costs to take the train."

"Tunnel vision!" Lance spat, unaware of his unintended play on words.

"Is it? Did you know the government has brought conspiracy charges against General Motors, Firestone Tires and Standard Oil of California?"

"No." The schoolboy yet a third time, feigning adult indulgence.

"It seems they've been arranging financing for some outfit that's buying up transit systems across the country—dozens of them. They rip up the rails and then sell or junk the trolleys, to be replaced by brand spanking new General Motors buses clad with Firestone tires and fueled by Standard Oil."

"They call that progress," Lance said. To him the elementary wisdom of his statement was obvious.

"Oh, I see. So what's good for the likes of General Motors is good for the general populace, is that it?"

"Damned straight!"

"And you tell me I'm shortsighted," I muttered.

"What was that?"

"Look, Lance. The government funds the construction of freeways—they take years to build. The first one in Los Angeles opened a few years ago and you know what? It was obsolete the day it opened!"

"So they'll build others."

"Oh, that's a well thought out argument," I said. "That kind of progressive thinking will turn this country into one big parking lot by the end of the century. Mark my words, in thirty or forty years cities like Los Angeles will be *begging* for a trolley, or some other form of mass transit, to alleviate the congestion on their freeways. In the meantime, the trolleys we sold abroad will mock us by moving the same people you just said we have to lead into a new era. They'll be laughing at us, Lance," I finished with one of my own.

"That's not funny."

"And a ten-mile trip to work taking an hour or more is?"

"Don't you think that's a little extreme?"

"No, I don't. Imagine New York City in forty years, population seven million or so, trying to get around town in their automobiles."

"That's insane."

"That's the first sensible thing you've said since this little debate began."

"You always disagree with me."

"Not always, Lance. Just when you're wrong."

"Aren't I entitled to an opinion?"

"Sure you are, pal. It's just that you don't always think things through, and you're far too trusting. I'd have thought the war would've remedied that."

"If you can't trust your own country, who *can* you trust?"

"You mean like Germany trusted Hitler to pull them out of their depression?"

"He led the globe into a world war."

"My point exactly. Look at some of the newsreels from before the war. He whipped up the German people into a frenzy; yet today you can't find a German anywhere who'll admit to supporting him."

I pulled the Ford over next to the curb and shut it off.

"Whenever someone tells you something is good for you, instead of taking them at face value, ask yourself, what do *they* stand to gain by championing such a view? Then trust your own gut feeling."

Lance laughed, the sound holding a note of irony—sarcasm's less humorous twin. Then in answer to my inquiring look, he relented.

"Buddy LaRue, my old tail gunner—coldhearted son of a bitch that he was ..." Lance looked ahead, through the windshield at some distant memory, then back at me. "Buddy once told me the seat of emotion lay not in the heart, but instead in the stomach. Buddy claimed he never listened to his heart, just to what his gut told him."

"Buddy was a wise man."

"He reminded me a lot of you."

"Then I know I would've liked him," I said, grinning.

"I know I'm too trusting. But I want to believe that people are inherently good. Is that so wrong?"

"I wouldn't say that's necessarily wrong, just riskier."

"It's a hard lesson for me. I want to believe there's benevolence in the world."

"There is, Lance. You and I and people like us wouldn't fight for what's right if there wasn't. We just have to look a little harder to find it nowadays. The fact that you just admitted to having to amend your thinking shows you've taken a step toward a higher level of maturity."

I reminded myself of why we were here and an image of

Ginger came to mind. Although she was a woman I'd never met, I trusted my overactive imagination to enhance Lindy's description to suit my own personal taste. For a moment I ogled the copious icon inspired by artistry resulting from my too often far too fertile ideality and smiled.

*If it so happens that you don't take the bait, Lance, I just might have to bite myself.*

"Now lighten up," I said as I opened the car door. "We're here to enjoy ourselves tonight. If you see anything you like, you just let me know and I'll make myself scarce."

"I don't know if I'm ready for this, Joe."

"Sure you are, pal. It's just like falling off a bicycle—the sooner you get back up, the better off you are. Now come on, let's not keep those bountiful Midtown dolls waiting."

# Chapter Two

The fourth incarnation of The Famous Door—all on 52nd Street—had recently opened. Lindy had suggested this latest venue of her favorite purlieu because Art Tatum was the featured artist.

Lindy, named for Charles Lindbergh—a man her father admired after having seen him during his barnstorming days in the mid-1920s, prior to his trans-Atlantic flight—sat in silent contemplation, Tatum's piano stylings a backdrop for her sensation of ominous foreboding. Ginger sat mercifully silent across from her sipping a martini, stirred, not shaken. Friends in high school, Lindy had graduated to mature, as the harshness of the real world had forced her to do; while Ginger—how she'd managed this, Lindy wondered aloud to me while we conspired, for Lance's sake, to arrange tonight's outing—had maintained the naïveté of her youth. Their conversations usually revolved around Ginger, the men in Ginger's life, Ginger's wants, Ginger's needs and Ginger's … well, suffice it to say that Ginger's life had become larger than life, to Lindy at least, to the point where it threatened to engulf her. Finally, in order to save her own identity, Lindy told me she had had to make herself inaccessible, leaving the phone to ring or, on those occasions when she guessed wrong or was expecting a call from someone else, feigning other commitments. Their correspondence grew less and less frequent, with Lindy's shame growing in direct proportion. That Ginger seemed indifferent to the why surrounding Lindy's aloofness served to fuel self-anger, the result of remorse, the product of her inability to effectively communicate at a level commensurate with Ginger's ever increasing needfulness. Lindy had her own reasons for setting up Lance with Ginger. Ginger's monopoly on Lindy's life seemed, to Lindy, to run in direct proportion with whether Ginger's insatiable appetite to have her needs met was being satisfied elsewhere, and so she hoped that her guilt would be appeased should Lance and Ginger hit it off.

The third member of their party sat next to Ginger. Shifting uneasily in her chair, she attempted a casual nonchalance as she took a sip from the glass—an item that served as a prop for her nervousness—that contained the rum and Coke she'd ordered upon arrival. A quick glance over her shoulder, toward the entrance, before returning her attention to the glass her hands toyed with, and Lindy again questioned the wisdom of allowing the stranger to accompany Ginger and her on this night on the town.

"Do you like Tatum?" Lindy offered as an icebreaker.

"He's a plagiarist," the woman said.

Taken aback, Lindy refuted the woman's unwarranted criticism: "I admit he's not much of a composer, but don't you think calling him a plagiarist is a bit strong?"

"Monk is better," the woman stated, matter-of-fact. She appeared bored with the conversation.

Lindy glanced at Ginger, who was just then signaling the waitress for another drink. It was a glance made out of exasperation, for Lindy knew intuitively that any support for her side of the argument wouldn't be found within Ginger's well-maintained self-involvement.

"I wish they'd hurry up and get here," Ginger said, more for her own benefit than that of her companions.

Lindy rolled her eyes and tossed her dark hair behind her before forging ahead.

"Monk is good," she offered, at once despising herself for the lie she told. Like many of Monk's derogators, Lindy didn't equate with music any of the dissonance Monk enthusiasts praised as inventive. Lindy once said to me, *Every town has its wayward child and Monk is the jazz establishment's village idiot.* "But Tatum's improvisatory talents are second to no one's," she finished.

Untouched by the potency of Lindy's retort, the woman merely affirmed her earlier assessment with the same uncorrupted apathy. "Monk is better."

"Is he very handsome?" Ginger asked. She had just finished her own glance-to-the-entrance-sip-from-her-drink replication, and for once Lindy was grateful for the interruption. Ginger's anxiety over having to wait had fueled her question. If she couldn't receive the immediate gratification of seeing the prize in the flesh, then someone would just have to reinforce her mind's image of what a decorated war hero looked like.

"I don't know," Lindy answered sharply. "I've never met him."

"How many medals does he have?"

"I don't know."

"Joe *does* know The Famous Door moved, doesn't he?"

"I'm sure he does."

"Nine o'clock, right? You told him to meet us at nine o'clock?"

"Yes, I told him nine o'clock," Lindy replied with feigned patience.

"Well, they're late," Ginger affirmed with a willful glance at her watch.

Ginger had been guilty of this sin many times herself, but somehow Lindy was certain her friend would make Lance pay dearly for his outrageous indiscretion.

"So they're late," Lindy chided. "Maybe Lance's flight was delayed. You have someplace else you have to be?"

The ensuing silence implied to Lindy that perhaps Ginger had taken her question literally, and so now was mentally checking her social calendar to see if she might indeed have overlooked something.

A moment ago Lindy had welcomed the distraction of Ginger's less than challenging repartee. Now she was grateful for the solitude with which her last question had left her. She took a sip from her gimlet—this was before Raymond Chandler popularized them in *The Long Goodbye* in 1958. It was the drink, in Victor's Bar, over which Marlowe and Terry Lennox bonded. Near the end of the novel Marlowe drinks a gimlet to the memory of Lennox, who supposedly committed suicide in Mexico, and the drink conjures up, for Marlowe, feelings of great loss. Lindy preferred her gimlet as Chandler later described them: three parts gin, one part

Rose's Lime Juice—no simple syrup, no bitters—shaken with ice.

Feeling alone in a roomful of people and lost within the intricacies of Art Tatum's impromptu playing, Lindy turned her thoughts inward, toward that glamorous life she was beginning to believe could not possibly exist anywhere but within her own fruitful imagination.

"Mr. January—"

"Miss Melissa MacIntyre," I said, dropping my hat onto the table. I noticed the youthful innocence I recalled from our previous encounter was gone, replaced by a sophistication that could only be the result of experience. I watched Melissa's demeanor take on a sudden affectation of self-importance; that I remembered her name after so many years impressed her, and so it seemed she expected her esteem to rise in the eyes of her two tablemates.

"Joe," Lindy said, "Miss MacIntyre showed up at your office late this afternoon. She said it was urgent. I had no way of getting in touch with you."

"It's all right, Lindy," I said as I pulled out a chair and sat down beside her. Lance grabbed a chair from a nearby empty table and seated himself at the end of the table nearest Melissa.

"You must be Lance," Ginger breathed, taken in by his compact stature.

Lance smiled and nodded.

"Mr. January," Melissa said, "I know it's been a while."

"Five-and-a-half years," I said. No mean feat since the encore to our first meeting had been the Japanese attack on Pearl Harbor the next morning. "Don't tell me you're still looking for your missing father?"

"Yes, I am." Again she seemed pleased that I remembered so much from our previous meeting.

Just then the waitress arrived to take our drink orders: me, my customary bourbon and beer chaser, Lance, Scotch over ice, while everyone else reordered their previous poison. As she left, I picked up where I'd left off.

"Miss MacIntyre, did it ever occur to you that after nearly six years your father might not want to be found?" The blank look that was her response was all the answer I needed. "Do you know if he's even still alive?"

"Yes."

"Oh?" My curiosity had been baited. Sensing my interest, Melissa quickly launched into her exposition.

"My father is an Associate Professor of Archeology at Columbia. He often leaves the country for Europe—the archeology-fine arts department at Columbia allows a small budget for research abroad. Occasionally my father purchases a relic or two. Something he hopes will ultimately leverage the facility to a higher level of prestige. But that sort of thing was more prevalent in the twenties. Then Hitler came to power. As the war in Europe escalated, my father began to fear for the welfare of some of the great archeological treasures in Europe. My father's last trip was made a month before the Japanese attack on Pearl Harbor."

"Didn't I read somewhere," I said, "of some committee organized shortly after we entered the war to help preserve the European cultural heritage from the ravages of the war?"

"Dr. Dinsmoor," Melissa replied with a nod, "Head of the Department of History of Art at Columbia was chairman. But that was nearly two years after my father disappeared."

"It seems your father had a little more foresight than Dinsmoor."

"I suspect his last trip was made in an effort to rescue some valuable artifacts."

"What sort of artifacts?" Lance asked. Then in response to my annoyed look, he added, "Maybe it's not important, but I'm just curious, all right?"

"Miss MacIntyre … Lance Cantrell," I said. Lance smiled and nodded, and I detected an interest behind his smile that was more than what mere cordiality required.

"Lance Cantrell?" Ginger gushed unabashedly, dismayed that more attention wasn't being lavished upon her. She wasn't used to being relegated to such a peripheral status. "The bomber-fighter?" she added, trying to draw herself into the conversation.

"Bomber *pilot,"* Lance said. His dissimulated embarrassment served only to promote how much he enjoyed the attention.

Lindy smiled, despite her abasement of her friend's faux pas. "Joe, Lance ... this is Ginger."

I'd been trying mighty hard, for Lance's sake, not to take notice of those attributes previously only described to me: large breasts forced together and pushed up by a bra perhaps two sizes too small, further enhanced by a sweater also too small. The sweater's divulging neckline exposed a tiny mole on the inside of Ginger's left breast that, when her elbows were on the table forcing her ample breasts together further still (as they were now), found itself quashed against the mass of flesh that normally stared back from across the gulf of her cleavage. That cleavage possessed a depth that had, until that moment, existed only within the confines of my own vivid imagination, and so a fantasy I fancied as potentially palpable began to take shape. I shifted in my chair to accommodate my growing nuisance.

"Sure, this is the famous Lance *Blades* Cantrell," I said.

"Joe," Lance began, suddenly toppled from his own, self-scaled pedestal.

"Blades?"

"Ginger, Blades is the nickname Lance acquired—*earned*—in flight school," I explained. "Why don't you tell everyone how you got it, Lance?"

Just then the waitress arrived with our drinks. After she left, Melissa took up her explanation:

"Mr. January, my father—"

"Your father, Miss MacIntyre," I said, quickly putting together into a plausible summation what few facts Melissa had provided. "Your father left the country at the height of Hitler's reign in Germany. If he's as highly esteemed as you imply, he probably had connections with a number of schools and museums throughout Europe. I can't imagine him conducting research without some local contacts. If he left a month before the attack on Pearl, then I agree, he undoubtedly hoped to play a part in preserving some ancient piece of art." I casually tossed down the bourbon and felt it sear my palate, my throat, and finally warm my stomach.

"If you had told me as much as you just did five-and-a-half years ago, I'd have told you your father was probably a casualty of the war. With tension as high as it was then, who knows? Maybe he stuck his nose where it didn't belong, stepped on someone's toes, or one of his friends turned him in to some unfriendly cabal. More than likely he was a fatality of the Luftwaffe's bombing raids. But now you come to me two years after the war has ended and claim he's alive and well. What makes you think so?"

"We received a letter from him."

I caught the look of discouragement on Lance's face and decided against referencing Melissa's older brother as the other person she had ascribed as "we." Although Melissa no longer held a physical fascination for me, my ego wouldn't allow that her preference might be for Lance.

"What was in the letter?"

"I really shouldn't say," Melissa said, absently toying with the clasp on her purse.

"If you had no intention of betraying its contents, Miss MacIntyre, you really shouldn't have brought it with you."

Melissa smiled uneasily a moment before she proceeded to hand me an envelope she procured from her purse.

I noted the postmark on the envelope: Indianapolis, Indiana, May 15—eight days ago. I pulled a single scrap of paper from the envelope and quickly scanned the script before returning my gaze to Melissa's blue eyes, hastily devising a line of questioning that would enable me to see through the veil behind which I suspected she would hide certain, pertinent information.

"Not much of a letter," I muttered, making a show of glancing at the back of the slip of paper. "I assume after you received this note, which was when—three days ago?" Melissa nodded. "I assume Benjamin ignored the warning and acted on his own." My statement was intended to throw Melissa off balance, and judging from her reaction I knew I had succeeded, my acute assumption diverting her own guess at where my line of questioning might begin.

"Yes," she said tentatively.

"And by your appearance here tonight, I presume you now have not heard from him either." I was leading her.

Melissa cast her eyes down, avoiding my penetrating gaze.

"Miss MacIntyre, your father states in his note that you should refrain from contacting him."

"He's our father, Mr. January," she protested. "What were we supposed to do?"

I detected a corner of Lance's mouth turn up; his concern over a rival now unfounded, he knew: "we" was a sibling. I was mildly disappointed the frontage had been penetrated so soon.

Across the table from me I noticed Ginger's scrutiny of me. Apparently my earlier analysis of those resources Lance had ignored had not gone unnoticed. The mole on the left breast was now kissing the right as she leaned toward me, her body language indicating that she was interested in far more than just what I was saying.

Blinking, I returned my attention to Melissa.

"Of course not." I sighed, a carefully placed cue designed to preface my next assertion. "Your father expresses that he is in good health," I said, flicking the corner of the paper I still held in my left hand with the middle finger of my right hand. I made a pretext of snuffling and then knuckled my nose, making certain that Melissa knew I knew the *why* behind my next contention.

"And I suppose I can understand why you didn't come to me at once. What I don't understand is why you waited so long after your brother's departure before seeking me out."

"Mr. January, I—"

"Don't play coy, Miss MacIntyre," I broke in, determined to not give her time to think. "Your brother might forbid you from contacting me, but after he left for Indianapolis there was nothing to stop you from getting in touch with me."

"Come on, Joe," Lance said. "Obviously she thought her brother had matters under control."

Melissa looked cool behind the auspices of her protector, the aegis that had deflected my assault.

"Maybe so," I snapped, unappreciative of Lance's encroachment, "but I think she's holding something back, else why would she tell Lindy it was a matter of life and death?"

"As I remember it, Lindy said it was urgent, not life and death."

"I *know* what she said. I also know what she meant."

Lindy had worked for me long enough for me to be able to read between the lines of what she told me, or in this instance what she had left unsaid. I rarely complimented her, the result of never having learned how to take one myself. But that particular compliment warmed her—to the point where she blushed. Blushed from embarrassment or flushed from our lovemaking, I always thought Lindy looked her loveliest with that little extra coloring. It always managed to arouse me, too; but that night I'd already decided with whom I was going home. Of course it was the wrong choice, but I was too foolish then to know the reason why.

"Joe," Lance began in a patronizing tone that immediately set me on edge. "This is Melissa's father and brother we're talking about. Why would she withhold anything that would endanger their safety?"

"Damn it, Lance," I countered, and stopped.

Lance had already forgotten everything we'd discussed in the car. His trust bordered on unconditional—something of which I had long ago learned to be wary. Having had my nose bloodied more than once had taught me the valuable lesson of looking beneath exteriors, especially where women were concerned, as well as asking questions before coming to the rescue of the proverbial damsel in distress. I wanted to remind Lance of what Buddy LaRue had said about trusting your gut and not your heart. I saw the way he kept looking at Melissa, Becky a forgotten commodity, a specter from another life; but this wasn't the time or the place. I should've been relieved that Lance was at least showing signs of pushing past the curtain of melancholia that had veiled his existence for so long. That Ginger held no interest for Lance was fine with me. I was more than willing to partake of the wealth of pleasure her not-so-discreet attire publicized lay in wait beneath. But why did it have to be Melissa MacIntyre? My gut told me she was trouble; my instincts had warned of that five-and-a-half years ago. Her appearance here tonight, under the circumstances—circumstances that *she* was dictating with vague answers to pointed questions—did nothing to allay my suspicion. I wanted no part of Melissa MacIntyre, or her brother, Benjamin Junior, for that matter. I would've liked nothing more than to walk out The Famous Door with Ginger and go back to her place where I could give that little mole much closer inspection and discover if it had any twins in other, more secluded places. But I knew that if I did Lance would only take it upon himself to offer whatever aid he could, which would be very little considering how little he knew about locating missing persons. While Melissa, a woman I viewed as very adept at manipulating people, especially someone as vulnerable as Lance was right now, would use that aid to satisfy her own mercenary ends.

I sighed yet again and decided to change tacks. Perhaps if I got her to hang herself Lance would see her for what she really was. A little practical experience to go along with the lesson ol' Buddy LaRue had tried to impart.

"Miss MacIntyre, did your brother instruct you what to do should he fail to contact you from Indianapolis?"

"No."

Lance was probably right: she thought her brother had matters in hand. But I didn't think for a minute that lack of instruction from her brother was what had driven her to contact me. She knew more than what this note let on or she wouldn't be here tonight. Her brother was in trouble, as was her father. This wasn't a simple case of missing persons.

Cursing to myself, I betrayed no outward sign of exasperation.

I still held the note Melissa had given me. I read again

the hastily scrawled words:

*I'm in Indianapolis. I'm well, but have no idea when next you will hear from me. Don't try to trace me!!!*

*Your father*

I noted the last of the three exclamation points was slightly smudged, leaving me to conclude that the composer of the note had been in a hurry—too big of a hurry to allow the ink from his fountain pen time enough to dry. I turned the letter over in mute consternation. After a moment of affected speculation, I played out my bluff.

"Miss MacIntyre, you don't by chance have the first page of this note?"

A look of perplexity passed over her features—features that in their forged innocence were maddening. But just before that I had seen something else: a look of alarm, that perhaps she hadn't been prepared for that question, or that she had been found out. But she was quick to cover up.

"Why, Mr. January, I don't know what you mean."

I held her gaze a long moment, my eyes narrowed.

"That's all there is," she added coolly before tearing her eyes from mine, confirmation, to me, of the lie she told.

"Miss MacIntyre," I pressed without bothering to mask my growing irritability. "I might be willing to help if I thought you were being straight with me."

"Joe," Lance said.

"No, Lance. Look at this," I said, pushing the note toward him. "Go ahead, read it."

Lance did. When he finished, he looked at me without comprehension.

"Now tell me, based on what that tells you, would you fly off to—" I broke off, already knowing what Lance's answer would be. "Don't answer that!"

"Yes, I *would.*"

"Yeah, I know you would. That's the difference between

you and me."

"Gentlemen's nobility," Lance said with a laugh. His comment was more of an aside for Melissa's benefit.

"Nobility has nothing to do with it!"

"Come on, Joe, where's your sense of adventure?"

"Damn it, Lance, don't you think she has an obligation to help me to help her?"

"I think she's a straight-shooter, Joe."

"Oh, you think she's a straight-shooter do you?"

"Yes, I do."

I could see Lance's admiration of the profile Melissa was presenting him while her attention was focused on me. Lance was already an advocate. He had been easily won over and would prove to be more easily plied in the future. But I was still the person she had to have at her disposal if she were to achieve her ambition, for good or bad. I couldn't shake the notion that her and her execrable brother's aspirations would only amount to no good for both Lance and me. I sighed.

"Tell me, Lance. Knowing what you know about all this—" I jabbed a forefinger at Melissa. "Knowing what she, who you've just met, has told us, what you *don't* know about her brother, who you haven't had the pleasure of meeting, and what you know of their father's mysterious communication after nearly six years in Europe … Knowing what you now know—which with the exception of Benjamin Junior, who I *have* met, is all *I* know, which doesn't amount to a hill of beans—what would you hope to accomplish by catching a plane to Indianapolis?"

"I don't know," Lance said, his fingers drumming idly upon the note he had neatly refolded. "I'd poke around."

"You'd poke around," I said. "Lance, in order to poke around, you first have to have something in which to poke around. Where do you suppose you'd start?"

"I don't know. You're the gumshoe, Joe. You tell me."

I threw up my hands. "No, don't go stroking my ego. I've been this route too many times before. Clients telling me only what they want me to know—usually just enough to get my balls busted because I'm in over my head with something I never even had a clue about." This last allusion elicited a snicker from Ginger, who apparently had been paying more attention to the discussion than I would've given her credit; or perhaps it was merely my reference to the male genitalia that had snared her short attention span. "'Help me find my father, Mr. January,'" I finished with distaste. "For all I know, her father's involved with contraband—or worse!"

"That's not true!" Melissa said. It was the first outward display of emotion exhibited in her otherwise placid disposition. "My father has *never* been in trouble with the law."

"Maybe not, but how would I know? Since what I've learned from you is sketchy at best, I have no choice but to fall back on a wealth of experience dealing with people like you and your brother."

"Jeesh, Joe, what have you got against the MacIntyres?"

"Gut instinct, Lance. I've met Melissa's brother. Besides, there's a mighty good reason why I don't take on missing persons."

"What's that?"

"Seven out of ten of 'em don't *want* to be found."

"What about the other three?"

"They're usually caught up in more trouble than I care to get involved with."

"He's a professor of archeology! What kind of trouble could he be in?"

"You tell me! And don't be afraid to use your imagination, Lance. Mine has served me well enough over the years. What if some foreign government *is* hot on his tail for something he did, didn't do, or didn't know he did?" In response to Lance's look of disbelief, I added, "Didn't we just have this conversation?"

"Don't you think you're being a little extreme, Joe?"

"No government is benign, Lance. Think about it. He's been gone nearly six years. What was happening in Europe six years ago?" I struck my forehead with the flat of my hand. "That's right, how could I forget? You were stationed in the *Pacific* arena, so it probably escaped your notice that Hitler was in a frenzy at that time, invading one country after another."

"That's not funny."

Undaunted, I continued my assault. "I don't doubt the plausibility that Professor MacIntyre may have been unable to correspond with anyone outside of Europe. How he managed to find himself in Indianapolis after nearly six years I can't begin to speculate, but the last time I looked at a globe, Indianapolis was a long way from Europe. I certainly don't doubt Miss MacIntyre's allegation that her father, and now her brother, are in some kind of trouble. But to me this reeks of something more than Professor MacIntyre's inability to make up his mind over which old relic he wanted to bring back with him to Columbia."

"Mr. January," Melissa said, her eyes meeting mine in what she hoped I would see as frankness. "How much would it take to get you to help me find my father and brother?"

"I can't be bought."

"What then?"

"The truth, for starters."

"You can be so stubborn sometimes, you know that?"

"Stay out of this, Lance." To Melissa I said: "What about it, Miss? There's nothing in that note that would prompt an intelligent person to go to Indianapolis halfcocked the way your brother did. There's more isn't there? A first page perhaps?"

"No," Melissa breathed. "There isn't a first page."

A moment passed before, unable to hold my probing gaze any longer, Melissa cast down her eyes in search of solace among the melting ice cubes that was all that remained of her rum and Coke.

"Joe—"

"That's all right, Mr. Cantrell," Melissa said. "Mr. January is very perceptive. There *is* more. Something I've been remiss to tell you. But it's not because I didn't want to."

# Chapter Three

"I was afraid to confide in you, because of the magnitude of the implications. I didn't think you would—or could—believe me. I didn't think you'd help me."

"I still may not," I said, "and not because of what happened at Minton's five-and-a-half years ago. Miss MacIntyre, I value honesty above all things. In my personal life as well as from my clients—*especially* from my clients."

"I know you do, Mr. January," Melissa said, bravely meeting my glare. "I'm impressed by your integrity. Why else do you think I looked you up again after all this time? It was because I knew I could trust you."

"Just not enough to trust with me all the facts."

Melissa looked down again, but try as she might, she just couldn't hide her shame in the glass she couldn't help but turn round and round in her hands.

"I'm sure she has a good reason, Joe."

I nearly blurted, *Any reason would be reason enough for you, Lance,* but bit back the rebuke. To Melissa, I prodded, "What about it, Miss?"

Melissa continued to toy with her glass, seemingly oblivious to my question, before, some weighty decision reached, she set the glass down with purpose, the tablecloth robbing the finality of the gesture of its effect. Whether her newfound courage was a result of that simple act or merely an act, I couldn't be certain. She looked me square in the eye, as if to challenge me to dispute the validity of what she was about to disclose.

"Mr. January, I didn't even know my brother was missing until last Friday."

"Yet you let me assume he flew off in search of your father a couple of days ago."

"My brother is often away on business, so I had no reason to question his whereabouts. But then last Friday …"

"Go on, Miss MacIntyre. What happened last Friday?"

Melissa looked at me, and something in her look told me that whatever information she was about to impart would be the truth—or at least some twisted part of the truth—and that she knew how much of that truth I believed would be paramount in achieving the business arrangement she so greatly desired. Without breaking eye contact, she withdrew a second envelope from her purse and handed it to me. I noted the postmark on the envelope—May 13. Two days before the note had been sent.

"I received a second correspondence from my father—last Friday morning."

"Which actually would've made it the first correspondence," I said.

Melissa said nothing, nor was she able to stare me down.

I removed a postcard from the envelope. The postcard depicted a hotel—The Severin Hotel the letters across the front identified. I flipped the postcard over and read it in silence, wondering at the oddity of sending a postcard in an envelope. A moment later I turned my scrutiny back to Melissa, a countenance of curiosity mingled with suspicion in residence. Having read the postcard, I could now see the wisdom of keeping its message secret from probing eyes.

"What is it, Joe? What's it say?"

"See for yourself." I pushed the postcard toward Lance, the gesture a duplication of our earlier exchange, and tried to discern why Melissa might have waited an entire week before seeking me out. Indecision? Perhaps she was waiting for additional correspondence; further instructions, which she'd received on Tuesday. And still she'd waited another three days before contacting me.

The letter she had showed me in itself seemed no puzzle; but in light of the postcard, which she'd received previous to the note, well, no wonder Melissa had been hesitant to share all the information she had. I surmised that having to wait several days after the original correspondence may have tried her patience to the point where she needed to take a proactive role in the face of the maddening ignorance of her father's fate.

We all sat in silence; even Ginger seemed taken by the importance of the moment. I was already considering the connotation of what Melissa hoped I might see portended in the message of the postcard while Lance perused its message. I could feel Melissa, Lindy and Ginger's scrutiny of me, their reasons for doing so worlds apart. Melissa, perhaps trying to gauge my reaction to what I'd just read; Lindy, in admiration of a profile whose nose boasted of Lithuanian origins; and Ginger, I hoped in anticipation of how I might go about fulfilling her desires. After Lance finished, he stared at me, uncomprehending.

"I don't get it," he said.

"They *do* tend to contradict one another, don't they—the note and that postcard?" I took a swallow from what remained of my beer before turning to Melissa. "What about the package that accompanied the postcard?"

"I followed my father's instructions on the postcard."

"Did you now?" I asked, trying to catch a glimpse of what might lie beneath her veneer of certitude. Perhaps Melissa would obey her father's wishes, but I suspected even I would be hard-pressed to refrain from opening a strange package, its contents unknown. Call it simple curiosity or a nose for investigating curiosities.

"Believe me, Mr. January," Melissa said with a laugh, "I wanted to open the package, but I ensured its delivery to Columbia." The laugh seemed evidence that she spoke truthfully.

"Your father's office—"

"Had been reassigned during his absence. I took it to my own office. Rest assured, it's quite safe locked in my desk."

I nodded and tried another approach, choosing my words carefully. "You received this package and the postcard that accompanied it last Friday?"

"Yes."

"Why wait until this morning to contact me?"

"Really, Mr. January, I had hoped to hear from my father within a day or two. Who knows what danger I may have put him in by taking action. And the note I received Tuesday did little to allay my concern. I now regret having waited even a day. By delaying taking action—any action whatsoever—I may have endangered him just the same."

Again I was forced to acknowledge Melissa's answer as marginally satisfactory. She was either being honest, or she'd had enough foresight to rehearse an answer to my question. I continued with my line of questioning.

"When did you first notice your brother was away?"

"Last Friday night, when he never came home. I assumed he was away on business."

"What kind of business?"

"Real estate."

I grunted. To me real estate meant a variety of ventures, and not all of them above board.

"Did any of your brother's real estate dealings ever take him to Indianapolis?"

"No," Melissa answered softly. "Not to my knowledge."

"Which is it, no or not to your knowledge?" I wondered how much Melissa might know about her brother's business ventures.

"Not to my knowledge," she said with more certainty.

*She's good,* I thought. *Whatever plot you have cooked up, Miss MacIntyre, it's well thought out.*

I shot a glance at Lance, who looked ready to buy anything Melissa might try to sell.

After a moment of simulated cogitation, I chuckled—the sound just as simulated—at a recollected epigram before, in response to Melissa's questioning gaze, I went on.

"I've never been much of a devotee of Sherlock Holmes, Miss MacIntyre." In all honesty, I'd always thought of him as queer; still, I needed to set the proper stage for my ploy. "But his author, Conan Doyle, wrote an adage for him of which I've always been particularly fond: 'Once you've eliminated all the possibilities, whatever remains, no matter how improbable, must be the truth.'"

"I'm afraid I don't follow you."

"Eliminate the possibility that this postmark was tampered with—that the date was deliberately set back to make it *appear* to predate the first one. Even I can't conceive of a reason why anyone would, or to what end such tampering could hope to accomplish." In truth that was the one piece of the puzzle I couldn't make fit. "Eliminate that possibility, Miss MacIntyre, and according to Doyle what remains, no matter how improbable, *is* irrefutable."

"I *still* don't get it," Lance carped, angry that he'd been left out of the loop.

"The postcard," I explained, "would seem, based on the envelope's postmark, to have been written first."

"But the gist—"

"The gist of the postcard," I interrupted so my train of thought wouldn't be, "seems to indicate by its reference to the first note to be just that, a second correspondence. But listen," I added, gesturing for Lance to return the postcard to me. Careful to keep any hint of cynicism out of my voice, I read: "This postcard supersedes all other correspondence."

"But the postmarks," Lance argued.

"I know, Lance, but look," I said, holding up the postcard. "Whoever penned this postcard hand-dated it."

Lance took up the postcard to prove that what I'd stated was valid. "I guess I hadn't noticed," he said.

"The first rule in detective work, Lance—observation. No detail is too small." *Especially this one since it was circled to draw attention to it.*

"But the postmark on the postcard's envelope predates the letter's postmark by two days."

"Right. Yet the evidence seems to indicate the postcard she received, despite its hand-date, was written after the first."

"Maybe he just wanted to make it look that way."

"Maybe," I said, impressed by Lance's skepticism. Perhaps there was hope for him after all. *Or someone else wanted to make it look that way.* I looked over to where Melissa sat, unflinchingly meeting my gaze. The innocence of her expression, which had so many years ago seemed naturally sincere, I now suspected was forged. "I've thought of that and it's a possibility I haven't yet ruled out, but first let's take a look at some other possibilities. Look, the hand-date on this postcard is circled. Why do you think that might be?"

"Maybe he was doodling."

"I don't think so. The penmanship here is of someone rushed. People in a hurry don't doodle. No, I think he"—*or someone*—"is intentionally drawing attention to that date."

"So you think it's a clue?" Lance had already decided we were taking the case.

"Yes, Lance, I think it's a clue. And its implications I must admit I find intriguing. What about the brother?"

Lance looked at me a moment before replying with his own question: "Do *you* think Benjamin Junior is with Professor MacIntyre?"

"Miss MacIntyre said she *believed* her brother to be away on business." I glanced at Melissa and asked, "Does your brother keep you apprised of his itinerary, let you know when he's going to be away for extended periods?"

"Not always. He often calls me for any messages he might receive while he's away, but usually only if he's expecting someone to contact him during his absence."

"So not hearing from him for a few days is not unusual?"

"No," Melissa replied casually.

I nodded but betrayed no sign of frustration that my line of questioning was leading nowhere.

"But the date on the postcard," Lance muttered under his breath, "as well as the postmark on its envelope, would seem proof that the postcard was written before the note—a note that warns both Melissa and her brother against trying to find him. And why circle the date?"

Apparently the seed that I'd planted earlier had gotten Lance to thinking, although he seemed a little impatient with my unwillingness to shed light upon what had become, to him, an imbroglio with no loose ends with which he could grapple in hope of untangling this enigma.

"And what, Lance?" I was interested in seeing where his supposition might lead him.

"But if the postmarks are accurate and the postcard—which in truth predates the note—references the note in past tense … well, that would mean …"

"What, Lance?" I teased. "We've eliminated all the possibilities so what remains now, no matter how improbable, *must* be the truth."

Lance thought a moment longer before, in frustration, he simply shrugged and confessed, "I don't know."

"What about you, Miss MacIntyre? What conclusion have you drawn from these two contradictory notes?" I could see she was still reluctant to provide any elucidation, which meant she was probably withholding information. Yet I could also see she was curious as to what conclusion I might have derived, the result of my own speculation over the conflicting dates.

"Come on, Joe, tell us," Lance urged impatiently. "I know that look. You know something, I know you do."

"All right, I'll tell you. But you're not going to like it. It's so simple you're going to kick yourself for not reasoning it out yourself."

"Joe!"

"The note and the postcard were switched."

I watched Melissa's face turn crimson—this was not at all the synopsis for which she was hoping—while Lance's eyes widened. Given my buildup, he'd been expecting something a lot bigger in scope.

"What do you mean they were switched?"

"I mean just what I said. Junior's been gone four days." *That's probably the only true statement in her whole story.* "Maybe he's away on business, maybe not. We have no way of knowing for certain. Maybe he *did* fly out to Indianapolis Last Friday, after receipt of the first note. Probably at his father's request since he couldn't have known where in Indianapolis he was staying. Professor MacIntyre's circumstances may have changed radically shortly after he'd sent the note … enough that he risked getting Junior involved. Then on Thursday, Professor MacIntyre wrote the postcard and sent it, along with the package, to Miss

MacIntyre. It would've been child's play to switch the envelopes after both had been received to make it appear the postcard had been written before the first. No doubt the envelope the postcard came in was attached to the package, making an additional postmark unnecessary. What about it, Miss MacIntyre, is that about it?" I waved my empty beer glass at a passing waitress.

"But …" Melissa's frustration appeared legitimate as she sought her rebuttal against my accusation.

"Joe," Lance said, once more coming to Melissa's rescue. "You said once we eliminated all the possibilities—"

"Whatever remains, no matter how improbable—"

"Well, what's so improbable about switching envelopes?" Lance was looking at Melissa, wanting desperately for her to confute everything I'd just construed as contrived.

Melissa fought back tears. Tears I identified as a sum of anger and frustration—that she hadn't been taken seriously and that I couldn't so easily be manipulated—and no doubt read by Lance as the resignation of someone who has just let her family down.

The mole on Ginger's breast beckoned to me, as did the smile she offered as she became aware of where my gaze had, for so brief a moment, alit.

While Lindy, lost in her own secret reverie, appeared to be listening to Art Tatum disguise a recently popular melody I knew but perhaps she could not readily identify.

"Why?"

I turned my attention back to Melissa. "What was that?"

"My father is in trouble, Mr. January. That's the truth. What reason would I have for manipulating the only evidence I have in order to persuade you to help me?"

I couldn't deny the truth behind her first two statements, and I only suspected she and her brother had their own agenda in all of this, but even with my vivid imagination I couldn't comprehend the *why* behind such a ruse.

"Come on, Joe," Lance said, "you've had all the answers to all the questions until now. This should be the easiest one yet."

"I can't answer that."

"You mean to tell me that with all your gumshoe savvy you can't come up with a motive?"

I bit back my anger. "I'll ask you once more, Miss MacIntyre. What other information do you have that might be helpful?"

Melissa shook her head. "You know as much as I do. I know it doesn't make sense, which is precisely why I was reticent about sharing it all with you. I knew it would make you suspicious."

I searched for the deceit beneath her confession but came up empty.

"You've changed since before the war, Joe," Lance said. "You used to thrive on challenges such as this. You used to fight for the underdog."

*Underdog? Is* that *how you view her?* I thought to myself.

Melissa looked on with renewed hope: that Lance might yet shame me into taking action on her behalf.

Lance was right about one thing. Like someone who can no sooner resist the challenge of a good crossword puzzle, if there were some subterfuge here, my inquisitive mind needed to uncover it lest it reflect unfavorably upon the aforementioned savvy.

"Maybe you're right, Joe. Maybe it is all some sort of deception. That doesn't mean Melissa's a part of it; it just means she was taken in by it—as I was."

Lance was stroking my ego again, something that a few years ago might have been an effective tactic. Hadn't I been willing to help this damsel with the auburn hair that had at that time been in similar straits? Grudgingly, I had to admit that perhaps I had become a slave of my own cynicism.

"And you can't deny you need the work."

I bristled at that. True, I still hadn't recovered financially since the war ended, but I resented having my financial needs discussed in the open.

"Lance, this is ludicrous. Where would I start?"

Sensing the flow of the battle was leaning in her favor, Melissa piped in. "Mr. January, I called The Severin Hotel—the hotel on the postcard. A Benjamin MacIntyre is listed as a guest."

"There, you see! A place to start," Lance said, reinforcing Melissa's suggestion.

*There, you see!* I silently aped. *What other information will she have at her disposal when she needs it?*

Rolling my eyes to the ceiling I asked, "Benjamin MacIntyre, or Benjamin MacIntyre, Junior?" Having met Melissa's brother, I was convinced the *junior* portion of his name would be important to him, if for no other reason than it set him apart from his father, provided him with a sense of his own identity.

"Benjamin MacIntyre," she said.

*Missing persons*, I sighed to myself. I didn't trust Ben and Melissa MacIntyre, but the maddening truth of the matter was that I didn't know why. Not that the why really mattered since I was certain I'd see the potential for deception no matter what. To quote Buddy LaRue, it was just a gut feeling. And I couldn't know where their father stood in all this. Associate Professor of Archeology. For all I knew he could be a traitor turned war criminal.

I looked across the table at Melissa, seated next to Ginger, who was, for some reason known only to herself, copiously ogling my hands. Melissa maintained her mien of candor and suddenly I couldn't be all that certain that it *was* manufactured, or that her motives were of ill repute. Maybe it was her brother, with whom I wouldn't be dealing, at least at the onset, who was the source of my distrust.

Furthermore, I knew that if I refused Melissa, Lance would only step in and offer to help, and he was too wet behind the ears in this business to do much except get himself hurt.

Lance. Looking back over the years, I can honestly entertain the notion that maybe it was Lance after all who had been behind my unwillingness to accept most of what Melissa claimed to be factual. I'd often played devil's advocate to Lance's axioms, sometimes for sport, other times for the sake of teaching him a valuable lesson. Yet there were also times, and even now I can't be all that certain that that episode in my life wasn't one of them, when I couldn't be certain what my motives for opposing Lance might've been. Certainly the notion that he might have gone home with the prize chafed my ego, despite the fact I no longer viewed Melissa as a prize to possess for a night's recreation. Although it was safe to say Melissa was no longer an object on which to spend my desire—especially since Ginger's own prized assets had ended up mine—the male ego is an unpredictable animal. So perhaps it was because of that beast that I managed, however temporarily and unknowingly, to put out of my mind the fact that Lance was at last showing signs of letting go of Becky.

Yet on another front, I considered that if the U.S. government, let alone some foreign government, was involved, it could only mean trouble for all concerned parties in the end.

Still, I couldn't deny that the mystery woven throughout Melissa's story intrigued me. I concluded that if it looked as if it were turning into something I no longer wanted a part, I could always opt out and return the unused portion of Melissa's advance.

Convinced that money would be no issue, I decided to let Melissa make the decision for me. I told her seventy dollars a day—that was twenty more than I normally charged—adding that the first five days were to be paid in advance, and that expenses were expected to be paid as incurred, which would start with a plane ticket to Indianapolis.

Later that night Lance saw Melissa home, via cab. The decorated war hero and gentleman nonpareil no doubt had sealed their business venture with a handshake and not a kiss. The kiss, he would anticipate, would come later.

I was mildly disappointed to find that the mole on Ginger's breast had no twin elsewhere; but the consolation her many other gifts provided helped to ease my disappointment. Still, I found Ginger to be a taker and not a giver, and so what pleasure I gained was the result of my own giving, which she was only too eager to take.

While Lindy, who drove home alone, was robbed of any chance to give, and therefore gained neither pleasure let alone solace from the image of where and with whom I had lain.

*Over the decades since that night, I've tormented myself over the fact that Lindy had suffered her disappointment alone, perhaps the previously unrecollected melody,* I Don't Stand a Ghost of a Chance With You, *echoing unsympathetically through her fading consciousness, her pillow taking the tears she could not help but give.*

*Tomorrow is forever. I should've held on for one more night.*

*Ah, so many regrets. What's one more?*

# Chapter Four

I was already sorry I'd agreed to take on the missing MacIntyres for pay.

First, I'd failed to convince Lance of the importance of leaving him behind as a sort of bodyguard for Melissa, not to mention the wisdom of sending a lone scout to Indianapolis as opposed to the entire cavalry. Lance had countered that a team of two, which in no way constituted an entire squadron, could work smarter and much safer. I doubted the acumen of Lance's first point; yet his second I couldn't in good conscience refute. Additionally, Lance had connections. He'd be able to charter a small aircraft at a fraction of the cost of plane tickets and fly the both of us to Indy himself. I reasoned the only person that arrangement would benefit was Melissa, and I was against anything that would make it the least bit easier for her, or more affordable.

Second, Melissa had refused to be left behind. I had my own reasons for keeping her in New York. I didn't want to be caught in a family crossfire should we manage to connect with her father and brother, if he was indeed in the mix. But she hadn't bought either of the reasons I'd given—that it was safer for her, and that she should be home for the reunion should her father and brother show up while Lance and I were away. "I wouldn't think of letting you and Lance take any risk I wouldn't take myself," she had argued.

*Any risk to you,* I'd postulated, *would be in staying home, unable to maintain control of your game until we hook-up with your father and brother.*

"And I can leave a note at home," she had argued further, "for my father to contact Lindy, and she can contact us through The Severin."

Lindy was the only person, no doubt because she was in my employ, who hadn't insisted on coming along. In frustration, I'd given up my argument.

That had been last night, and just before we retired from The Famous Door it was decided we would all meet at nine o'clock the next morning. My office is located in the upper end of Hell's Kitchen, that formerly tumultuous part of New York City that had, at the turn of the century, housed penurious migrants. From there we'd depart for the Teterboro airfield, just south of Hackensack in New Jersey.

I arrived just before nine. Lindy, who seemed somewhat detached, had already put on coffee. With all of my powers of observation, I failed to notice her eyes—or perhaps I did but chose to attribute their puffy state to the lateness of last night's hour.

My original intent last night had been to bury my misgivings, among other things, within the soft confines of Ginger's irriguous flesh; but she had done little other than lie there to take my mind off my presentiment over the MacIntyres. So I kissed the mole one last time, as well as the two jutting nipples that stood erect in their arousal from the twin torpedoes that were her breasts, thanked her for her hospitality, and excused myself as I dressed, blaming the late hour coupled with a need to get a good night's rest prior to our early departure. Ginger in turn thanked me because that was the courteous thing to do. Her indifference further disappointed me. Her body was an altar at which I'd be only too happy to worship sequentially. I knew there would be no conditions set and no expectations to be met. Still, it had been just that aloofness, Ginger's inability—or unwillingness—to appease (as Lindy could) that certain something in my male ego I had always refused to acknowledge existed, that affirmed to me that I would not again enjoy the pleasure of this woman's body.

Lindy had opened the window in my office and was now making her customary rounds watering the plants. She had brought them in of her own accord to brighten up the stark dreariness of the office. I'd said nothing, but Lindy understood their care would be her responsibility. She had just finished tending to her personal favorite, an African violet that sat atop the file cabinet nearest the window—it needed lots of sunlight—when I arrived.

The previous night I imagined Lindy had clung to what

little comfort her dampened pillow might offer her, perhaps very nearly conceding defeat. But that had been the previous night. The next day was a brand new one—bright with sunshine, born of the renewed hope borne upon the fresh breath of spring. Such was Lindy's youthful ideology.

I could feel Lindy's discreet scrutiny of me as I hung my jacket on the tree by the door and then dropped my hat on the corner of her desk as I made my way through her office and into mine, where the coffee pot was. My inhalation of its strong aroma was long and audible, and I recalled the nights I'd spent with Lindy.

My appetite was very nearly insatiable. We'd spend long hours lost in the throes of our passion with nary a word spoken between us, another far more pleasurable sort of oral communication taking precedence. I was convinced, or perhaps my ego was, that her soft whimpers, the effect (yet they hardly seemed affected) of my soft caresses, as well as my own quick intake of breath as she touched me in secret places, spoke more than an encyclopedia of words.

When something special happens between two people, they each know it. I felt it, both in myself and from Lindy. I had my own, at that time, good reasons for refraining from sharing my deeper feelings with her, and I can say now that they were never good enough reasons. And when it became clear that I'd never see her again, I had good reason to add to my ever-growing list of regrets all those wasted nights during which I kept silent and went home early.

Lindy was always careful to keep our private life private; that is to say, separate from our working relationship. Yet mornings after, her own unobserved observation must've shown her a tired-looking Joe January. Tired, yes, but also in residence she must've noticed something else. Something more than just the warm afterglow of our tryst … and whenever she caught me looking at her, which had happened more than once, I would be quick to look away, as if in denial of my thoughts. What else could it have been?

That long ago morning she must've thought I looked well-rested. I had refused to meet her gaze as I stood blowing at the steamy contents of my cup of coffee, and the scowl I wore could only affirm to a woman of her intellect that last night's foray into Ginger's gregarious flesh had left me less than satisfied. Small consolation for Lindy, then and later, and if what happened hadn't happened, I wonder how much longer she'd have been willing to accept that consolation. The next day might have been questionable. Perhaps by the following week she might have had her fill; yet in those days she seemed content to accept it. That hardly makes what I did right. Not then and especially not now, now that I can't make it right.

Certainly she must've been disappointed that my preference the previous night had been for Ginger—I sensed it in her demeanor that morning. But I now know, or perhaps I only want to believe, that her disappointment would've paled beside what she would've felt had my contentment that morning been a doppelgänger of the repletion she'd provided on those nights when she'd quenched my desire. Small consolation for me these many years later. Minuscule.

"Damn," I whispered. I'd moved to the open window that looked out onto 59$^{th}$ Street. Across the street stood the Church of St. Paul the Apostle, its Gothic brownstone looking irenic in the midmorning May sunshine.

"What is it?"

Lindy had joined me at the window; all had been forgiven and she now could take comfort in standing so near me, aware perhaps, as I forever would be, of our height differential. Discreetly she inhaled the scent of my after-shave.

"How long has that Packard been there?" Our third-story vantage prevented us from seeing into the vehicle, but an arm protruded through the open window, resting on the edge of the door. The car had been vacant when I'd parked the Ford.

"It was here when I got here, but empty." Lindy said. "You think it's a stakeout?"

I imagined a paper cup filled with coffee in the hand of the car's occupant, maybe purchased from the breakfast diner around the corner.

*Did you set this up, Miss MacIntyre? Or is someone acting independently, tailing you here yesterday, and now hoping to pick up your trail again this morning? Or perhaps that someone has in mind deterring me from taking action on your behalf, courtesy of your brother.*

"Maybe," I said. "We'll know for sure when we leave for Jersey."

"Good morning," Melissa said, her voice sounding bright and cheerful from behind us.

"That it is," I said, turning.

*Let her go on thinking we were standing here admiring the sunrise,* I thought wryly.

"Set down your suitcase and help yourself to some coffee, Miss MacIntyre," I added, moving to my desk.

Lindy left my office for her own unaware, as Melissa stepped aside to let her pass, of the blue eyes that were attempting to gauge just where her responsibilities as my gal Friday might end.

"Thank you, no," Melissa said. "Coffee's something I never acquired a taste for. My preference is for tea."

"What a pity," I said, although my tone betrayed none. I sat down and, once again inhaling deeply of the aroma from the cup I still held, added, "The morning cup of coffee has an exhilaration about it that the cheering influence of the afternoon or evening cup of tea cannot be expected to reproduce."

"Why, Mr. January! I had no idea you were a reader of Oliver Wendell Holmes."

"I'm not, Miss MacIntyre," I said flatly, unable to recall where I'd heard or read the adage I had just adduced. "I just don't care for tea."

Melissa laughed, the sound taking me by surprise. Yesteryear's child was gone, I noted again, replaced by this more cultivated, ripened, much more sophisticated woman, her teeth just as straight and just as white as I remembered from that long ago night at Minton's. For a moment I softened, and a different image of Melissa played itself across my mind, this one naked and squirming in ecstasy beneath me—

"Mr. January?"

"I'm sorry," I said, embarrassed by the fictive vision of a moment ago. "You were saying?"

"I asked if it were necessary that we maintain such a formal arrangement."

*No,* I told myself, refusing to allow the remnants of that other Melissa to reassert itself. *It's best to keep business separate from pleasure—at least until such time I can be certain for whose side she's playing.*

To Melissa, I said, "I'm in your employ, Miss MacIntyre, and until we sever our business arrangement, I prefer keeping our relationship strictly business."

"You weren't working for me last night," she said, baiting me. When I wouldn't bite, she added, "Have it your way, *Mr.* January."

I ignored her jest and pulled from one of my desk drawers the shoulder holster that housed my Colt Detective Special .38. Melissa's eyes went wide.

"You don't think you're going to need that, do you?" She sounded as if she were having second thoughts about accompanying Lance and me to Indianapolis.

"You never know," I said, slipping the holster over my head. "I'd hate to get all the way to Indianapolis just to wish I'd brought it along."

After I finished adjusting the holster, I picked up the envelope that Lindy had left on my desk. I very nearly put it into the drawer vacated by the Colt, to be opened upon our return from Indy, but its lack of an address stopped me.

*Hand-delivered,* I guessed, *yesterday afternoon or last night, after Lindy locked up. Or maybe early this morning, before her arrival.*

I thumbed open the gummed flap and pulled out the single scrap of paper. A moment later I stashed the note in my shirt pocket and cast a wary eye at Melissa. Leather creaked as I leaned back in the chair, while Lindy's typewriter sounded faintly from the outer office. I allowed the tension to lengthen a moment longer. When I felt certain Melissa understood what was expected of her, I invited her to sit down with a quick motion of my head.

From her purse Melissa procured a stack of bills. I'd been right—money would be no object; apparently her brother had profited quite handsomely from his real estate ventures. Silently she counted off four bills, returned the unneeded portion back to her purse, and set the four bills on the desk.

"The first five days," she said. "In advance."

"Lindy," I called. The typing stopped and a moment later Lindy appeared.

"Yes, Joe?" No doubt our familiarity with one another was not lost on Melissa.

"Lindy," I said, handing her the four bills. "Write out a receipt for three-hundred-fifty dollars … and bring Miss MacIntyre her change, would you?"

"Certainly, Joe," Lindy said as she left for the outer office. I watched her shapely legs, sheathed in their silk stockings, the straight seams following the gentle swell of her gams before disappearing under the hem of her skirt. From there I imagined them continuing on up the backs of her thighs, to be clasped by the garter belt I knew she wore.

The ensuing silence broke me from my vagary. I glanced at Melissa, who quickly averted her eyes, and I silently cursed myself for my transparency. I'd always prided myself on my stoicism. At that moment Lance made his entrance, saving me from further embarrassment.

"Morning, Joe," he said without bothering to make eye contact. "Melissa."

I noted the familiarity of the second half of Lance's salutation—the slightly prolonged sibilance of the middle syllable.

"Good morning, Mr. Cantrell," Melissa said, rising and offering her hand to Lance.

Lance laughed. "I thought I told you last night to call me Lance."

"Mr. January kindly informed me this morning that

while you are in my employ I should maintain a professional formality."

I felt my face heat at her good-natured revenge. I'd always despised being the target of someone's sport. That it was Melissa MacIntyre only served to stoke my anger.

"How Lance conducts himself with his business associates is his own business," I blurted.

"Then Lance it is," she announced, beaming her smile up at Lance.

"Great!" Lance said, unable to suppress his infatuation.

"Help yourself to some coffee, Lance," I said, not bothering to mask my irritation. "I want to get going." I made my way back to the window, where the Packard still waited, its occupant flicking a cigarette butt onto the street.

"Nothing like a cup of coffee—hot, strong and black—to get you going in the morning," Lance said as he poured himself a cup.

I couldn't recall the last time I'd seen Lance so chipper, let alone this early in the morning, and I dreaded seeing what a cup of Lindy's coffee might do to him.

*All the result of Miss MacIntyre,* I concluded. *If I* ever *act so goofy over a woman, I hope to god someone has the good sense to kick my ass.*

"Oliver Wendell Holmes couldn't have said it better," Melissa said.

I still stood at the window with my back to her, but I could sense her scrutiny of me—men's intuition.

"Who?"

"You'll have to forgive Lance, Miss MacIntyre. Very often some real thought on some real subject knocks the wind out of him." My thinly veiled coinage of the only other Wendell Holmes axiom I knew. I turned and noted Melissa's upward turn of her lip, the slight raising of her right eyebrow, the ever-so-slight tilting of her head—as if to keep my ever-rising esteem within her field of view.

Just then Lindy came in with Melissa's change, which she gave her along with the receipt she had written out for the four bills I'd given her. "Your change, Miss MacIntyre," she said, formalizing the transaction.

"Thank you, Lindy," Melissa called to Lindy's back. Then to me she said, "I'm sorry but it's the only name I know her by."

"Grab your bag, Miss MacIntyre," I said, striding past her. "It's time we got going."

"Wait a minute!" Lance protested, still oblivious to my affront. "I haven't finished my coffee yet."

"Bring it with you," I called from the outer office.

"He's always like this in the morning," Lance said to Melissa.

Apparently he had missed, or perhaps simply failed to recognize it as such, Melissa's admiration of his chief rival. But then, he no doubt also failed to recognize me as such.

"Here, I can get that for you," Lance said, exchanging his cup for her suitcase.

I'd already donned my jacket and was thumbing the lip of my hat.

"Did you remember to bring the photograph I asked for?" I said. Melissa nodded. "Give it to me."

Melissa complied and I found myself looking at the features of a professor whose appearance lacked any of the attributes one might associate with someone of that profession. Standing in front of a sizeable bookcase, he appeared to be somewhat tall and slender, with dark hair. No beard adorned his cheeks, and the glasses were the only item that might lend an air of bookishness to his features. I darted a glance at Melissa to confirm the family resemblance.

"When was this taken, Miss MacIntyre?"

"The summer before his disappearance."

"I'll hold onto this," I said, stuffing the photograph into my inside breast pocket and adding, "Make sure you leave Lindy the phone number to The Severin."

I sensed Lindy's relief that I hadn't reverted to referring to her as *Miss Parquette*. No doubt to her it meant I didn't care what Melissa thought might be going on between us.

I watched Melissa copy the number from the back of the postcard onto the steno pad on Lindy's desk. "Better leave your home number, too," I added as an afterthought. "Just in case."

"In case what?"

"Just in case," I iterated, suspicious of any suspicion her question might betray.

While Melissa acceded, I gave final instructions to Lindy. "Lindy, you're working late tonight. Stay by the phone—don't go out for dinner, have it delivered. We'll check in when we get to Indianapolis. Any idea when that might be, Ace?" I finished with a scowl at Lance.

Lance thought a moment before answering. "There's a big racetrack on the northwest end of Indianapolis. Before the war they used to hold a race there. A real big affair." He was talking to Melissa now, trying to sound knowledgeable.

"They call it the Indianapolis 500," I said brusquely, bursting Lance's bubble, "and they still hold it—as of last year. As a matter of fact this year's race is next Friday—Memorial Day. Now *when* did you say we might get there?"

"Well, I can put us down at the track. From there it'll be a snap to find out where The Severin is. I'll bet my captain's bars it'll be within walking distance."

"Not that they're of any value to me," I said, my patience wearing thin, "but that's a pretty safe bet. Now for the last time, when are we going to get there?"

After a moment of silent calculation, Lance declared: "No later than six o'clock—Central Time."

"Lance."

"Yeah, Joe."

"Indianapolis is on Eastern Time, just like New York."

"I don't think—"

"Lindy, we'll call in between seven and eight." Then, with a disparaging glance at Lance as I strode past him and out the door, I added, "Local time."

"Are you sure they're in the same time zone?" Lance called, slinging his flight bag over his shoulder and hurrying to catch up with me.

On the street I opened the trunk of the Ford and, as Lance

arranged his flight bag and Melissa's suitcase alongside my own overnight bag, cast an unassuming glance in the direction of the Packard. Its denizen was well-hidden behind a newspaper, its improbable angle intending to do just that.

*Well, he's no pro, whoever he is,* I reasoned, *or he would've parked up the block a ways, to be less conspicuous.*

*Then again, maybe he just doesn't care if he's noticed,* I argued to myself.

An image of a government agent on the other side of the newspaper, peering at us through a carefully cut out hole in the business section, played across the movie screen that was my imagination. With a grunt and a shake of my head, I scattered the pieces of the picture; with the slamming of the trunk the remnants vanished completely.

"What's so funny?"

"Never mind. Get in the car. Miss MacIntyre … you're in back."

I'd just fired the ignition as Lance slid in beside me.

"You know if we're going to be business partners, I wish you'd treat me—"

"Partners! Listen, pal, the *only* reason you're along on this one is your piloting skill, and I've got to tell you, your knowledge of this country's time zones has left me more than a little skeptical of those—*Blades.*"

"I resent that! During the war I flew in conditions and under circumstances that would leave you without your breakfast."

"I know," I placated. "If I *ever* meet one of you flyboys who hasn't landed a dinged up airplane in the middle of a rainstorm with enemy fire erupting all around you I'd—"

"Excuse me," Melissa said. "Maybe I'm under the mistaken premise that you two are friends."

In the Ford's side mirror I casually noted the newspaper still being used to obscure its reader. The Ford had idled long enough. Not wanting to alert my passengers to the presence of our tail, I teased out the clutch, fed it gas, and eased out away from the curb, more than a little irked that Lance had failed to notice anything suspicious.

*Some partner!*

"We are," Lance said, his anger suddenly defused; that Melissa might think him refractory was unthinkable. With a laugh, he added, "If we weren't, I'd have punched him in the chops for saying that."

*Yeah, we're friends all right,* I thought. *If we weren't, I wouldn't be risking my neck by letting him come along. I must be nuts.*

I checked the mirror again at the intersection of 59th and Amsterdam to see the Packard pulling away from the curb.

A few years ago I would've rounded the corner with a squeal of tires and in a cloud of dust in an effort to lose my tail; but with maturity had come wisdom. Curious, I was content, for the moment at least, to let whoever was following us play out their hand.

The three of us headed north on Amsterdam, toward the George Washington Bridge.

A moment later, so did the Packard.

# Chapter Five

"So how did you come by your nickname?" Melissa asked sweetly, totally unaware of the embarrassment her question would create for Lance.

"That's a long story," Lance said.

"It's a long way to Indy," I said, "and I *never* tire of hearing the story. Go ahead and tell her, Lance."

"Ah, it's not much of a story."

"Really? A moment ago it was a long story. Now it's not much of one. Which is it?" The Packard, I noted in the mirror, was complacent in maintaining its distance.

*Certainly the driver knows our intent to leave the city—he watched Lance load our baggage. Will he be hell-bent to stop us and, if so, when will he make his move? Or is he just using us to lead him to Professor MacIntyre?*

"Joe, you know I don't like to—"

"Like to what, boast?"

"Cut it out, Joe."

Ignoring him, I went on. "Lance was on approach in the middle of a rainstorm, Miss MacIntyre. At a hundred and ten knots, windshield wiper blades tend to shear off when they're turned on; hence the nickname *Blades.*" Then, with a glance over to Lance, whose deportment was one of anger tinged with a healthy dram of embarrassment, I added, "That wasn't such a long story now was it? And we're still on the island."

From the backseat I heard Melissa's laughter, light and mellifluous.

"Very funny." Lance said, gripping tightly the reins of his ire; I felt certain that if it weren't for Melissa's presence he'd be standing toe-to-toe with the perpetrator of his humiliation.

"Why didn't you serve, Mr. January?"

"Too old," Lance said, his revenge for my incommodious revelation.

I laughed and said, "Yeah, well somebody had to stay

behind to turn off the lights at night."

I slowed to catch the light at Broadway, forcing the Packard to a much closer proximity so that I could make out the features of its driver.

"Well I bet Lance has a hundred stories to tell."

"He sure does," I said as the Packard came to a halt behind us, the admiration in my voice feigned. "But none compare to the one I just told you."

For the first time I could see the driver—middle-aged and bespectacled—hunched over the big steering wheel. I concluded that he was probably no government agent.

The light turned green; I let out the clutch and accelerated, veering left onto Broadway, shifting up through the gears. The Packard maintained its distance behind us. I was dimly aware of Lance and Melissa's conversation, centered about Lance's flying antics during the war, as I tried to reason out who might be piloting the Packard.

"No, I wasn't aboard *Enola Gay*, nor was I in the 509th. But I met Colonel Tibbets when we were both stationed on Tinian. I saw him off the morning *Enola Gay* dropped *Little Boy,* although at the time I had no idea their objective."

*Namedropper,* I grumbled to myself; my pun did little to improve my rapidly deteriorating disposition. I hated playing wait and see, reacting to external stimulus like a lab rat in a maze. My preference was for taking initiative. Having to ignore our tail was a direct affront to me. Not trusting Melissa's purpose and not knowing where her father stood in all of this mystery and intrigue, or what threat her obnoxious brother might yet render, and having to wait for the cards to be played out before I could take action chafed me. I refused to admit that Melissa's interest in Lance's stories was also in part responsible for my sudden moodiness, preferring instead to believe her attentiveness merely topical.

In the rearview mirror I could see her blue eyes fixed on Lance, who had turned in his seat to relate one of the many stories in which she earlier hinted a fascination. Her singular goal, I was certain, was to solidify her hold over Lance so she would be able to more easily manipulate him should she need his support in the future.

The Packard loomed large in the rearview mirror, larger still in my imagination. I briefly considered the possibility that its driver had delivered the note this morning, perhaps at the professor's petition.

"Talk about bringing it in on a wing and a prayer," Lance said in summation of some anecdote he obviously thought more amusing than Melissa, as evidenced by what I regarded as her contrived laughter.

Traffic on Broadway at this hour on a Saturday morning was light and moving briskly. As a result of timing the lights I was able to make good time through the Upper West Side, the Packard in tow.

Zabar's, a combination grocery-deli I frequented, flashed by on our left. An absurd image of the Packard pulling over, the temptation of a J. J.'s Special, a sandwich named for its creator—hot pastrami with grilled onions and Swiss on rye—or some other delectable deli delicacy too great for its driver to resist, crossed my mind.

My mood, already darkened to an extreme by my inability to solve any aspect of the puzzle of the missing MacIntyres or the mysterious person residing in my rearview mirror, I now found myself forced into a position that precluded any action on my part save reaction. Angry at Lance but in denial over the *why,* suddenly angry at Lindy for *not* being angry with me about last night—and ignorant of the wisdom behind her understanding—I found no amusement in the farcical vision of a moment ago.

The Packard refused to be swayed by the lure of Zabar's.

Lance continued to chat incessantly about his wartime heroics.

Sighing aloud, I chose that moment, precisely the wrong moment, to check on Melissa's interest in Lance's boring saga of how he acquired the tattoo of a tiny American flag he bore on his left forearm. Perhaps it was the sound of my exhalation, long and audible, that drew her attention away from Lance, but when I found her eyes in the mirror, I found them staring back at me …

… While Lance's voice droned on.

The potency of my earlier proclamation regarding the length of our upcoming trip suddenly hit home. We'd been in the car but ten minutes, we had yet to leave the city, and with several hours to look forward to aboard a small aircraft as we made our way to Midwestern rural America, I found myself already at my wit's end.

Glancing over at Lance, whose infatuation with Melissa continued to grow at an alarming rate, I somehow resisted the urge to tell him to stuff a sock in it. Instead I muttered, "Tattoos are permanent proof of temporary insanity."

"What was that?" Lance shot back, daring me to repeat what I'd just said, although I was certain he'd heard my admonition.

Already sorry for provoking my friend but unwilling, due to Melissa's presence, to fully retreat from his counterattack, I opted to alter my original angle of assault.

"I said I once knew a girl who had a tattoo of a bluebird on her right breast." Melissa, I saw in the mirror, was hiding her mirth behind her left hand; she had no way of knowing how much truth my parable might contain. "She told me she regretted having had it done. 'But,' she explained to me, 'that was a long time ago, and you know the follies of youth.'"

"Did you find it attractive, Mr. January? The tattoo."

The directness of her question startled me. Still, in all honesty I could only answer, "No. I mean, she told me it was a bluebird, and I suppose while she was lying down it looked just like what she said it was. But when she stood up, I couldn't help but think it looked more like a pelican."

Melissa laughed. That she didn't instead blush, betraying youthful bashfulness, further served to contrast that other, less mature Melissa I recalled from nearly six years ago. Not that the frankness of my reply had been intended to cause her discomfit. Yet her laughter was genuine, not manufactured as it had been for Lance's sake, and so a part of my male ego was pleased at the authenticity of her amusement. While another part of my ego—the part that was Lance's friend—

resented her for misleading someone as vulnerable as Lance was right now. But to forewarn Lance would only result in malice toward the messenger. Lance was seeing only what he wanted to see, and any effort on my part to put into perspective that which he was allowing his skewed vision to show him would only backfire.

*Well, Lance is a big boy now,* I reasoned, finding comfort in the hum of the Ford's engine, the sound magnified as a result of the uncomfortable silence that existed amidst its three occupants. *And I'll be damned if I'll take responsibility for protecting him from himself.*

Lance was angry, his withdrawal into himself was proof, and I was certain he would go out of his way to vocalize that anger later, when the two of us were alone.

*Just my luck he now thinks I'm competing against him for Miss MacIntyre's affection.*

That I couldn't in good conscience deny I was angered me. Over the years we'd known each other, Lance and I had competed over a lot of things, but never a woman. That I'd been attracted to Melissa many years ago I freely admitted to myself; that she wasn't today without her charm, I wouldn't argue with anyone. From whence my distrust of her stemmed, I couldn't be certain.

The Packard continued to emanate hostility through my rearview mirror. Yes, even Zabar's had been unable to stay it from its present course in the wake of the Ford. Lance had failed to take notice of it when he loaded the trunk—not surprising since he had eyes only for Melissa. As for the object of Lance's adoration, now busy touching up her makeup, if she knew of its presence behind us, then she was very good at feigning incognizance. Much better than I was.

Suddenly unable to maintain any longer an air of ignorance so contrary to my nature, anxious to teach Lance yet another lesson in the fine art of observation, and yearning to impress Melissa for reasons I would deny, I reacted in the only way my instincts, coupled with my years of experience in such matters, would allow: on impulse. If the Packard had been sent to prevent us from leaving New York, then I would prevent that prevention. If on the other hand the Packard's intent was to tail us all the way to Indianapolis, using my talent to locate the missing MacIntyres for its driver, well then I would prevent that, too.

I stood on the brake pedal. The front brakes bit harder than the rear brakes; a high-pitched squeal sounded as the tires fought against the car's forward momentum. I heard Melissa's quick inhalation of air and her single syllable exclamation "Oh!" underscore Lance's "Jee-sus, Joe, what are you doing?" as he braced himself against the dashboard.

The rear tires lost traction amid blue smoke and the back end of the Ford started to pass me on the right. I allowed the car to come around ninety degrees before correcting into the skid. A moment later the Ford came to a halt in a position perpendicular to the flow of traffic.

Through the windshield I watched traffic flow past in the southbound lane, across the median. In the rearview mirror I saw Melissa's surprised face. A ragged line of bright red streaked her right cheek; she had been applying lipstick when I'd locked the brakes. Beyond her face, through the rear window, I could see the Mapes Gates of Columbia College, and beyond them, University Hall. Grunting my amusement at the irony, I glanced at Lance, who looked somewhat shaken.

"What's the matter, Lance?" I asked. "You look like you're about to lose your breakfast."

"Huh?"

Ignoring Lance's question, I looked to my left to find the surprised face of the bespectacled driver of the Packard staring at me over the steering wheel he still clutched. Due to the Packard's close proximity I was unable to open my door.

"Huh," I grunted in contempt, suddenly aware of the many different uses of the three-letter interjection Lance had used but a moment ago. Had he intended interrogation, or had his response been simply reflex, an expression of surprise the result of shock?

"Hold this," I said, handing my hat to Lance.

"Where are you going?" Lance asked dumbly, the color

drained from his face.

"To make an acquaintance," I said, hauling my bulk through the window frame.

I stepped one leg out, then the other, landing lightly on the Packard's bumper. From there I bounded down onto the brick that was Broadway and made my way around to the driver's side of the Packard. Flinging open its door, I reached in, grabbed the still startled driver by the lapels of his cheap tweed suit, and shook him violently several times. The last of the repetitions partially dislodged the pince-nez from the bridge of the nose it spanned. The blue eyes, now just inches from my own, swam beneath water that wasn't tears. One eye, the left, focused its terror on me while the other, due to a weakness of its tendon an optometrist would diagnose as strabismus, seemed to focus furtively on some distant object behind and to my left. I resisted the urge to turn around to see what it was that held that other eye's interest.

"Now that I have your attention," I rasped, "maybe you'd like to tell me just what it is you're doing tailing us."

The great eyes blinked; yet the pools of water still threatened to spill over their levees.

"I haff no idea vat you are talking a-bout." The man spoke, his high tenor surprising me, in a carefully metered pace that betrayed an uncertainty of the English language and I felt my stomach sink. We had yet to leave New York and already my worst fears were confirmed.

*The man's a Nazi!* I concluded.

"Shit!" I said. An image of the man whose lapels I still firmly held dressed in the black of the German Gestapo flashed before my eyes.

*And to think I was concerned over the likelihood that he was an agent of our own government. Damn!*

"You always make a point of enjoying a cup of coffee while reading *The Wall Street* in front of my office on 59$^{th}$ before following me uptown?"

"I haff no idea—"

"Yeah, yeah," I broke in, giving him another violent

shaking. The action provided a release for my slightly trembling hands, the result of my surging adrenaline. "I've already heard that."

I snorted aloud and a new strategy began to take shape. I released my grip and fussed over the rumpled lapels.

"Obviously you're a tourist," I said, righting the glasses that still teetered precariously near the end of his nose.

"Ja, a tourist," the German answered with a slow nod.

I watched the conspiratorial gaze that had been residing in the right eye make its way none too stealthily to the good eye. In the vacancy left behind, I thought I detected a certain nonchalance that surely was intended to disarm me.

"Ja," I mimicked. "Well, being a local maybe I can help you find whatever landmark it is you're looking for, Herr Tourist."

"Land-mark?" the big German enunciated carefully. Neither eye looked like it comprehended what I was talking about.

"Ja," I repeated. "You know ... sightseeing." I watched the light come on in the cerulean of the left eye and the thin lips parted in a good-natured smile to reveal a good-sized gap between the two front teeth.

"Ja, sight-seeing," the stranger acknowledged with a nod, and his smile broadened.

"Ja," I repeated a third time with a nod of my own. "What would you like to see?" The smile inverted itself. Neither eye met my penetrating gaze. "The Statue of Liberty?"

Silence.

I nodded. "I see. Been there already. Well how about the Empire State Building, then?" Like all native New Yorkers, I slurred into one syllable the second and third words of the proper name that identifies New York's most famous landmark. The stranger brought one eye to bear on me while the other stared off into the distance. I wondered if any object it might focus on would register an image for the German. "No? Well what about Columbia College? You seen that yet, Herr Pal?"

"Co-lum-bia Col-lege?" The German enunciated each syllable carefully, uncertainly.

"Great!" I said, allowing my own manufactured smile to break out. "I know just where Columbia College is. Why don't you slide on over and I'll have you there in no time."

"No. I do not vish to … trouble you. I vill find landmark."

"Oh, it's no trouble at all," I said with finality.

I stared hard at the one blue eye and saw it consider several alternatives, discarding each of them in turn. With a nod, the German, resigned to his one and only option, the one that had been forced upon him, relinquished his place behind the wheel of the Packard, and I hauled myself in beside him.

Firing the ignition, I stuck my head out the window and called to Lance, "Go ahead and park the car, Lance. I'll be back in a few minutes."

"But, where are you …?" I heard Lance call back as I brought my head back inside the Packard, just in time to see my unwilling passenger fumbling with the catch on the glove compartment. With catlike quickness I grabbed the German by his wrist.

"I don't believe you'll be needing that tour guidebook for this one," I said.

With that, I dropped the Packard's automatic transmission into reverse, glanced over my right shoulder, and backed up the few feet I needed to steer clear of the Ford. A moment later, with the Packard in drive, I slowly accelerated past my own car, giving a wave to Lance and Melissa, and on up Broadway.

"You know," I said as the automatic transmission smoothly shifted from first to second gear, "you rubbernecks would get around our city a whole lot easier if you just kept in mind that the Avenues"—I glanced over at the German's profile, a mask of contrived sincerity on my face— "you know avenues—Park Avenue, 5$^{th}$ Avenue. Avenues?"

"Ja, avenues."

"Right, avenues. The Avenues in New York all run north

and south, along the length of the island. Now the Streets," I continued patiently. "The Streets all run east-west. Now if more of you tourists understood that concept—that the Avenues run north-south while the Streets run east-west … well, you'd all have a helluva lot easier time finding landmarks and such and you wouldn't have to pester us locals. You understand what I'm saying, Herr Rubberneck?"

"Ja."

"Ja." I noted our speed had crept up to thirty miles per hour.

"Now take Broadway for instance—the street we're on now? It's not a Street, so it doesn't run east-west. It runs north-south—like an Avenue. But it's not *really* an Avenue, I mean like Park Avenue, see? But avenue *is* another name for a broad roadway. Which is where Broadway derives its name."

Our speed had risen to thirty-five miles per hour by now, well above the limit for the city. I kept a close lookout for any police cars that might be patrolling.

"So you see, Broadway really *is* an avenue, which is why it traverses the island in a more or less north-south direction. Just a little something for you to keep in mind while touring the sights here in our fair city, ja?"

"Ja."

Even from his profile I could tell the German was more than a little edgy.

The speedometer now registered forty miles per hour. The traffic light at West 130$^{th}$ Street was red. I sailed right on through it—as I had the red at 129$^{th}$ Street.

"Oh, what *am* I thinking?" I said, pressing the palm of my right hand against my forehead. "You know I got so carried away with my advice, I didn't realize we just passed Columbia College fifteen or so blocks back."

With a glance into the rearview mirror, I slammed the gear selector into reverse. The Packard came to a stop in a hurry and filled up with smoke, as much from the tires as from the transmission. Reverse was stripped out but that was no problem; I had allowed the Packard to do a tight one-hundred-eighty-degree spin in the middle of Broadway so we'd be facing south. Pale as a ghost and staring straight ahead, the German clutched the dashboard as I crossed into the southbound lane at 131st and drove back down Broadway.

"Well here we are, Mac, none the worse for wear," I said once I'd finished parking the Packard across from Columbia, just a few yards from where we'd started our little jaunt.

Nose-to-tail with the car in front, the German would effectively be dead in the water. With no reverse, he would have no choice but to wait until the car in front was moved before he could continue his pursuit, and by then we'd be miles away.

"Sorry about all the confusion," I said. "I guess I'm just not used to driving one of these new automatic transmissions. Although," I added as an afterthought, "I've got a buddy who tells me they're turning them out like hot-cakes in Detroit."

Opening the glove compartment, I reached in and removed a German Luger. "Tsk, tsk, tsk. I haff no idea vat you intend to use dis for." Then, in my South Bronx dialect, I added, "We Americans don't take too kindly to Gestapo straight-arm tactics. What do you say I hang onto this for you?"

The German continued to stare straight ahead.

I got out and slammed the door of the Packard, gesturing for Lance, who along with Melissa had gotten out of the Ford when they saw me park the Packard, to join me.

"Here you go," I said, tossing Lance the Luger as he trotted up with Melissa struggling to keep pace. I noted the ragged streak of lipstick was gone from her cheek; I guessed vigorous rubbing with a tissue was responsible for the pink mark that now resided in its place. "A little souvenir for you, from the European arena."

"What's this all about?" Lance asked.

"German tourist," I said, gesturing at the Packard. "He's been following us since we left my office. I'm happy to say he won't be any longer. I hope that doesn't trouble you, Miss

MacIntyre."

"Mr. January, I have no idea—"

"You know he kept telling me the same thing. It's uncanny how you two even sound alike, despite your ethnic differences."

"What's that supposed to mean?" Lance was quick to come to Melissa's defense—not that she needed it.

"But then again, it's not how you said it that compares as much as what was said."

"Is that supposed to be funny?"

"Relax, Lance. The thought crossed my mind that Miss MacIntyre may have been responsible for our tail, but now that I've met him I've reassessed that notion. Somehow I can't conceive that she or her brother would associate with Nazis."

"Nazis?" Melissa breathed in disbelief.

"You in the car, get out," I said, walking around the back of the Packard. The German complied. "Lance, Miss MacIntyre, let's go."

"Where are we going?" Melissa asked.

"To your office to pick up a certain package."

"But—"

"Don't argue." I handed her the scrap of paper from my shirt pocket and watched her eyes widen in disbelief as she read the note.

"When … but where did you—" Melissa said once she'd finished reading, before recalling, "This was in that envelope on your desk. Why didn't you show this to me then?"

"Didn't see any reason to," I answered with indifference. "Come on, we've got an itinerary to keep, remember?"

# Chapter Six

We'd just passed through the Mapes Gates, the mute German rounding out our foursome, and were heading toward University Hall, beyond which was the Avery Repository, where Melissa's office was housed. Melissa had just finished rereading the letter for what seemed to be the fifth time.

"It was hand-delivered to my office, either late last night or early this morning," I said.

"Hand-delivered? By whom?"

"The envelope contained no handwritten address or return address," I said. The message had been made up of individual letters cut from a magazine—arranged and pasted to a plain sheet of paper to compose the simple one-sentence message: *Bring the package to Indianapolis.*

"But who would've delivered it?" Lance asked.

"A more important question is who constructed it?"

I couldn't conceive of any reason why Professor MacIntyre would maintain anonymity in his request to have the package returned to him. Which meant that another party was involved, unless of course Benjamin Junior had put together the letter. But why the secrecy? He couldn't possibly know I was involved, unless Melissa had managed to get a message to him. But why not just ask his sister outright to bring the package? I considered that she'd lied to me last night, about his business trip; the possibility that another party had just dealt themselves into the hand. Too many choices, none of them very good.

"Can you think of anyone your father might have contacted here in New York, Miss MacIntyre?" I asked. "Someone he trusts enough to get them involved?"

"My father hasn't been in touch with anyone in New York for years," Melissa said. "Everyone at Columbia thinks he's dead."

"To your knowledge he hasn't been in touch with anyone," I said. Then to Lance I said, "Maybe this latest correspondence *was* mailed at the same time as the package, but to someone else, maybe a trusted colleague of the professor's at Columbia."

"But why? That doesn't make any sense."

"It does if he wanted to protect the contents of that package for a few days and then have it returned to him. Think about it, Lance. By sending the package and the letter at the same time, he ensures its return to his possession. Two more pressing questions though are how did he know I'd be bringing Miss MacIntyre to Indianapolis, and how did the letter come to be delivered to my office?"

I tried to picture Melissa last night, after she and Lance had said their goodnights, taking a cab back to my office to leave the envelope under the door, to be found when Lindy opened up. Better still, why not this morning? I imagined her dropping the envelope through the mail slot in the door before adjourning to the breakfast diner around the corner from my office—perhaps the same one from which our German friend had gotten his coffee—to await Lindy's arrival as she breakfasted on scrambled eggs and toast.

*No*, I amended. *No scrambled eggs for Miss MacIntyre. She'd order her eggs sunny side up.*

"What about it, Miss MacIntyre?" I asked. "Any suggestions as to how he might know I'd be your escort?"

"How could she know, Joe?" Lance said.

"If you don't mind, I'd really rather hear it from her."

Melissa shrugged. "I know you're suspicious of me, Mr. January, so there's nothing I can say to assuage your cynicism. I really am just as confused by this note as you are. And how it could have been delivered to you is beyond me."

I sighed. *Why doesn't that surprise me?* Yet I couldn't argue against the sincerity with which she had spoken. Indeed, the mystery continued to compound.

We were crossing the upper quadrangle and the Avery Repository was now in sight. I saw Melissa looking at the big German, guessed at what she might be thinking, and answered her unspoken question.

"Not all Germans are Nazis, Miss MacIntyre, but it's my guess your father has managed, either knowingly or by chance, to get the attention of some elite overseas group."

"Just as you suspected last night."

"But as I also speculated last night, I wonder if our own government is embroiled. Probably they're not," I added, watching the German for any sign that might betray the accuracy of my speculation. "If they were, chances are they would've contacted you by now. Have any Feds been in touch with you, Miss MacIntyre?"

"No," she answered, and for once I believed her—another *gut* feeling.

"And if they're not involved …" I pondered aloud.

"If they're not, they *should* be," Lance announced loudly.

"Why, because our government stands for truth, justice and the American way?"

"That's right!"

"The classic battle of good and evil, eh? The Fascist oppression of a fallen dictatorship versus the greatest democracy the world has ever known and *their* dictate, Government of the people by the people?" I sighed and glanced at the German, who maintained an air of indifference.

"If there's a Nazi movement in this country, don't you think the government should be made aware of it?"

"The key word is *if,* Lance. We have no proof yet of anything nefarious. If our own government is deaf and dumb on this, I prefer keeping them that way, at least for the time being. There's no reason to put ourselves in the awkward position of having to fight a battle on two fronts—at least until I can determine what it is we're dealing with. On the other hand, if they *are* in on this, chances are we'll be caught, if we're not already, smack dab in the middle of the fracas. But that can't be helped."

After a moment of silent speculation I added, "Still, unless I'm totally off the mark, I can't imagine our German friend here not working in tandem with someone else."

"That someone else could be in Indianapolis," Lance

said, his tone bordering on histrionic.

*And,* I postulated silently, *that someone else* could *be responsible for the professor's inability to contact his offspring directly. Certainly Professor MacIntyre wouldn't want to endanger his family. His need for stealth probably prohibits any conjecture on his part that their identity and whereabouts have already been uncovered.*

"Agreed," I said. My own muted tone had been designed to contrast with Lance's angst. It was a long way to Indianapolis and we'd be safe while we were in the air. There would be plenty of time for concern once we landed.

Melissa unlocked her desk's file drawer and pulled out a square box about eight inches a side wrapped in brown paper. I took the package from her and began to open it.

"Mr. January, my father said I wasn't to open the package."

"I'm not you."

Once the brown wrapping was gone, I used my car key to slit the taped seam that held the boxes' lid closed. A moment later I held a curiosity.

Crumpled newspaper stuffed into the box had delayed the item's discovery while offering protection during transit nearly halfway across the country. I heard the German's quick intake of air as he caught sight of it: a cube, small enough to fit in the palm of my hand, each side composed of nine squares, each square a different color. Each color seemed to randomly change at equally random intervals.

"What is it?" Melissa breathed.

"I've never seen anything like *that* before," Lance added.

"Nor have I," I said, looking from the German to Melissa to Lance, and then back to the curiosity I held.

Indeed the mystery continued to escalate, and for the first time I found myself thinking I was in over my head on this one. In over my head, perhaps, but unable to bring myself to walk away. The intrigue had intensified to the point where I couldn't bring myself to do that just yet.

"What about it, Herr Mac?" I said, stepping toward the German. "You know what this is?"

The German nodded, unable to take his one good eye away from the cube's flashing colored squares. "Ja," he said, "I know vat dat iss."

"Maybe you'd like to share it with us?" I said.

The German shook his head, left to right, once. "Its secret, I know. But dis secret iss hidden from me. I cannot make it show it-self."

"Don't talk in riddles."

"You vould be vise to give dat to me and let me be on my vay."

"I don't think so," I said, handing the cube to Lance. "And since you refuse to be of any help, I regret to tell you we're going to have to leave you behind."

With that I landed a punch to the German's midsection, heard the big man's "oomph" as he doubled over; then I landed a right cross that sent the foreigner past Lance, who had been quick to step back, and into unconsciousness. I flexed my right hand.

"Mr. January!" Melissa said. She seemed abashed yet impressed by my display of brutality.

"Sorry, Miss MacIntyre," I said. I marginally adjusted my hat and bent to rifle through the German's pockets and added, "But I don't want this goon following us any further than he already has, although we'd be wise to assume he already knows our destination. Besides, we don't have a lot of time for asking questions he had no intention of answering … ah, here we are," I finished, pulling passport papers from the inside breast pocket of the German's jacket and reading, "Werner Von Bahl, from Berlin. Why doesn't that surprise me?" I glared at Melissa. "Still think your father hasn't gotten himself mixed up in some sort of international scheme?"

Melissa didn't answer, but from the look of concern on her face, I felt my resolve to distrust her begin to weaken.

"Well, Hairball," I said to the inert body on the floor, "you're going to have a helluva time doing anything without these." I dropped the passport along with the key to the Packard into the file drawer that had housed the strange cube. "Lock it up, Miss MacIntyre."

"But he won't—"

"He won't be able to leave the country. Nor will he be able to follow us anytime soon. Which is the way I prefer it."

"But we can't just leave him here."

"Why not? We've got what he wants, and what he needs will be locked away in your desk. Believe me, he's not going to cause any commotion when he comes to. Without his papers he's not going to want to draw attention to himself. Now lock it up and let's get going. Lance, give me the cube. We've got a flight to catch, remember?"

Once we were on our way again, Lance pulled the Luger from his pocket, removed its cartridge, and began admiring the piece's craftsmanship. As a flyboy he'd had very little contact with the more intimate weapons of war.

After a moment of silence, her curiosity getting the better of her, Melissa ventured, "Mr. January, what happened in the Packard?"

"What happened?"

"Yeah," Lance said. "Where did you go?"

"We saw a cloud of smoke up Broadway."

I smiled mischievously. "Well, I offered to take our visiting foreign friend to see any New York landmark he wanted to see. He opted for Columbia College."

"But—" Melissa said.

"I know, we were in front of Columbia when we left. But our fair friend, not being from around these parts, had no idea where he was, and when I confessed to him that we had missed the landmark he wanted to see so badly, he seemed disappointed," I said with a laugh.

Melissa, I could see in the rearview mirror, seemed amused, surprised and somewhat taken by the sound, and I realized it was the first time she'd heard my genuine laughter. Danger always had a way of doing that to me. By keeping me loose it allowed me to do what I did best: improvise.

"What's so funny?" Melissa asked.

I detected a tone of admiration in her voice. That earlier image, the naked one, reasserted itself in my imagination, while the remaining adrenaline made its presence known elsewhere.

"You should've seen the look on his face when I dropped the automatic transmission into reverse at forty miles an hour."

"But you're not supposed to be able to do that," Lance said, his eyes wide with disbelief.

"Really?"

"It's supposed to have a lockout mechanism to prevent people from accidentally doing that."

I laughed again, but this time I was joined by Melissa, and a moment later by Lance, who, I deduced, did so only so as not to be left out. "Well that just goes to show what you can do when you don't know any better."

The George Washington Bridge loomed ahead.

I began to reacquaint myself with the familiar apprehensive anticipation of imagined events to come I always experienced in the face of adversity and had to admit, if only to myself, that I was becoming further drawn in by the additional intrigue of all that was unfolding. There was mystery here, and I fully intended to unravel that mystery. I only hoped that someone wouldn't get hurt before I did.

Forty minutes later, a lit cigarette in my mouth, I stood alongside Lance in the hanger lounge. We watched in silence as the ground crew—a man on a tug and two others that were on foot—pulled an aircraft out of the hanger. A tow bar joined the tug's front-end to the nose wheel of the Stinson Tri-motor that would be our transportation to Indianapolis.

Once clear of the hanger, the tiny craft was pushed slowly down the line of other craft tied down on the ramp and subsequently pushed into a space between two smaller planes. I thought the craft's fabric construction made it look awfully small and fragile.

Once the Stinson was in place, one of the wingmen left

to procure a fuel truck, while the other disconnected the tow bar from the nose wheel. A moment later the tug backed away and slowly made its way back toward the hanger.

Melissa was down the hall in the lady's room, attempting to make right with her makeup what I had earlier managed to undo. I could feel Lance's wrath, which had been growing steadily since we'd resumed our jaunt to Jersey after our encounter with the German, emanating in waves, like heat from the radiator in my office.

"Why do you have to embarrass me like that?" he said.

*Here it comes,* I thought.

In an effort to defuse his anger, I replied, "I don't have to. You do a fine job by yourself." My foray into flippancy failed.

In exasperation, Lance sighed. "That's not what I mean."

"Then say what you mean."

After a pause, he said, "I thought we'd outgrown that."

"Look, Lance, I'm not competing with you on this one, believe me. It's just …" I trailed off, uncertain of the validity of my claim. Lance filled the silence.

"I thought you'd be happy that I'm letting go of Becky."

"Hey, I'm delighted you're finally putting that to rest, but, well …" I'd never been very good with words, but at least, unlike Lance, I couldn't be faulted for skirting the issue. I always said what I meant, even if it meant stepping on someone's toes. But Lance was my friend. Sighing, I began again.

"Well, you know about last night—"

"I know," Lance said with a laugh. His previous anger had dissipated. In that we were very much alike: neither of us could stay angry at the other very long. "Last night was a setup. And I appreciate what you did, I really do. I'm sure Ginger is a swell kid."

"Lance, I had no idea Melissa was going to be there."

"I know! That's what makes it all so perfect."

"Perfect?"

"Yes! It's like I've known her all my life. She and Becky are like night and day. They're so different and yet …"

"And yet what?" I couldn't believe what I was hearing.

"I'm not the same person I was before the war," Lance said. "And who's to say if Becky hadn't done what she did, I wouldn't have come home to find we no longer had anything in common? She did me a favor, Joe," he finished, placing a hand on my shoulder.

I could only stare my disbelief into Lance's eyes.

"Don't you see, Joe? I wouldn't have hurt Becky for the world."

"So by dumping you first, she spared herself the pain of your rejection."

"Exactly!"

"Lance, believe me, the last thing I want to do is involve myself in your love life, but don't you think you're a little vulnerable right now?"

"Of course I am," Lance said. "If I weren't I wouldn't be able to leave myself so open to Melissa."

"Lance, you're on the rebound."

"No I'm not."

"You've known her less than twenty-four hours!"

"Joe, haven't you been on me to trust my gut feeling?"

"Your gut, yes, not your gonads!"

"I resent that."

My penance for my vulgarity was to turn from Lance and watch the refueler drag a hose from the cylinder on the side of the truck around which it was coiled out to the ladder he had set-up between the fuselage and the starboard engine. From there he made his way up the ladder, hose in tow, where he inserted the nozzle into the fuel tank opening that resided on the topside of the wing.

Suddenly I couldn't be certain the war *had* changed Lance. Certainly the years he'd been gone had aged him. That much was obvious in the way he carried himself, the weight he'd put on and the lines on his face—crow's feet and frown lines. But the foolish, childlike trust was still there. The war had done nothing to alter that.

I pictured Lance blindly following the orders handed down to him by his superiors, his trust in those superiors implicit, and at that moment I realized that that trust would always be there. It didn't matter how many conversations like yesterday's I could have with him, or how many friends he had like Buddy LaRue who would advise him to trust his gut feeling and not his heart, Lance would forever choose to see only the benevolent side of those who touched his life. Even after they had proven otherwise, he would but excuse their actions and accept the hurt they inflicted upon him as just, justifying their cause as righteous, as had been the case with Becky. Not that she could be considered in the same league as the MacIntyre siblings. I nearly shuddered at Lance's blind trust of the government.

"Look, Lance," I said, turning back to meet his gaze. "Have you given any thought to how *she* feels?"

"You mean about me?"

"Don't give me that 'Isn't it obvious?' look, Lance. I know her type. She'll stop at nothing, including playing you for a sucker, in order to achieve her goal." Although I was beginning to rethink my original distrust, I was still mighty wary of her. Wary enough to warn Lance of the potential for getting himself hurt, especially since it was so obvious to me just where her romantic interest lay.

"And just what do you think her goal is?" Lance snapped, avoiding the plausibility of what I was suggesting.

"I haven't figured that out yet, but trust me," I said. "That woman's a sweet-talker. She'll give you the big eyes, but when her sweet talking is done, you'll see she's a two-face—a worrisome thing who'll leave you at the drop of a hat."

I'd been dimly aware of the two men seated behind where Lance and I were standing. Although the two hadn't been eavesdropping, apparently they couldn't help but overhear my philosophy on women, prompting one of them to hurriedly scribble the adage I'd just voiced onto a piece of paper over which both he and his associate had been deliberating. By the time the song they'd write—*Blues In the Night (My Mama Done Tol' Me)*—became popular, it would be years and a lifetime before I would recognize my wisdom paraphrased in the lyrics of Johnny Mercer and Harold Arlen.

"So you don't trust her."

"Isn't that what I just said?"

"Jeesh, Joe, what is it with you and women?"

"Not women," I said. "Just that one."

"No," Lance argued. "This goes beyond Melissa. For as long as I've known you you've had a distrust of women."

I felt my right eyebrow rise a fraction of an inch, the only surprise I'd betray over Lance's perceptivity.

"Is that right?" I said, ignoring a long-ago image from my youth. The years may have dimmed its clarity, but I would never forget it. "I'll have you know I've tasted the flesh of more women in my lifetime than you could ever—"

"That has nothing to do with trust," Lance said. "Just lust."

"Maybe so," I conceded. "But at least I don't let my avidity for the pleasure women offer get in the way of my ability to judge their trustworthiness."

"And who are you to judge Melissa's trustworthiness?"

"Who do I have to be?" When Lance refused to back down from my defiant glare, I softened and added, "Look, Lance, it's not like I'm making her jump through hoops. Can't you see the potential for subterfuge here?"

"No, I can't."

I could only throw up my hands in frustration. Lance had always professed in the inherent good of mankind, and now it looked like no one—not Adolph Hitler, not Emperor Hirohito, or a hundred other tyrannical despots—would be able to emend that credo. When I didn't further my argument, Lance continued.

"Who's to say *your* gut feeling is right and mine is wrong? You haven't really known Melissa any longer than I have."

"You weren't there that night at Minton's nearly six years ago. Her brother—"

"She's a grown woman, Joe. You can't hold her accountable for her brother's actions," Lance said.

"Maybe not, but he's family, Lance. And if you think that when the time comes to chose sides she'll pick you over him, you've got another think coming."

Now it was Lance's turn to watch as the refueler scaled the ladder to add fuel to the tank located in the portside wing. A long moment passed as he considered the implications of what I was forewarning before he asked, "What if you're wrong?"

"If I'm wrong," I said, doubting while at the same time hoping, for Lance's sake, that I would be, "if I'm wrong, then you'll have my blessing."

"So you're really not interested?" he asked, his somberness brightening.

I bade goodbye the libidinous image that had plagued me at various inopportune moments. I valued Lance's friendship far too much to put it at risk over the affections of a woman, especially when so many others could be had.

"No," I answered, blinking away the picture of lips, ruby red and moist, shaping themselves around the single vowel of my name as I imagined Melissa's pelvis moving against me to meet my thrusts. "I'm really not interested."

Lance smiled his relief.

"But what if I'm right?" I asked.

The blank look that replaced Lance's smile was proof the notion that Melissa might indeed be guilty of some treacherous involvement had never crossed his mind.

"You don't have to answer," I added. "Just think about it. And try to keep an open mind, will you?"

# Chapter Seven

"You two handsome gentlemen wouldn't be talking about me, would you?" Melissa asked, joining Lance and me at the window.

Her makeup repaired, the sunlight highlighted her complexion to near perfection. I'd never seen her look more radiant. Despite the brightness of the late morning sun, I thought I detected a slight dilation of the pupils that resided at the center of her blue irises as they widened to welcome my image. I wondered if she might recognize the same reaction in my own eyes and found myself questioning the conviction behind my covenant with Lance that she no longer held an interest for me.

"As a matter of fact," Lance began, smiling.

"I was just telling Lance," I said, focusing my attention back on the Stinson, where one of the ground crew was now adding oil, by the quart, into the port engine, "that our transportation looks awfully small and fragile, and now it looks as if it's an oil burner, too."

Lance laughed. "With the power those engines generate, it's impossible that they wouldn't burn *some* oil." Then, to Melissa he added, "Joe's afraid to fly."

"If God had meant us to fly we'd have been born with wings."

"But we weren't, so technology enables us to go where before only eagles soared."

"You can't fly like an eagle with the wings of a wren." Thankfully Lance missed Melissa's look of estimation. "To me the wings of your Stinson there look more like those of a wren."

"It beats driving."

"Only if we get there in one piece."

Lance laughed again: my weakness was his own strength—while we were in flight he would be in his element, another way in which to impress Melissa.

"Listen," Lance said, "it'll be a few minutes yet before

they finish servicing the Stinson. In the meantime I have to do a preflight. The Civil Aeronautics Administration requires it nowadays. The good old days of barnstorming are over."

"Yeah, the government," I said. "They sure know what's good for you."

Lance ignored me. "Peg," he called to the woman behind the counter as he made his way toward the lounge exit. "How about some coffee for my two friends?"

"Sure thing, Lance," Peg replied to Lance's retreating back, before acknowledging the intensity of my perlustration.

I saw a dusky complexion that vaunted Italian descent, complemented by dark, shoulder length hair and just as dark, mysterious eyes.

"How do you take it, Mr. …?"

"January," I finished for her with a wink that betrayed I would take it any way she liked.

"I believe," Melissa said, "Mr. January likes his coffee black."

Peg blushed in embarrassment and looked away.

Nonplused, I offered introductions: "Peg, this is Melissa MacIntyre, who if I'm not mistaken doesn't care for coffee."

"I'll be but a moment," Peg said and departed for the pilot's lounge.

I took notice, not caring that Melissa might take notice of my notice, of the silk stockings with their straight seams that adorned Peg's legs, and the three-inch heels that accentuated the well-sculpted swell of her gams, and I resolved to remember Peg if I ever again found my way back to this part of Jersey.

I ignored Melissa's inspection as I strode past her to the center of the lounge, where I took a seat in front of the window to watch the planes take off and land. A moment later she joined me; upon taking the seat to my left she crossed her right leg over her left, letting her skirt rise to just above her knee.

Five-and-a-half years ago I had judged her legs too thin

and shapeless for my liking. Even today, with her youthful immaturity behind her, they lacked the shapeliness I found so alluring in Peg's and that had driven me to sequential excursions between Lindy's. Still, I couldn't help but imagine the pale flesh of Melissa's upper thigh, left bare by her silk hose, and was forced to cross my own left leg over my right.

As the silence between us threatened to go on interminably, Melissa finally ventured, "Why didn't you ever marry, Mr. January?"

The question caught me off guard. I answered her question with one of my own, designed to turn the tables, to put her on the defensive, where I preferred having her.

"How old are you, Miss MacIntyre?" From her reaction I knew I had succeeded. "Not yet thirty, are you?"

"I'm twenty-nine-and-a-half."

Her answer, along with the slight indignation I detected, elicited a laugh from me. Her use of the half-year reminded me of a child and the importance that half-year held in terms of maturity.

"What's so funny?"

Just then Peg arrived with my coffee.

"Your coffee, Mr. January."

"Please, call me Joe," I said, rising to take the ceramic cup from her. I couldn't help but notice she had unfastened the second button of her blouse, exposing the proud swelling of her breasts, where a scattering of freckles ornamented the cleft between. Last night's mole was quickly forgotten. Peg smiled, pleased that I'd taken the further notice she had hoped I would take. "And thanks for the coffee, Peg." I wondered briefly if, in lieu of Melissa's desire to be on a first name basis with me, the casualness would be lost on her.

*Not a chance*, I concluded.

"You're welcome … Joe," Peg said, trying on my name for size. She seemed pleased with the way it fit. "If there's anything else you need, please, don't hesitate to ask."

"I won't," I said, acknowledging her offer as well as her

departure, which was, I was certain, a little more affected than usual.

Peripherally, I noticed Melissa staring straight ahead, out the window, her complexion betraying the heat of some hidden passion. Was it embarrassment, that I was so clairvoyant with my intentions? Or perhaps it was anger or envy, both for the same reason—that her own overtures continued to be ignored.

"Forgive me, Miss MacIntyre," I said, and a moment later specified my apology. "I didn't mean to laugh at you."

She ignored me. So it was envy.

I watched a DC-3 hurry toward the far end of the runway, where it attained enough speed to acquire lift. I watched it leave the runway and saw the landing gear retract as the plane banked steeply to its right while gaining enough altitude to clear the trees it was fast approaching. When Melissa refused to engage me with conversation, a custom to which I'd become accustomed, I took up the conversation where we'd left off, prior to Peg's intrusion.

"You know, I could ask you the same question. An attractive young woman in her late twenties, with marriage on her mind." A deduction predicated upon her earlier question of my marital status. "How have *you* managed to escape the restraints of such a commitment?"

Not surprising, my compliment was just the right thing to say. I'd yet to meet a woman whose vanity would prohibit her from being touched by the type of felicitation I'd just offered, or pass up the opportunity to talk about herself. Melissa warmed and smiled demurely, completing her compliance to my avowal of her attractiveness.

"Education, Mr. January. My father nurtured in me during my childhood his love of fine arts and archeology. As a little girl I'd go with him to Columbia on Saturdays. After grading papers or working on his lesson plan, he'd take me to the Avery Repository—my father's interest was largely artistic rather than anthropological—where he'd show me the latest sculptures the college had acquired. He'd explain to me where the pieces had come from, how old they were, their history, and what they'd meant to the people who had created them. Then he'd take me to the library; it would be afterhours, so we'd be the only ones there. All the lights would be off, except for the one above the table at which we were seated. My father would pore over some reference book that provided more background on the pieces we'd just seen." She sighed at the pleasantness of the memory. "Just the two of us, bathed in a halo of light, while the rest of the denizens of that great hall looked silently on, patiently waiting for the day when they might be called upon to reveal to us their vast wealth of knowledge."

Melissa seemed lost in some secret reverie, baring a part of herself that I'd never seen or suspected existed. A part, I was certain, that even Lance had not yet glimpsed. I couldn't help but be taken by the passion with which she spoke of those past years and of the relationship with her father.

"I fell in love with the passion my father had for his work," Melissa said, as if our thoughts were cognate. "And he taught me—although at the time I had no idea he was doing it, or even if he knew he was doing it—how to learn."

"Knowledge is of two kinds," I said. "We know a subject ourselves, or we know where we can find information upon it."

"Samuel Johnson," Melissa said. "You're a very learned man, Mr. January. Much more learned than you let on."

"There is sometimes power in feigning ignorance."

"Who said that, Mr. January?"

"I think I did," I said, glancing over my right shoulder.

Melissa laughed, and again I couldn't help but notice her teeth, so straight and white, framed by lips red and moist with freshly applied lipstick. A moment later her eyes told me that I had let my guard down, and I cursed myself for my weakness. Turning away I changed the subject.

"I assume then that you work for the College?"

"I'm an archivist in the Department of Special Collections. Don't look so impressed, Mr. January. Opportunities for women at Columbia, even in 1947, are limited. I'm just fortunate that the archeology-fine arts department is more accepting of women than elsewhere on campus."

"And what is it that an archivist does?" I asked.

Melissa smiled, seemingly embarrassed by my question.

"Most of my time is spent preserving manuscripts from the horrors of climatic changes, bugs, unconscionable visitors who would see their own private collections enhanced by say, Serlio's sixteenth century architectural treatise, and of course that ancient foe we all fight a losing battle with—time."

"All things flow," I muttered. "Nothing abides."

"Heraclitus, Mr. January?"

*"New York Times* crossword puzzle," I said. "*Abides* was the six-letter word missing from the quote cited."

Melissa giggled, a childlike sound that recalled for me that other Melissa, the girl from almost six years past, when we were both different people, younger: Melissa, more naïve; me, less cynical. To prevent her from taking advantage of the lull in our conversation, I asked another question.

"Do you plan on following in your father's footsteps?"

"It was a childhood fantasy," she said. "Then, when Margarete Bieber fled Germany and became an Associate Professor at Columbia, it became an ambition. I idolized Doctor Bieber—not only for her love of fine arts, but for the places she had been, what she'd seen. She never let her womanhood stand in the way of her achievements. But the war changed everything. Now I'm afraid it's just a dream."

I knew many people who could subsist on dreams, living day-to-day on the hope for a better tomorrow; but I couldn't believe Melissa MacIntyre was one of them.

"So how has all this," I said to control the conversation, "prevented you from finding a marriage partner?"

Melissa laughed. "The fine arts department is *not* well suited for what I'm looking for."

"I would've thought it ideally suited. Chock full of well educated young men, all sharing your passion for art."

"The fine arts department, Mr. January, is filled with stuffy old men who refuse to give credence to a woman whose ambition was at one time to see her own research published."

"What of this Bieber?"

"That's different. Not that her addition to the staff wasn't met with some obstruction. But mostly they view her as a colleague. After all, she had already established herself. Look at the work she did at Kassel," she explained discursively, as if I were a colleague in possession of the knowledge of Bieber's efforts to separate statues that had been improperly restored during the seventeenth , eighteenth and nineteenth centuries. "By the time she finished, they very nearly doubled the number of display pieces. Even those that had been reduced to a mere remnant of their former self now find themselves in possession of the beauty originally intended by their creators. No, I'm afraid," she said, finding her way back from the digression she had taken, "their only interest in me is what I can do to help them further their own careers, which consists primarily of the more mundane aspects of research and wading through worthless donations."

"Patience and persistence, Miss MacIntyre," I said. "Perhaps in time—"

"Of those two virtues, I'm afraid I possess very little of either."

"What a shame then, that you would allow the very thing you say Bieber never allowed to stand in her way to bar you from attaining your life's ambition." From the look on her face, I realized Melissa had never viewed her inability to acquire her goal from the perspective I'd just brought to light.

Melissa looked down at her hands, which lay on her lap, seemingly unable to meet my, in her mind, judgmental gaze.

"Anyway," I continued, "there must be some young men among the student body whom you would find to your liking."

Melissa laughed, grateful for the diversion from a truth she could not discredit to one she could. "Enrollment was down during the war," she said in jest, but I suspected her humor was intended to cover up what was really an excuse.

"I'm sure it's rebounded by now."

"They're just *boys,"* she contended, and something in the way she was now looking at me convinced me she was about to plunge the conversation into uncharted waters.

"You never mention your mother," I said before she could.

"My mother died during childbirth," she answered, matter-of-fact.

"I'm sorry."

"Don't be. It would've been different had I known her, but it was in giving me life that she died." Melissa looked pensive, as if she were considering what she might've missed by not having a mother.

My discomfort grew in direct proportion with the prolonged silence, so I again changed topics—to the only other commonage we shared.

"What about your brother? Where do his interests lie?"

"My brother and I were never really close," she said, disappointed that she hadn't seized the moment to take control of our conversation.

"Really?" I said, recalling the scene from Minton's.

"Although," Melissa answered, as if she were privy to the same recollection, "he *is* very protective of me. We're different as night from day. While my love is for knowledge and its pursuit, Benjamin's nature is more suited for business."

"Business," I mused aloud. I equated business with the pursuit of money, money with power. And money, when enough of it was accumulated, more often than not corrupted the power it spawned.

"He became involved in real estate."

I concluded I'd been right about Benjamin Junior, and as a result of those first impressions, I resolved to continue to be wary of him in the future.

"The war was very hard on his business ventures, but he's very astute—he had to be. Columbia eventually declared my father a casualty of the war in Europe. My salary is meager at best, so without the income Benjamin generated, we surely would've lost our home in Gramercy Park."

"Didn't your father have insurance?"

"Certainly, but I forbade Benjamin from cashing it in. I refused to believe my father dead, and now of course I'm glad we didn't."

Her tone once again betrayed the great love she felt for her father; nor was she able to hide the expectancy of being reunited with him after six years.

Had I been too harsh in my assessment of her intentions? Could I be mistaken about there being something more than just her desire to see her father returned home safe and sound after his long absence? Despite Benjamin Junior's bizarre behavior that long ago night at Minton's, I really had no hard evidence suggesting anything iniquitous was at stake. Just a gut feeling.

*Predicated,* I reminded myself, *upon two mysterious letters and a third correspondence, seemingly directed at me.* Were *the contents of those first two envelopes switched?* I asked myself yet again. *If so, why? And if not?*

Stir in the mysterious cube we had in our possession and I couldn't disavow the potential for a recipe guaranteed to leave behind a whale of a bellyache.

Yet I judged Melissa would not allow her father to take a backseat to any man. So it would be best, at this juncture, to continue to assume those intentions, whatever they might be and however much they might encompass, were entirely self-serving, and that she cared little about the risks others, namely Lance and me, would be taking on her behalf.

I'd waited too long to phrase my next question. Now it was Melissa's turn.

"But enough about me," she said as a preface. "What about you? And don't give me that 'What about little ol' me?' look, Joe January. You know what I'm talking about—I know virtually nothing about you."

"You know all you need to know, considering I'm in your employ."

I couldn't deny, although I would've had I been asked, that I enjoyed hearing her say my name. I imagined her whispering it into my ear as I ran my hands all over her naked body and blushed at the eroticism of the image I couldn't refrain from conjuring up, and hoped that Melissa mistook my misplaced passion for anger, my remark as reprobation.

"I'm sorry," she said. "I know I'm paying you, but I fail to see what that has to do with making small talk."

"This is business," I said.

"Yes, I know, you prefer keeping business separate from pleasure, you've said that before. But you didn't always feel that way."

That she remembered my flirtation so many years later flattered me, that she'd kept alive the memory of my comments on her behalf as well as an image of what might have transpired between us … but that was my ego inflating.

"That was a long time ago," I said.

"Can you deny you're not attracted to me, or has your taste changed so drastically over the years?"

"I'm attracted to a lot of women, Miss MacIntyre," I said. I was surprised by her straightforwardness, but able to hide it.

"Yes, so I've seen."

Her statement was an accusation, one from which I refused to back down; to do so would be to expose weakness. I said nothing in my defense, choosing instead to fortify that defense with a reluctance to look away.

"And from what I've seen, you pursue with diligence that which attracts you."

No denial.

"So what is it that keeps you at bay?" she murmured to herself. Then, to me she affirmed, "You're motivated by pleasure—your own, specifically—so surely your distrust of me has nothing to do with it."

I laughed. "Nice to see you think so highly of me."

"But you don't deny it," she alleged.

"No, I won't deny it. But I also know your type, Miss

MacIntyre. If I weren't such a poseur to you, I'd venture that your interest in me would be strictly professional."

"Poseur? I'm afraid I don't follow you."

"Don't deny it, Miss MacIntyre," I said, borrowing her allegation of a moment ago. "I perplex you. To you I'm a puzzle. You accuse me of being motivated by pleasure, a charge I won't contradict. So why do I remain unaffected by your charm? I'd guess you're used to having your own way. I think you're a user, and that you think that by pushing the right buttons you can control and manipulate me to your own ends. Well I have news for you. I can't be controlled, nor will I allow anyone, including you, to manipulate me."

"It's nice to see you think so highly of *me,* Mr. January."

"Don't take it personally, Miss MacIntyre. I've met plenty of others, men and women alike, with your penchant for vanity. But let me tell you, the only reason I'm in on this is Lance."

"Lance?"

"That's right. If I had walked out of The Famous Door last night, Lance would've taken it upon himself to help you find your missing father and brother. That's the way he is. As far as I'm concerned, he's far too trusting. But in spite of that flaw, I think far too highly of him to allow him to get in over his head in something that might get him hurt."

"You and Lance go way back, don't you?"

I nearly sneered—to me the obviousness of her query was affected. Surely our friendship was unmistakable.

"Yes, we do," I said. "And let me make it clear to you, I have no intention of competing against him for your affections. He's sweet on you, Miss MacIntyre—no, don't deny you haven't noticed. There are some things a woman doesn't miss, and a man's attraction to her is one of them. Lance has been disappointed once already, so all I ask is that you don't mislead him."

"I have no idea—"

I waved her off; I'd heard that denial far too many times today.

"Have it your way, Miss MacIntyre. Just don't be too

surprised when it all blows up in your face."

# Chapter Eight

"Have you ever been in love?" Melissa asked.

*My god, she changes gears smoothly,* I thought. *Too smoothly.*

"I suspect you've had many lovers," she continued before I could reply. "But have you ever been *in* love?"

"You know it's funny," I said. "You can ask a hundred people to define what love means to them and no two answers will differ all that much. Every answer will evince ideas about chemistry, butterflies in the stomach, and sex appeal—all things purely physical."

"That shouldn't surprise *you,"* Melissa said with a laugh.

"It doesn't. But the one element they share in lacking does."

"And what might that be?"

"Obligation." I watched Melissa's eyebrows rise.

"Obligation, Mr. January? As in, 'I'll do something for you, but only in return for something you've done for me?'"

"No," I said. "An obligation born of a commitment. A commitment given freely, born of a want not a need. The obligation is a product of that commitment, the result of years—a lifetime of years—that breeds a familiarity that no wrinkling of the skin or graying of the hair, no sickness or disease can weaken."

My response was the only response that could have astonished Melissa since it was the one response, if she were capable of conceiving it herself, she least expected.

"What about trust?" Melissa asked.

"You mean between a man and a woman?" I didn't know whether Melissa was referring to my own personal distrust of her or the general trust that should exist between couples pledged to one another but most often does not; yet it didn't matter, for my opinion on that subject was the same.

"Yes."

"Trust is earned, not given unconditionally."

"I always trust," Melissa said, "until the person proves

untrustworthy."

"Yes, I suppose there are some people who trust that way," I said. Then, with a shake of my head, I added, "but blind trust, trusting in someone's trustworthiness, is at best naïve, at worst, foolish."

"So you believe trust to be a flaw."

"Trust in itself is not, but a willingness to trust without limits or conditions, as Lance is inclined to do, is."

"From what I've seen, you seem to trust your lovers, and potential lovers, without provisions."

"You're wrong, Miss MacIntyre." I didn't miss her advertence to Peg. "My trust in my lovers is that they place no expectations upon me."

"A provision easily spotted."

"It requires no special talent, just a little practice in the art of observation."

"You seem to hold no hoops out for them to jump through."

"No, I don't. Just so long as they are of a certain type and temperament. And might I point out that you're mistaken in putting yourself in their company."

"What a pity," Melissa said. To me her statement sounded somewhat pretentious. "What about Lance?"

"What about him?"

"Has he ever been in love?"

"He thinks he has," I said. Melissa nodded to show she understood; I went on. "Don't get me wrong, Miss MacIntyre. Lance has a heart of gold and a lot to offer the right woman. It's just that he …" I trailed off.

"Has yet to meet the right woman."

"Just about any woman is the right woman for Lance, that's his problem. Like most men, he responds to sex appeal, which he misinterprets as love."

"Why is that a problem for Lance and not for you?"

"Lance's problem lies with his willingness to give too much of himself too quickly."

"It's rare that two people move through the stages of a courtship at the same pace."

I waved aside her observation. "His expectations are too high, and he believes himself capable of loving enough for two—until the woman he's set his sights on comes to recognize the value of his worth."

"Is that a fault, Mr. January?"

"Perhaps not a fault, but it is a risk."

"A risk you've never taken?"

"I've seen firsthand the results that kind of risk can inflict."

"Lance? He seems to be rebounding quite nicely."

"Rebounding is right, Miss MacIntyre, and I have you to thank for that. But as I said earlier, all I ask is that you not mislead him. A second disappointment so soon wouldn't be good for him. And no, I wasn't referring to Lance. It's something I don't care to discuss."

"Because you're in my employ?"

"It's something I've never discussed with anyone," I said. "Not even with Lance. Let's just say I don't believe that love exists, not within the parameters I defined earlier."

"Perhaps you haven't been looking in the right places."

"Perhaps I don't wish to."

"I find that surprising for someone with your depth of character."

"Be careful," I warned. "You're setting me up on a pedestal—one from which I'm destined to tumble."

Melissa ignored my self-deprecation: "Why wouldn't you want to?"

"What, fall from your pedestal?" I said, knowing all too well where her question was leading. Melissa ignored my humor.

"But the rewards are—"

"The inevitable disappointment is far greater."

"Isn't it better to have loved and lost than never to have loved at all?"

"A poet's deception. In my own way, Miss MacIntyre, I *have* loved many women. Yet never have I suffered the disappointment of what Tennyson terms loss. Nor have any of my lovers suffered from that infirmity. Like mine their expectations are minimal, save for the physical. With minimal expectations come no conditions. And conditions are what spell doom in any man-woman relationship."

"But no conditions is in itself conditional."

"Semantics," I said, dismissing her assessment of my principle.

"So you don't believe in unconditional love?" She seemed unable to hide her disappointment.

I felt relief. Perhaps I had finally toppled from the proverbial pedestal, and now she would come to accept our business arrangement.

"I would rather place my trust in non-conditional love," I said. "I won't deny that in not pursuing love to the degree you suggest I may have missed out on something. But I would be quick to add that I've found happiness with the life I've chosen, and that's enough for me."

"Your pursuit of variety would seem to indicate otherwise."

"Variety is the spice of life."

"I suspect, Mr. January, that you hunger for something more but choose to ignore that hunger, preferring instead to hide your loneliness behind solitude bred by diversity."

"And what do you know of loneliness, Miss MacIntyre? Not the definition but the authenticity of its pain? The most wretched outcast can choose to hide his aloneness behind a façade, or he can bare his exigency for all the world to see. If what you say is true, that I'm hiding my loneliness behind an assortment of sexual encounters—which I beg to disagree—then that is my choice. Not the best choice perhaps by your standards, but the choice *is* mine to make. As for my hunger, that is purely biological, and like all hungers, it can be easily surfeited."

Melissa sat staring at me, beaten by my logic and unable to refute the strength behind my truth. I couldn't help but be touched by the disappointment on her face—I would've guessed her incapable of disappointment—but was unable to respond to it, at least not in the manner in which she would wish, because I was incapable of responding in that way. I wanted to ask her if she had ever been made love to, but my desire to maintain a business relationship, if only for Lance's sake, prohibited such forthrightness. To ease her disenchantment, I made her own earlier question my own.

"Have *you* ever been in love, Miss MacIntyre?"

Melissa smiled weakly, perhaps wanting to discern something more in my query than what had been intended.

"Sadly, no, I haven't," she said, and without understanding why, I believed her. Yet my acceptance of her admission surprised me, for her answer—the only one that could educe sympathy points—was certainly the answer I would've expected from a woman with an agenda. "I know you don't believe me," she continued, blushing, and the answer to my other question, the one I'd been unable to ask, was answered.

"Perhaps you haven't been looking in the right places."

Melissa shook her head, chewed her lip. "No, I'm afraid you may be right, Mr. January. I may have to reassess my belief in the legitimacy of what I seek."

"And just what is it you seek?"

"Everything you defined earlier as love—commitment and obligation, yes. But I want the excitement of being *in* love, too. The butterflies, the chemistry. I want it all and more."

"A tall order to be sure," I said. "But just because I've chosen a different credo doesn't mean I'm right and you're wrong. Perhaps what I define as love doesn't exist for me simply because, in my disbelief, I choose not to seek for it; whereas your search will result in the discovery of that which you believe exists."

"Believing in something does not make it so. Perhaps I seek the notorious needle in the haystack."

In her sudden cynicism, I found her statement strangely reminiscent of something I would say.

"Never underestimate the power of your convictions." While in my optimism, I sounded remarkably like Melissa. Recognizing the levity of our sudden role reversals, I managed to keep my amusement to myself.

"If you mean I should take solace behind the pretense of a false belief, well then I would prefer the life of a spinster."

"That wouldn't become you." My compliment broke her from her musing; she brightened, a mischievous glint replaced the dolor that had a moment ago resided in her eyes.

"Are you flirting with me, Mr. January?"

Infinitely more comfortable and confident conducting myself in the presence of women who desired the simple physicality my company afforded, I wasn't used to women pursuing me on the presumption of such high suppositions.

"Miss MacIntyre," I said. "Surely you must know you cannot hope that I will meet your lofty expectations?"

"And what of Lindy's expectations?" Melissa countered. "You must know that one day she will come to desire more than you are willing to give."

I was taken aback by Melissa's candidness as well as her perceptivity; but then I cursed myself. I couldn't attribute Melissa's statement to a guess. I had allowed her to see, not only through my informality and transparency but by a show of ego as well, what was going on between my gal Friday and me. I couldn't deny the accuracy of Melissa's charge. That Lindy would someday come to demand more from me was something I had already determined.

"Perhaps," I acknowledged because I had waited too long to deny her indictment, and to do so now would only avow that I was lying.

"What will you do then, fire her?"

I could only look away; it was rare that I found myself at a loss for words.

"You must know she cares for you very much."

I glared at Melissa. *As if I don't know,* I thought. It had been a mistake hiring Lindy. Certainly she took her job seriously, was good at it, did everything I asked of her—and more. But I hadn't hired her for just her clerical skills. I hired her as much if not more for her physical appeal—the soft, wavy dark hair that complimented her dark eyes, her smooth complexion and dimpled chin, her hourglass figure with its narrow waist, and especially for her shapely legs.

I brushed aside the erotic image.

It hadn't taken me long to discover that Lindy's sweet disposition, a contrast to my own volatile nature, was also an attraction I couldn't deny. Yet I knew her to be the type of woman whose expectations would one day come to exceed my willingness for which to provide.

But since I was a man ruled by my physical need, when the opportunity presented itself I could only take advantage—of the opportunity, not Lindy.

Shy though she was, Lindy seemed to know instinctively what pleased me; while I, my own pleasure stemming from that which I gave, tried to convince myself as I lay spent still inside of her, that it was indeed only my own pleasure I had sought.

Unconvinced and confused by my conflict, I knew then that what was for me the simple act of copulation would be infinitely more meaningful for her.

From that moment our working relationship changed. I found I couldn't fire Lindy any more than I could stop myself from enjoying the comfort I found within her embrace. So I returned, time and again, to the warmth that was more than just her body, and cursed myself for my honesty. That I enjoyed the pleasures of others I did not keep secret; my only consolation was that Lindy's choice in sharing me with those others was her choice.

Yet I cursed myself for my *dis*honesty as well—that I could not admit, to myself as well as to Lindy, what she had come to mean to me.

I believed that women, like men, pursue for the sake of pursuit. Take Miss MacIntyre. The more I retreated, the further she advanced. But I was convinced that should she ever win the prize, it would be a prize she no longer coveted.

Of course, I trusted Lindy. I just didn't know it. I'd always found her to be open, honest and trustworthy. Perhaps it was me I couldn't trust.

"... It would seem, Mr. January, whether you choose to acknowledge it or not, that you have found your needle in a haystack."

"Why trouble yourself to look for the needle," I said, more for my own benefit than Melissa's, "when you can content yourself with the whole haystack?"

Melissa looked appalled. "How can you be so dishonest?"

"Dishonest? I've been nothing but honest with you."

"Not me—"

"Lindy, too. She knows I have others."

"I was referring to you," Melissa said softly.

I only stared, astonished that my well-placed veneer had so easily been pierced. I waited a moment before saying, "If what you say is true, then who, other than myself, does my dishonesty harm? Would you rather I was dishonest with you? Tell you what I think you want to hear in order to control and manipulate you, to take advantage of you?"

"Of course not, but don't you see?" When she saw I didn't, she went on. "Hasn't anyone ever told you that they loved you?"

"Never," I replied without hesitation. My tone betrayed neither disappointment nor suggestion of loss. "But I've had many women tell me that they wanted me."

"And so you give yourself to them." Melissa's simple statement.

"Far be it for me to disappoint." My simpler philosophy.

Melissa refused to be put off by the size of my ego. "If you've never heard those three words—"

"Easily said, more easily taken back." No cynicism, just fact.

Melissa found her youthful romantic ideality no match for my pragmatism; yet it seemed she also found herself unwilling to concede her argument.

"A few minutes ago," she said, "I would've given anything to have you look at me the way you looked at that woman behind the counter."

I turned away. "Well now you know," I muttered.

"But I know now," she continued, ignoring my self-chastisement, "that Lindy is the one to be envied."

I looked back at her to discover I had not fallen from her pedestal; quite the contrary, I saw my value had somehow risen.

"I've no doubt that when you two are alone you look at her the same way you looked at that woman. Certainly you've slept with more attractive women than Lindy," she said. "No doubt some of them have been more experienced. Yet it *is* to Lindy you keep returning. That she allows you to indicates she sees in you what I see."

"And what might that be?" I said, daring her to tell me something I could refute.

"You don't need me to tell you. And your denial of its existence doesn't mean that it doesn't."

# Part Two

# Chapter Nine

Lance applied full throttle; I felt my weight thrust back against my seat, listened to the engines whine their protest, thought about voicing my own, and watched the trees at the far end of the runway hurtle menacingly towards us.

Moments later those same trees, which moments ago had appeared so tiny with distance, seemed to dominate the field of view allowed by the Stinson T's windscreen. Lance would tell us later that it had been necessary to use every available foot of the short runway because of the full load of fuel we were carrying. "Best to exceed our takeoff speed by five or six miles per hour," he would say, "to ensure enough lift, otherwise there wouldn't have been enough runway left to bring us to a stop." What had been offered as assurance carried little as far as I was concerned.

I held my breath as Lance pulled back on the yoke and felt my stomach sink to a place just above my testicles—a feeling so reminiscent of an elevator ride, yet somehow different.

I watched the horizon of trees disappear below the horizon of the instrument panel, to be replaced by blue sky and white clouds—"cumulus clouds," Lance later identified, explaining that they were formed by the ascent of thermally unstable air masses. I fixated on that word, *unstable,* and wondered how it might affect our flight.

The ache in my hands reminded me just how tightly I was clutching the armrests of my seat. Remembering to exhale, I glanced down, forced myself to relax my grip, and watched the color return to my hands.

*So that's where the term* white knuckling it *comes from,* I thought.

I removed my hands from the armrests and placed them, now balled into fists, onto my knees.

Looking out the window to my right, I noted the rapidly receding ground and tried to come to terms with the fact that the physics of flight—our forward momentum against an invisible gas I could neither see nor touch—was what kept us aloft.

I became aware of a distinct pressure building against my diaphragm and remembered to exhale. With a conscious effort I released my aching hands from their fetal-like positions and pressed them, palms down, against my thighs.

I felt helpless, and helplessness was a feeling I despised. I detested entrusting my safety to someone else, even if I'd known that someone else for nearly half my life. I recalled Lance's earlier accusation of my distrust of women. Never had it been more apparent than at that moment that trust was a term I couldn't associate with another human being. I trusted only myself. If someone else insisted on driving, I would opt to walk or take the tunnel train, and I always questioned the resources of any self-professed authority. And why not? It had served me well over the years.

Lance had just finished receiving final instructions from the control tower and I felt his gaze on me.

"What's the matter, Joe? You look white as a ghost." He was enjoying every moment of my discomfiture.

"Unnatural way to travel," I protested meekly. My ears were ringing and I felt the onset of airsickness. I began to wish I'd taken Lance's advice to take the dimenhydrinate.

"How are you doing back there, Melissa?" Lance called over his shoulder. This was her maiden voyage, too.

I heard her voice as from a distance, yet it seemed loud in my left ear as she competed against the roar of the engines, as they in turn competed against the irresistible lure of gravity. "This is *so* exhilarating!"

"Now you know what it's like to be a bird—to feel the freedom of its flight. There's no experience like it."

"Let's just hope we don't experience what it's like for a rock to plummet to the ground from ten thousand feet," I said, closing my eyes against the onslaught of nausea.

Nearly seven hours later, Lance banked the Stinson T steeply to the right and began our descent, affording me my first glimpse of the Indianapolis Motor Speedway. Even from an altitude of several hundred feet the sight was impressive. I watched, fascinated, my ears popping, as race cars circled the track, practicing for the race which was now just days away. From this altitude they seemed to crawl at a snail's pace, but I suspected, although I was no motor sports enthusiast, that their speeds must be well in excess of a hundred-fifty miles per hour.

Lance approached the infield from the north end of the track, into the wind. I reminded myself to inhale as we cleared the trees on the inside of the track's apron, but was unable to talk myself into releasing my grip on the armrests until after we'd touched down—a rough landing made rougher still by the unevenness of the ground.

"There, that wasn't so bad, was it?" Lance asked me as we taxied back toward the north end of the track, where a number of other aircraft were parked. "You never even threw up."

From behind me I heard Melissa titter.

"Very funny," was all I said, fumbling with my seatbelt. I wasn't about to concede just how close I'd come.

Fighting airsickness the entire trip, I'd been silent and only dimly aware of Lance and Melissa's conversation: Lance again boasting of his flying heroics, no doubt embellished for the sake of impressing Melissa; while Melissa talked shyly of her work at Columbia. She had promised not to mislead Lance, and while she had done nothing to encourage his flirtations, she certainly had done nothing to *dis*courage him either, further fueling my suspicions over her intentions.

I had never considered myself claustrophobic, but I was scrambling for the exit before Lance finished setting the brakes and shutting down the engines.

Opening the door, I was at once greeted by a ground attendant wearing a pith helmet. The man was short and perspiring heavily despite the mild seventy-degree temperature. I concluded the man's bulk was at least in part responsible for the rivulets of sweat coursing their way down his sun-browned face, as well as for the dark stains under his arms. The man adjusted an armband on his left arm—I saw the letters *IMS* and, as the man removed his hand, the word *Security* embroidered on the band—and then proceeded to hike up his pants in a gesture I took as one of self-importance.

"Here for the big race?" he asked. He removed the helmet and began wiping the sweat from his bald pate with a dirty black and white checkered handkerchief. I took note of the dead peeling skin and the raw pink beneath it and wondered how, despite the helmet, he'd managed to get so sunburned.

"Nope," I answered as I jumped from the Stinson, my own hat in hand. I was glad to have my feet firmly on the ground again. The drone of a finely tuned racing engine, its revs well into its power range, sounded from off in the distance somewhere behind me. "We're here on business."

"There's a five-dollar landing fee," the attendant said, stuffing the handkerchief into a pocket on the backside of his pants, "and it's five dollars a day to park," he added as he hitched at his pants again.

*God bless capitalism,* I thought as I donned my hat.

"Don't look at me," I told him. "I'm not funding this trip, she is." I threw a thumb over my shoulder at Melissa, who was just then making her way from the door of the Stinson.

"Ma'am?" the attendant asked as Melissa swung around. He had doffed his helmet again, this time in deference to her gender.

"I beg your pardon?"

"How long will you be staying?"

Melissa looked at me and I told her we'd be here at least overnight and to pay the man ten dollars.

The sound of the engine had moved to my right, its high performance pitch wavering as the driver backed off the accelerator, and advanced to somewhere in front of me. I caught a glimpse of a white car with red and blue trim as it came into view from beyond a thicket of trees before disappearing again, this time behind a row of outhouses, as it rounded one of the broad sweeping turns I'd seen from the air.

"You sure you won't be staying for the race?" the attendant asked. The helmet had been replaced yet again.

I wasn't used to Hoosier hospitality. Having grown up in the Bronx and living my whole life in New York, the attendant sounded as if he were trying to sell a bill of fare in which we weren't interested.

"Why not?" Lance called from the fuselage, his bulk framed by the open door. "They say it's quite a spectacle. We're here and with your aversion to flying, Joe, there's no telling when we'll have another opportunity."

"This isn't a vacation, Lance," I said. I thumbed the lip of my fedora before adding, "Besides, I thought you wanted to keep Miss MacIntyre's expenses down." Of the attendant, I asked, "How do we get to The Severin Hotel from here?"

"By train," the fat man answered cheerfully, happy to be of assistance.

"So much for walking distance," I muttered, darting a glance at Lance. "Where do we board?" I asked, suddenly impatient for a shower and a meal.

"You just take the bridge over the back-stretch over there," the attendant said, pointing. "Head south and follow the perimeter of the track around to the main gate. From there the train'll take you to Union Station, downtown. The Severin's right across the street."

"Thanks," I said. "Lance, make arrangements to have that thing gassed. And make sure it's got plenty of oil, too," I added as an afterthought. "Toss down my bag. I'll head over to the hotel and get us checked in. You think you can find your way or should I send a bellhop for you?"

"Don't you worry about me."

"I hope I won't have to. Miss MacIntyre—"

"I'm going with you," she said.

"Fine," I said, noting both Melissa's surprise as well as Lance's disappointment. "Just make sure you leave Lance enough cash to pay for service of his airplane."

"Aircraft."

I ignored Lance's rebuke, which was just as well since he'd disappeared into the tail section of the Stinson, where our baggage was secured. I reached inside my jacket for my cigarettes.

"Who's this year's favorite to win?" I asked the attendant once I'd finished lighting up. The attendant had just finished exchanging a ten-dollar bill along with a receipt for the twenty Melissa had offered him. I couldn't have cared less who the favorite to win the race was, but I thought it best we maintain a façade of being enthusiasts—which I guessed most of the patrons of The Severin would be—and the best way to maintain that façade was by being able to namedrop.

"Well," the attendant said, giving his pants another tug, happy to have been asked his opinion. I saw the waistband of the attendant's pants was soiled where he habitually hoisted them up whenever they threatened to slip down and wondered at his choice to dress sans a belt or suspenders. "Ted Horn's on the pole at a hundred-twenty-six plus. He's driving the car Shaw won with back in '39 and '40. New equipment's at a premium due to the war, doncha know? Bergere's Novi's been quick in practice, but its reliability is doubtful. Rex Mays is a threat, if he can keep it off the fence. Rose is the sentimental favorite to win his first 500 and he's starting third. Who do you like, mister?"

"Well," I said in thoughtful imitation of the attendant. "Rose gets more out of his cars than most, and he's patient, too. Remember, the 500's a marathon, not a sprint race."

"Mister, I like the way you think."

I caught my overnight bag as Lance tossed it from the Stinson.

"Go ahead and toss down Miss MacIntyre's, too," I said.

"I'll bring hers."

"She's not paying us to carry her bag, Lance. She'll do fine unless she over-packed."

"It's all right, Lance," Melissa said, cutting off any potential debate, "I can carry it."

Lance eyed me with disgust as he handed Melissa her

suitcase. I took another drag from my cigarette.

The sound of the engine, on which I'd been keeping an ear, was fast approaching again on my left. This time I caught sight of the car about a third of the way down the long straightaway. I had no idea how fast the cars could negotiate the turns, but if the average speed around the circuit was over a hundred-twenty-six miles per hour, as the attendant had just informed me, then the speeds down the straightaways must be a hundred-sixty or more. The engine wavered, signaling that the driver had lifted his foot from the accelerator prior to entering the turn; I wondered if the driver had been perhaps a bit premature, that a truly fearless driver would drive deeper into the turn before backing off the gas pedal.

I turned to see Melissa hand Lance another C-note and, recalling last night, wondered how many more her purse might yet contain. Somehow I'd known that money would not be an issue; yet a part of me had hoped Melissa would decline my services once I'd revealed my terms. But she had not, and I recalled her statement that were it not for her brother's business dealings they might have lost their home in Gramercy Park.

"Real estate," I muttered to myself. "I'm in the wrong business."

"You can arrange to get your bird gassed up over there, behind the pagoda," the attendant told Lance. He was pointing at a ramshackle wooden structure about a half-mile distant, its direction opposite from that which Melissa and I would be taking. Its architectural design, rooted in Chinese origins, looked to be out of place in rural Midwestern America.

"Great," Lance said. "Which way was that train?"

"Southwest corner," the attendant said.

"Southwest is that way," I added, pointing.

"I *know* which way southwest is," Lance said.

"Let's go, Miss MacIntyre," I said, checking my watch. "I've got to check in with Lindy."

"What time is it here, anyway?" Lance asked the

attendant, checking his watch in a gambit to show me up.

"Nearly six o'clock."

"Dinner's at eight," I said, shouldering my overnight bag. "Eastern Time. Don't be late."

I didn't wait for a response, and as I made my way past Melissa, I noted discreetly that it was an effort for her to keep a straight face. Nevertheless I was grateful for her success. I had a tendency to speak sometimes before thinking, and I would've felt bad for Lance had his new ideal failed to keep from laughing.

# Chapter Ten

"Please, slow down," Melissa said once she'd caught up with me. I slowed my pace without apology.

After nearly a minute of silence, Melissa said, "I had no idea you knew so much about this race."

"I don't," I said around the cigarette clenched between my lips.

"What you told that man back there about that driver."

"Rose." I took a drag from the cigarette and exhaled.

"You mean you just made that up?"

"Not made up, Miss MacIntyre. He provided me with certain information. I took that information, chewed on it, ingested it, and then spat it back at him. In a sense I just regurgitated the same information he'd given me."

"And that's what you came up with?" she asked.

I shrugged. "He told me Rose was the sentimental favorite. From that I figured this Rose has been around a while—longevity tends to breed sentimentality. That he was patient I deduced from his longevity. In a sport that's hard on mortality, he must be very good or very patient—probably both since he's starting third. Drivers who aren't very good probably aren't very patient. They usually end up in the hospital, or in the cemetery. That bit about the race being a marathon, you have to finish in order to win, and to finish five hundred miles you have to pace yourself. That's just logic, pure and simple."

"But you made it all sound so believable," she said.

"What's to disbelieve?"

We continued walking. I wasn't nearly as uncomfortable with the silence as Melissa, since another half-minute later she ventured to ask, "Are you two always so competitive?"

"Lance and me?" I pulled one last drag from my cigarette.

"Yes."

"Nearly," I replied. The one-word answer was a sort of exclamation point as I flicked away my cigarette butt.

Melissa waited for me to elucidate; when I didn't, she went on. "Well I'd sure hate to see what might happen if the two of you *were* competing for me."

"That would never happen."

"Really? Is that by agreement, or is it part of the Marquis of Queensbury rules?"

"Neither," I said, refusing to bite. I adjusted my hat, thumbed its lip, and added, "There was a time when perhaps we would have. But as we've gotten older our tastes where women are concerned have gone in different directions."

Melissa laughed. When I failed to prompt her for an explanation, she took the initiative and volunteered one.

"I haven't noticed that men's taste in women varies all that much. Aside from hair color, I'd say all men covet someone slender and pretty."

"Ah, but that's where you're wrong, Miss MacIntyre. In my youth I had a buddy who, whenever we went out drinking, always went for the homely, overweight dame. While the rest of us were competing for the slender, pretty type, and often coming up empty, he was almost always assured of scoring."

Melissa laughed again. "Somehow I can't picture you coming up empty, Mr. January." Apparently, since my tale of the bluebird on the woman's breast, she couldn't be at all certain just how much truth any of my stories might contain.

"I was young and—"

"Inexperienced?"

"Hadn't yet learned how to read women."

"You make it sound like a science."

"Not a science," I said with a quick shake of my head. "But it *is* a knack."

"Why do you insist on turning something so simple—something that should come easily and naturally—into something so complex?"

"If it's so simple, Miss MacIntyre, then why have you thus far been unsuccessful in obtaining your heart's desire?" When she couldn't respond I went on. "What I seek in my relations *is* simple."

"Simple complication."

"If by that you mean uncomplicated, then, yes. But even finding something simple requires a certain percipience on the part of the seeker."

"So you admit to being a game player."

"We all play games, Miss MacIntyre. Even you do."

Melissa seemed surprised that I hadn't denied her accusation; in return she seemed to accept my own.

"We have to, in order to get what we want. But getting back to my friend—"

"I think your friend either lacked the confidence to compete with the likes of you, or else he was smarter."

"You mean because the homely type, not having to fend off the advances of the masses, would be less likely to shoot down the overtures of the occasional admirer?"

"Exactly."

"Whether there's truth to that I won't argue. But as I started to say, he was attracted to a certain type of woman I, on my worst day, would never consider pursuing."

"Because she was overweight and not very pretty?"

"It could just as easily have been that she was too short or had the wrong hair or eye color, or that her nose was too big, or a hundred other reasons."

"All of them physical, no doubt," Melissa said. "Maybe your friend had lower standards. Was he very handsome?"

"No less handsome than Lance."

"I think Lance is very handsome," Melissa said, not because she thought so, or so I reasoned, but instead to get a reaction from me, which I was only too happy to withhold; I sensed her disappointment.

"Why is it so difficult for you to comprehend that some men resort to dishonesty rather than spend the night alone?" I said.

"Dishonest? To whom, the woman they've chosen?"

"Themselves, for lowering their standards. Although now that you mention it, I imagine the dame probably lies to herself, too, allowing herself to imagine herself desirable. A ruse to which I can't conceive you having to resort."

"Are you complimenting me, Mr. January?"

"Just making a comparison."

"Why can't you admit that you find me attractive?"

"Because I don't. At least not for the reasons you would want to hear."

"And what woman doesn't want to be physically attractive to her man?"

I suddenly realized that Melissa had taken control of this debate and was relishing the upper hand she had gained. I decided I didn't care for the direction she was going. It was time to wrest back control and put this discussion back on course in a direction with which I'd be far more comfortable.

I noticed that with my growing frustration our pace had picked up. With a conscious effort I slowed to one that Melissa, in her heels, would be able to more easily match. I took a deep breath and waited for the sound of the engine, much louder now due to our closer proximity to the track's edge, to subside as it sped past us before beginning anew.

"Look, about last night."

"I know all about last night," Melissa said in a tone that revealed she had spent an inordinate amount of time in speculation. Certainly Lindy wouldn't have filled her in about our plan to fix up Lance. "You don't really think Lance would've gone for Ginger had I not been there?"

"I had hoped he would, yes."

"But he didn't and you did."

I ignored the thinly veiled accusation her second statement held. "I never expected he'd fall in love with her. She was only supposed to help him forget someone else."

"You don't forget someone you truly care for so easily."

A dozen or so steps later, Melissa offered her assessment of last night's events: "I would venture that after we left The Famous Door, you wound up with Ginger." When I didn't refute her account she went on. "I wouldn't have thought her your type."

"What do you know of my type?" I said.

"I know *I* was your type five-and-a-half years ago."

"Is that why you contacted me after all these years, Miss

MacIntyre? To renew an old acquaintance, to see if I might still be available for you?"

"Of course not," Melissa said, and then amended her answer. "Not entirely. But then, you know the reason I looked you up again. You know how I feel about my father."

"Do I?"

"You trusted me five-and-a-half years ago, why don't you trust me now?"

"I was younger then. Younger and far more trusting."

"Less cynical."

"Have it your way, Miss MacIntyre." Then, "I also had different tastes in women back then."

"I was younger then, too," she agreed, "but …" she trailed off, inferring that despite the passage of time I still held an attraction for her.

"If I were to chase you with all the vigor that Lance is showing, I suspect you would maintain yourself as unattainable."

"So you're not spurred by the chase." She spoke as if this was some sort of revelation; yet I doubted that this point had baffled her.

"That, Miss MacIntyre, is one game I don't play. There's far too much other game—no pun intended—to be had to waste my time chasing after that which doesn't wish to be caught."

"Nor do you like to be chased."

"A mutual interest," I explained, "allows me to take the initiative. A woman who continues to pursue despite my lack of interest leads me to believe she must have an agenda."

"You must be talking about me," she said.

"I will admit, Miss MacIntyre, that you are as much a poseur to me as I am to you. I don't trust you, although I can't be certain yet as to why. Maybe it's your aggression; maybe it's your brother, plain and simple. I won't deny I'm intrigued by the mystery of your missing father."

"So you *are* pursuing, if only for sake of the mystery."

"Don't read too much between the lines," I said. "Yes, there was a time when I would've been all too happy to enjoy the pleasures your body could offer me. But with you, as with all women of your type, there would've been conditions and expectations, two things I won't tolerate."

Melissa's silence indicated that my suspicions were correct: she would never concede those two issues—she would never give herself freely merely for the pleasures of the flesh.

"So you see, while it's true that every woman needs to be found desirable by her lover, it's equally true that not every woman will give herself away simply on the premise of that desirability."

"Did you want her?" Melissa asked. The sweetness of her tone seemed unaffected. "Ginger," she clarified.

"Let's just say she satisfied my need for the moment."

"Ah, yes, your insatiable appetite for the salacious."

My ego bristled, but I managed to keep my umbrage to myself. "Are you judging me, Miss MacIntyre?"

"Not at all. It's just I've never known anyone who professes to be driven solely by their needs."

"Needs are much easier to tend to," I said, "whereas wants …" I trailed off, certain that the obviousness of my comparison made unnecessary a conclusion to my rationale.

"I'm afraid I don't follow you."

"It's very simple, Miss MacIntyre. For an hour or so last night Ginger and I shared a mutual need. Neither of us *wanted* anything from the other, other than the moment. To people like us it's more important to need what we have than to have what we want. You, on the other hand, want something from me. Something I'm not able—"

"Or not willing."

"Something I'm not *able,"* I reiterated in order to assert that this was nonnegotiable, "to provide you. So you see, I equate *wants* with that which cannot be had. And no matter how much you might want something, if that something—or someone—doesn't wish to be had, well, then I'm afraid you are left merely wanting."

"And if I were to say that I needed you?"

"You cannot substitute one for the other. Besides, I

know what you want."

"Really?"

"Not by definition perhaps, but I know your type. You've admitted to me, although you may not be aware you have, that your expectations—a word that *is* interchangeable with want—far exceed those for which I'm able to provide."

Melissa thought about that for a moment, a gentle breeze cooling our faces from the warmth of the late afternoon sun, before posing her next question.

"Did she please you?" and I knew to whom she was referring. "Or did you find yourself thinking—wanting—of Lindy?"

"What happened last night and with whom is no business of yours." Because she was right, and because she was right, I could think of nothing to say to make her wrong.

Indeed, I *had* felt the culpability to which Melissa referred. I'd felt it this morning as I thought about the tears Lindy must have shed as she lay awake, waiting for sleep's mercy, haunted by images of me and the recipient of all that she desired me to lavish upon her. My remorse, I knew, had been born of the pain I had knowingly inflicted upon Lindy. I had later seen that hurt embodied in her eyes, yet had chosen to ignore it, pretending it was something else. Finally, I'd wondered at her capacity to forgive me my transgression as well as her reasons for doing so.

Melissa: "She sees in you what I see."

*Even now I'm uncertain what it was that Lindy saw in me. Perhaps it was nothing. Then again maybe it was something she only thought she saw, or worse, merely something she wished to see.*

*Wanting to do right for the clients who hired me did not make me a righteous person. Perhaps in time I'd have done right by Lindy. But that time was taken from me. From us. Perchance it's only through this regret that I feel the way I do. Had I not disappeared from her life in the manner I did, who can say what further disappointment I might have caused her? I can only speculate over how she took my sud-*

*den disappearance. Did she sense loss? Eventually she got on with her life, as I would later discover. But did she ever give any thought to me and to us throughout the remainder of her life? It pained me greatly to learn that she had.*

*It's funny, although I'm not laughing, what losing Lindy did to me. It made me realize what she meant to me. Maybe it's only a result of guilt, the product of so much that was left unsaid.*

*Guilt? Perhaps. But I don't believe that. Especially now, I'm adamant about that.*

"Forgive me, Mr. January," Melissa said. "I sometimes forget your desire to maintain a business relationship. But you must understand, just because a woman keeps secret her wants doesn't mean they don't exist."

I said nothing and was grateful for Melissa's compliance as we walked on in silence, approaching the bridge to which the attendant had directed us. The silence was now magnified by the absence of the car that had, until just a few moments ago, been buzzing in circles around us as it lapped the ribbon of brick that surrounded us. I hadn't realized, until I missed it, how much of a comfort it had been.

I strode through the lobby, past the seated man hiding suspiciously behind the evening edition of *The Indianapolis Star,* while Melissa struggled to keep pace.

*Does he actually think he's inconspicuous?* I thought, and wondered if the man behind the newspaper knew our identity, or rather Melissa's. Perhaps he'd been in touch with his New York cohort and been informed of our presumed departure. If that was so, then it was a stroke of luck that the trio he had been alerted to be on the lookout for was now a duo, although I knew I'd be a fool to assume we could function with anonymity under that presumption.

"Are you here for the big race, sir?" the desk clerk asked.

"We sure are," I lied, carefully modulating my voice to be overheard by the man with the newspaper. I was playing the part of the tourist.

"But—"

"We'll need the room through next Saturday," I said, cutting off Melissa, who looked as confused as she sounded. "Melissa here will take care of the arrangements." A glance at my watch and then, "Where can I find a phone?"

"Just the other side of the elevators, to your right, sir."

"Wait here, will you?" I said to Melissa. "I'll be only a minute."

"What about—"

"Not now," I said, heading her off, my voice a whisper. And then I was gone, precluding further protest.

Moments later, after I'd finished dialing the phone, I cast an unassuming glance in the direction of the man with the *Star.* He hadn't moved, but he *had* shifted the newspaper, still held at an unnatural angle, in an effort to keep it between himself and me.

*It's a wonder these guys were ever a threat to win the war,* I thought as I waited for the operator to put my collect call through to my office in New York.

"Hello, Joe." Lindy's voice sounded thin and hollow with distance, but I thought I heard, or rather missed hearing, something else as well.

I recalled last night, and of Melissa's question of whom I had found myself thinking while with Ginger. There was no denying it: my thoughts *had* been of Lindy. Although Ginger had taken care of my need, albeit in a somewhat less than satisfying way, I couldn't argue myself out of the truth that it had been Lindy I *wanted* beneath me. Feeling her movements against me; her soft sighs, her whimpers that I wished to hear. And so last night I had closed my eyes against the vision that was the moment, desperately wanting to *need* Ginger more than I desired Lindy.

So it was at that precise moment, nearly a day later, that I realized it had been just those thoughts and images that had moved me to an ecstasy I found, at the time, to be lacking. As a result, I knew my disappointment had been born out of a need, and yes a want, to exhaust my passion with the one woman I refused to acknowledge had come to mean so much to me. For an all too brief moment, I thought about apologizing. Not that it would have done much good since actions speak louder than words, and unlike words, once an action is taken it can never be taken back.

*Regret: unwanted companion of the aged.*

"Hello, Lindy," I said into the phone, and wondered whether she might hear something in the tone of my voice that, despite the hundreds of miles that separated us, she had never heard before. "Lindy," I said in a tone with which she would be much more familiar. "We've just checked in at The Severin. It's eight or ten miles from the track."

"So much for being within walking distance," she said, and I was dimly aware, not for the first time, of how very much alike we thought.

Freud would say we are attracted to mirror images of ourselves. If that's true, then it could also be said that I viewed myself as unattractive, for it seemed that mirror image was an attraction I continued to deny.

"I should know better than to trust Lance. I should've known the track wasn't near to downtown and had you call." It was the best I could do in terms of a compliment. "Still, it's only a minor inconvenience." A misnomer, I knew, for I'd never known an inconvenience to be minor; but as small talk went, again, it was the best I could do. "Did you call the MacIntyre residence?"

"Yes, and there was no answer."

Lindy had known when I'd asked Melissa to leave her home telephone number with her, *just in case,* what I'd expected of her. No doubt she wished there was something more in terms of results she could offer.

"That's not surprising," I said, "but don't give up. Try again in the morning."

"Who do you expect to answer?"

"I don't know, probably no one. I just don't want to leave any stone unturned."

"The father, the brother?" she offered to keep me talking, because she didn't want to hang up. Nor did I.

"Maybe. But then Miss MacIntyre left instructions for them to contact you should they arrive while we're away."

"The man in the Packard?" Lindy asked. In my mind's eye I watched Lindy watch its departure in pursuit of my Ford this morning, wondering how I would deal with its presence. I imagined her question had had to wait for the appropriate moment.

"I don't think so. If he'd wanted to prevent us from leaving New York, he would've made a move to do so. He seemed more content to tail us, hoping that maybe—and this is just conjecture on my part, assuming they haven't already found him—we'd lead him to the professor. Fortunately we got rid of him before we left the city, but I figure he's working with someone here. Assuming they've managed to tail MacIntyre this far."

I glanced out to the lobby and discovered the man with the *Star* was gone. Perhaps I'd been too suspicious, read too much into an innocent tourist bent simply on reading the evening edition of the local newspaper, but then I noticed that Melissa had left the front desk and was nowhere to be seen within the lobby. Instantly my suspicions were aroused.

"At any rate, it's my bet they'll try to pick up our trail with the hope we know something about his whereabouts."

Silence.

I didn't wish the call to end; perhaps Lindy didn't either. Yet neither did either of us know what else should or could be said to continue it.

"Lindy …"

"Yes, Joe?"

A pause and then, "I don't know what we'll turn up here. Maybe nothing. If that's the case we'll be back in New York tomorrow. No sense staying any longer than we have to." Another pause—this one much longer—and then, "And Lindy?"

"Yes, Joe?" Her words were the same, but somehow the way she said them held a different meaning.

"Stay by the phone," I said, my voice once more rife with its more traditional bluster. "Even after you've gone home. In case I need to get in touch with you." Because it comforted me to know she would be but a phone call away.

After I hung up I realized how easy it would have been to substitute the word *need* with *want.*

# Chapter Eleven

I strolled over to where the mysterious man had been sitting. *The Indianapolis Star* had been left behind. I sat down and picked up the section the man had been reading; it had been left on top of the remainder of the newspaper. It was section one, and from the condition of the rest of the newspaper, the only section that had been read. The front page contained a follow-up story to a brutal murder that had taken place last week near the train station across the street from The Severin. I quickly scanned down the column and found no mention of a name. I imagined a foreigner with an expired visa murdering for money and perhaps an ID and exhaled: maybe Professor MacIntyre; more than likely a stranger.

I regretted missing my chance to espy the reader of the *Star* prior to his departure; now the mystery man would be able to maintain his anonymity.

*Maybe I'm reading too much into this,* I thought, grunting, amused by my unintentional pun.

"Well, you certainly have your nerve, *Mr.* January," Melissa said as she sat down beside me; she was referring to the single room we'd checked into as husband and wife. Her tone was anything but serious.

"Relax, Miss MacIntyre. I have no intention of taking advantage of you."

"No? What a pity," she replied.

"I thought I told you to wait for me at the desk."

"I'm sorry, but after that interminable walk and then the train ride, I had to use the little girl's room."

I'd already gathered as much. While she hadn't touched up her makeup, it was apparent she had run a brush through her hair. But that didn't preclude the possibility that she and the owner of the *Star* had exchanged room numbers for a more clandestine meeting later.

"Why didn't you ask that man behind the counter about my father?"

"What could he know?"

"That's what I'm paying you to find out."

"Then let me do my job. Now come on," I said, getting up. "Let's get a room for you."

A moment later I told the desk clerk that after talking to my business associate on the phone we'd need a second room, right next to the first if it were possible.

"Put it under the same name," I added.

As I watched the clerk write the name, *MacIntyre,* Melissa asked, "Are there any other MacIntyres on your guest list?"

I glared at Melissa, but she ignored me.

The clerk quickly scanned his list for a match and shook his head. "Sorry, miss."

"Anyone by that name check-in prior to this week?" she pressed.

I was beginning to lose patience, but when the clerk conceded a moment later that no, no one by that name had checked in or out of The Severin during the past two weeks, I found myself a little taken aback. Melissa had said that when she called The Severin yesterday morning, she'd been told that a Benjamin MacIntyre had been listed as a guest.

"You're certain?" Melissa asked.

The desk clerk checked his records a second time. "Yes, miss."

"But—"

"Never mind, Melissa," I said. To the desk clerk I added, "A little hobby of hers I'm afraid. Wherever we go she likes to see how many others might share our name. She'll even introduce herself to strangers if the opportunity presents itself, find out if we might share family origins. MacIntyre's a fairly common name in Scotland. Not like Smith or Jones here in the States, of course. It's unusual that there are no other MacIntyres on your guest list."

"Well, I'm sorry, sir … miss."

"No need to apologize. Come along, dear," I urged Melissa. "Let's get ourselves unpacked and ready for dinner."

I hoped all that I'd said hadn't sounded as pathetically

phony to the desk clerk as it had to me. Not that I thought we had anything to fear from the clerk, but I'd learned long ago that it was best not to ask too many questions. Questions, when not subtly posed, arouse suspicions. Then later, if someone else were to pose questions to the clerk about the tall man and the auburn-haired woman, the clerk, better armed than ignorant, might be more than willing to offer more detailed information than was appropriate.

Once inside the elevator I pushed the disk marked "7", watched the doors close quietly, and felt my stomach sink as the elevator began its rapid ascent.

"Why did you cut me off?" Melissa said. It was the first time since I'd questioned her father's integrity last night at The Famous Door that I'd seen her this angry.

"You'd do well," I said, "to remember our discussion from Minton's. I don't need you meddling in how I conduct this investigation."

"I'm sorry, but obviously that man was lying."

"And just how do you propose we go about proving that?"

Melissa's long exhalation was indication that she had no response.

"Look," I said, "it's obvious what your expectations are. You think we can just waltz into town and through a few well-placed questions find out where your father's been holed up, rescue him from whatever circumstance he may be mired in, and have Lance fly the reunited MacIntyres back to New York where they'll all live happily ever after."

"Well maybe you should've told me how it's supposed to work."

Melissa's anger was spent; this was her apology. I realized that, like me, she would never hold a grudge. She would vent her anger and then all would be forgiven.

"Perhaps I should've at that," I said, "but I thought you trusted me." There was no accusation in my statement.

"Like you trust me?" No hostility, just a note of irony.

"I deserved that."

"We're far from even," she said teasingly as the elevator

door parted. A moment later we exited and started off in the direction of our rooms.

"Do you have any theories?" After my display of deductive reasoning concerning the racer, which she thought brilliant, Melissa seemed anxious to hear my theory concerning the disappearance of her father's name from the hotel's guest list.

"Well," I began, "based on what I already know—that another party seems just as interested in your father's whereabouts as you are—I'd say it isn't entirely out of the realm of possibility that someone from that other party paid off that desk clerk, or whoever was on duty at the time, to remove the name *MacIntyre* from the guest list."

"Wouldn't the clerk have wanted to know why?"

"Not if he'd been paid enough. Everyone has their price." I unlocked the door to the first room Melissa had rented and held it open.

"You don't," she said, recalling that last night I had denied her my services at any price, relenting only so that Lance wouldn't go it alone.

"Even I do, Miss MacIntyre," I said as I followed her in. "But I'm no thief, and as I started to point out, the possibility that the desk clerk has been paid off is reason enough for us to be more discreet in our probing. Any *good* payoff will include a provision that the payer be informed of anyone nosing around."

Melissa set down her suitcase alongside the dresser and turned to face me.

"Joe, I'm sorry, I guess I didn't …" she trailed off, perhaps conscious of her breach in etiquette. She seemed to be waiting for the reprimand she was certain would follow.

"Know any better," I finished for her. Her momentary lapse in formality had caught me off guard, although it shouldn't have, considering the informality of our surroundings. To hide my discomfort, I strode past her to the window and drew the curtains wider. I wondered about my choice to ignore her faux pas; yet she seemed grateful that I had, and so she picked up where she'd left off previous to her quick apology.

"What would they hope to accomplish by removing my father's name from the guest list?"

"Who can say? I'd only be speculating."

I remained by the window, my overnight bag casually slung over my shoulder. Melissa's open blouse invited me to closer inspection; she had undone the second button at some point during our long trek from the plane to the train, the result of the heat. I refrained, but not before noting the pale flesh between her breasts, turned crimson pink from the sun, glistening with perspiration.

"But," I continued, shifting my weight from one leg to the other, "since our German tail in New York made no real effort to prevent us from leaving, I would guess they had hoped we would lead them to their objective."

"But?" Melissa prompted. Looking up at me, she had guessed that I'd had to reassess that supposition.

"Removing such evidence would seem to indicate they don't wish us to be able to trace his whereabouts."

"But that would mean …"

"That they're already onto him."

"Or they already have him." Melissa's tone was a combination of fear for her father's safety and frustration, that despite all her hopes and efforts to find him, she would fall short of her goal by a matter of hours.

"I wouldn't be too concerned about that," I said to reassure her, although I was far from sure myself.

"Why?" Melissa asked. After the disappointment in the lobby she needed to hear some good news.

"There may have been someone staking out the lobby."

I hated giving up that bit of information. If Melissa was not to be trusted, then I might've been wise to hold onto any advantage I might come across. But I despised the look of despair she now wore, preferring instead the straight white teeth born of the childlike innocence of youth that I had, several years ago, found so tempting.

She was waiting for me to continue.

"Whoever was reading that newspaper I was going

through when you came out of the lady's' room. Perhaps our German friend back east alerted his accomplice to be on the lookout for our party."

I could see from the renewed look of hope in Melissa's eyes what she was thinking. All we had to do was find the man who had been reading the newspaper and he would tell us where her father was. If he became belligerent, well, that was part of what she was paying me for, too.

"Unfortunately I never got a look at him before he left," I added.

Melissa's previous demeanor of triumph now turned to one of defeat, and I wondered what it might be like to live a life of such extremes.

"Well then, what's left for us to do?" she asked.

"There's not much we *can* do except wait for our adversaries to contact us."

"Do you really think they will?"

"They most certainly will if your father has somehow managed to keep a step ahead them. They can only presume what knowledge of his whereabouts we might possess. If they run into a dead-end themselves, then they'll have no choice but to further presume we know more than they do. And don't forget, we have that cube in our possession."

I assumed the cube was as much the target as Professor MacIntyre.

"What if he hasn't managed to elude them?"

"Then there might be one or two things we can do to get their attention," I said with a grin. "Remember the cube. Hairball back east seemed to think it was pretty important."

Melissa laughed at my pronunciation—the honorific preceding the name intentionally contorted to conjure up an image of something the family cat would cough up.

"But for now," I added, making my way to the door, "I'd say a nice, long shower is on the agenda before dinner. I'll knock at eight."

"Mr. January," Melissa called before I could get through the door, her tone again puckish. "I know it was for the sake of appearance, but it was nice to hear you call me Melissa."

I blushed and managed to blurt, "Just don't forget the reason behind it, Miss MacIntyre."

And then the door was closed and I breathed a sigh of relief, grateful that she hadn't teased me over my usage of the term of endearment I'd also affixed to her while in the lobby. I was certain that she'd heard it, and fearful she might yet use it against me in the future.

Moments later, in my own room, I unzipped my travel bag and removed the cellophane tape I'd packed.

A few minutes later, through the wall that separated our rooms, I faintly heard Melissa turn on the shower. I waited a minute longer before cracking my door and peeking out into the hall, finding it empty. I slipped out the door and stepped over to Melissa's door, where I bent to apply a piece of cellophane tape about two inches from the floor so that it spanned the slender crevice between the door and its jamb. Then I returned to my own room for the much anticipated, long awaited but much shorter than I'd told Melissa, shower.

# Chapter Twelve

Twenty minutes later I left my room feeling refreshed. The cellophane tape I'd placed on the door to Melissa's room was, as I'd expected, undisturbed. I put my ear to the door. From the proximity of the bathroom I heard the clatter of what I guessed to be cosmetics and pictured Melissa, with naked flesh still damp from her shower, rummaging through her makeup bag, her wet hair hanging limp, adorning her breasts, its curls caressing her nipples—I imagined large aureoles—their pale pink a complimentary contrast to the tarnished copper of her hair. I ignored the message the icon sent to my groin and took a deep breath, and let it out slowly.

*Good,* I thought. *She'll be awhile yet.*

Turning, I made off in the direction of the elevators.

When the elevator door opened, a portly middle-aged woman with huge breasts began to push a cart toward me. I stepped aside to allow her egress while politely holding the door to prevent its closing. The various plates and utensils aboard the cart rattled noisily as it crossed the elevator's threshold. The badge affixed above her left breast identified her as Katherine.

"Thank you, sir," Katherine said automatically, without making eye contact. She evidently was used to not being noticed by guests. She spoke with an Irish brogue.

"You're welcome, Katherine," I replied, startling her.

Katherine peered up at me for a moment, a questioning look in her eyes, before her hand went to the badge. She toyed with it absently as she blushed from the simplicity with which I had discerned her identity.

"Something sure does smell good," I said.

"Frog legs," she offered with a smile that lit up her face.

"Never tried them," I said, making a show of hiding my distaste. An image came to mind of an unsightly aquatic amphibian squatting atop a lily pad croaking its midnight song in some sweltering swamp.

"You should," Katherine said in her melodic cadence.

"They're delicious. They taste just like chicken."

I laughed and added, "Why order something that tastes like chicken when you can have the real McCoy?"

Katherine looked hurt that I'd scorned her unsolicited suggestion.

"No, Katherine," I said. "I'm more of a meat and potatoes man. And now that you know that much about me, what would you propose I order from the menu downstairs?"

Katherine immediately brightened.

"Well sir," she said, running the two words together, as all people from the Emerald Isle are prone to do, "if it's meat you like, I'd recommend the porterhouse. But don't order it well done, not unless it's shoe leather you like. The chef will broil all the flavor right out of it."

I smiled. "So our chef's a real literalist, is he?"

"And if it's rare you like," Katherine went on with a nod, "well then, be prepared to chase it down with your knife and fork."

"And what will I get if I order it medium?"

"You'll get a slab of beef cooked just the way I like it—cooked through, with just enough pink in the middle to allow for the proper flavor."

"Then medium it is," I said, basking in the warmth of Katherine's smile. "Thank you, Katherine," I added and stepped into the elevator.

"You're welcome, sir."

"By the way, Katherine," I said, straddling the threshold of the elevator, my left foot outside, my right foot inside; the door retreated from the obstruction that was my back.

"Yes, sir?"

"I was supposed to meet a business associate here at The Severin. He should've arrived several days ago."

"Did you ask for him at the front desk?"

"Well, you know that's the funny thing. They told me he hadn't checked in, but then, they were awfully busy. Maybe they just overlooked the name. I'll ask again on my way to dinner. I'm sorry to have troubled you."

"Oh, that's no trouble at all, sir."

"You know," I said, stepping out of the elevator and reaching for the photograph Melissa had given me. The elevator door closed behind me. "Maybe I can trouble you to tell me if you've seen him." I handed the photograph to Katherine, who looked at it a moment before answering.

"I'm afraid I can't say I've seen this gentleman around, sir. But The Severin's a big hotel."

"That it is," I said, "but take another look, would you, please? That was taken about six years ago, so try to imagine someone a little older."

Katherine peered again at the image of Professor MacIntyre and shook her head. "I'm sorry, sir."

I made a show of looking at the photograph before suggesting, "Oh, and how could I forget? He's wearing a beard now."

I was fishing, but I was also trying to get what I hoped was a fertile imagination in Katherine working. That Professor MacIntyre had grown a beard to better maintain anonymity was a possibility that had already crossed my own fecund imagination.

Katherine looked at the photograph yet a third time; a moment later, forgoing a verbal denial, she simply shook her head.

"Well, thanks anyway," I said cheerfully and pushed the button to summon the departed elevator.

"You're welcome, sir."

Katherine leaned forward and her great bulk, seemingly supported by the cart in front of her, propelled the inert frog legs back into motion. A gentle whoosh-whoosh filled my ears as her immense thighs, encased in silk stockings, chafed one against the other.

I recalled the discussion I'd had earlier, with Melissa, regarding the allure obesity held for some men and shook my head.

The lobby was considerably more crowded than it had been earlier when Melissa and I had checked in. I quickly scanned the faces of its denizens: the man who had been reading the newspaper could be anyone. The notion of a potential adversary maintaining obscurity burned me. Now I could only wait for that adversary, who may or may not have a penchant for reading the local newspaper, to make the first move, then in turn react. That first move could be days in coming. My hope that we'd be back in New York tomorrow waned.

Glancing toward the front desk, I saw the clerk had vacated his post, however briefly, to take care of whatever other duties his job might encompass.

I made my way to the guestbook, spun it around on its pedestal and turned the page over, glancing at the date to verify yesterday's date—May 23. I followed my finger down the page of names looking for the one I already knew I would fail to find. The twenty-second also provided no proof that the professor had checked into The Severin, as did the twenty-first. On a whim, I turned the pages back one at a time, scanning each day all the way back to Monday, the twelfth, only to discover that neither MacIntyre, senior nor junior, had checked in. Had Melissa lied to me about her call to The Severin revealing a Benjamin MacIntyre on the guest list just to get me to agree to fly out here?

I sighed, frustrated that my acumen continued to fail me. That I was unable to solve the puzzle of the missing name from the hotel registry stirred my ire.

I'd just finished rotating the guest list back to its original facing when the desk clerk appeared from the back room.

"Can I help you?" the clerk asked glancing at the guestbook before turning a suspicious eye at me.

I'd been leaning forward, elbows on the counter, toward the bank of mail slots behind the counter. Melissa had said the operator had told her that her father had been staying in room four-eleven.

"As a matter of fact you can," I said. "Let me have an envelope, will you?"

The desk clerk promptly complied and momentarily left to cater to the needs of another guest. I pulled the photograph of the professor from my breast pocket and, using the fountain pen attached to the guestbook by a long chain, scribbled a quick note on its back. I then sealed the photograph in the envelope and wrote *411* on the envelope's front.

When the clerk returned, I handed him the envelope and said, "For the guest in four-eleven."

"Anything else, sir?" the clerk asked once the envelope had been deposited into the proper mail slot.

I shifted my weight and pivoted on my right elbow, facing away from the clerk. Lance was just now coming through the front doors. I waved at him. "No, just waiting for my associate."

"Ah, yes," the clerk said, not bothering to hide his disdain. He paged the guestbook forward, to where the latest lodgers had been recorded. "Another MacIntyre, perhaps?"

"Yeah," I said with a savage glance at the perpetrator of the antagonistic remark, "another MacIntyre." I pushed myself away from the counter to close the distance between Lance and me.

"Where's Melissa?" Lance asked, sounding like a lovestruck puppy.

"Upstairs in her room primping herself for you," I answered sourly with a look at my watch. I noticed the look in Lance's eyes and was immediately sorry for the lie I'd told.

"Come on," I added, steering him toward the elevators. "It's nearly eight o'clock; she should be ready by now."

As we stood side-by-side waiting for the elevator, Lance pumped me for information pertinent to his cause.

"Did she say anything to you about me? Ask you any questions about me?" He was barely able to contain his excitement over the prospect that I was about to provide him a wealth of information. Everything he wanted to hear, all of it positive, as if Melissa and I had talked of nothing but him on the train ride from the track to the hotel.

"No."

"No?" Lance's one unrehearsed answer to the only unexpected response.

*Decades have elapsed since that exchange, yet I remember it as if it had taken place yesterday. At the time it meant little to me. Even in retrospect I find it difficult to explain. One word, a single syllable, spoken once each by two men, its meaning to each of them undeniable—the first, simple, unquestionable in its certitude, sounding almost clipped in its resolution; while the second, a barely audible exhalation of the long* O *sound lingering just short of infinity as the tone raised its question, revealing a certitude just as simple, just as unquestionable, yet so contrary to the first. Contrary in that unlike the first, which was devoid of any color, the second was laden with the shade of despair.*

"No," I reiterated as the elevator door slid open.

Inside the elevator, a moment after the door kissed itself shut, Lance pressed on in desperation as I pressed the disk marked "7."

"Is she seeing anyone?"

"No." The same timbre: opulent with truth, barren of compassion. The elevator began its ascent.

"But … what did you talk about on the train?"

"Her missing father," I said in an effort to refocus Lance's attention. "Remember, that's the reason we're here."

I watched the lit number "2" above the door go dark, and a moment later the number "3" next to it flashed on with a self-importance that seemed to speak in favor of a surety that that information was a necessity to all passengers of all elevators everywhere, as if not knowing which floor they were traversing would make a difference in their lives.

"That's all?" Lance asked.

I groaned inwardly and realized that watching each ascending number flash on in its turn would not bring our vertical jaunt to an end any sooner.

"She said she's still looking for her needle in a haystack," I said with indifference.

"Well, then …" Lance began with confidence.

"I *said,*" I affirmed with finality, glaring at Lance, "she's still looking."

We finished the ride in silence, me in contemplation of

what few facts I had concerning the mystery that continued to spur me on. While Lance, driven to win the approval of a woman who had no intention of bestowing upon him what he sought, no doubt considered various options that would ultimately lead him to his conquest.

Moments after Lance had deposited his flight bag in our room, he and I stood in front of Melissa's door. I casually noted that one end of the tape I'd placed earlier had come undone: the seal had been broken.

I considered whether she had left her room or allowed someone entry. Not that it mattered since either occasion amounted to the same conclusion: Melissa had a contact at The Severin. I cocked an ear toward the door, straining a moment in an effort to hear voices from within. Before I could be satisfied she was alone, Lance, in his impatience, rapped sharply on the door.

A moment later the door opened and Melissa stepped out. Her room, I noted, was dark. The curtain I'd earlier drawn wide had since been closed.

"Hello, Lance, Mr. January."

Despite her intended informality, I detected a distinct formality in her greeting of Lance, a lack of warmth that she failed to withhold from her greeting of me. I scoffed at the notion that Lance might have noticed it. Perspicuity was a gift with which Lance had not been blessed.

"Hello, Melissa," Lance said loudly to draw attention to himself.

Melissa acknowledged Lance's greeting with a casual nod and a smile, which no doubt was misinterpreted, and I couldn't help but think that maybe Ginger would have been a better choice for Lance after all.

"I just knocked on your door," she said, looking up at me, and I was forced to reassess my assertion that she'd secretly met with someone else. I cursed myself that I'd been so ready to jump to such a conclusion.

"I was downstairs in the lobby waiting for Lance."

"Well, I must have just missed you then."

“No doubt,” I said. “Anyone else hungry, or are we just going to stand around jawing in the hallway all night?”

“Let’s eat,” Lance agreed. “I’m starving.”

# Chapter Thirteen

In the dining room, once the waitress had taken our orders, I sat in silent consternation. I'd ordered the porterhouse, medium, as Katherine had suggested, while Lance had also opted for the porterhouse, but rare. When Melissa couldn't make up her mind, I recommended that if she liked chicken she should try the frog legs. Melissa laughed at my homology and promptly made my suggestion her choice, missing the piercing look Lance gave me. For all I knew, he'd been ready to suggest the pasta primavera.

I leaned back in my chair, nursing my beer, while across from me Melissa engaged Lance in idle conversation that Lance had initiated. Contrary to my posture, Lance was leaning forward, elbows on the table, making his intentions overtly obvious.

*Ah, Lance,* I mused silently.

It was rare that I felt sympathy for anyone, but Lance was my friend. I had tried to warn him, and he'd agreed to keep his eyes open. Unfortunately, both were filled to capacity with images of Melissa MacIntyre, blinding him to the truth. Anger flared: she had promised not to mislead him.

But then my anger diffused. The distraction that Lance was providing allowed me to take note of Melissa's wan complexion now tinged a healthy pink, compliments of the sun. I was grateful, for her sake, that we hadn't made our trek around the track at midday, or the pale rose I now found so alluring might've been an angry red that would've been very painful to her. With an effort, I forced myself to look away from Melissa and take in our surroundings.

I was looking for anyone suspicious, and it didn't take me long to find that someone. At the table in the far corner, beyond Melissa's right shoulder, dining alone—which is what first caught my attention—a fair-complexioned, just as fair-haired gentleman in a tweed suit. But where Hairball, the similarly attired man who had tailed us in New York, had been homely as sin with his skewed eye and gap-toothed smile, this gent was about as handsome a man as I'd ever seen. His features and perfect complexion reminded me of the face of a porcelain doll I'd once seen in an antique store.

Looking away at the precise moment our eyes met, he now was perusing the bill of fare the menu provided. I wondered if he had a penchant for local news, too.

Melissa laughed at something Lance said and favored me with a quick glance before saying, "No, I'm afraid I'm still looking for my knight in shining armor."

"Really?" Lance asked in mock surprise with a glance at me. He had missed, or perhaps had chosen to ignore, the pleading look Melissa had given me.

*Serves you right, Miss MacIntyre,* I ruminated, relishing her discomfiture. *Maybe now you'll realize that by not being up front with him you've been misleading him.*

"Well maybe after we reunite you with your father and we get back to New York we can have dinner, at my expense instead of yours." Lance laughed at his own humor. Neither Melissa nor I joined him.

*Jesus, Lance,* I thought, *throw yourself at her much harder and she'll have to duck.*

Melissa blushed, looked to me for help, saw none would be forthcoming, and surprised me by saying, "I don't think that would be such a good idea, Lance."

"Why not?" Lance asked, trying in vain not to divulge any hint of surprise as well as his obvious disappointment.

"I just think …" she began, her discomfort just as obvious.

For a moment I felt sorry for her, but the moment passed quickly as I realized it was best this way, that Lance be made to suffer this minor disappointment now instead of a major one later, after he'd gotten more attached to her. I felt Melissa's eyes on me but kept mine averted. I heard a quick intake of air and a brief pause during which I imagined her licking her lips in preparation of finishing that which she had begun.

"That Mr. January is right," she finished quickly. "That maybe we would be wise to keep our relationship business."

"I see," Lance said, toying with the glass that contained his scotch; it was a gesture I thought strangely allusive of Melissa's from the night before, when I'd backed her into a corner and forced her to reveal the existence of the postcard. "Since when did you acknowledge the wisdom of *Mr.* January?" he finished with a savage glare at me, perhaps beginning to think more had been said on the train ride than I had let on.

"Look, Mr. Cantrell—" Melissa said before realizing it was too late to revert to such formality. "Lance," she began anew, and discovered that her decision to return to her former familiarity merely served to further enhance her discomfort. Ignoring it, she forged ahead. "I think you're a very nice man …"

"But," he finished for her. It was a line he'd heard before.

"No buts," she said. "You're very handsome and it's very noble of you to come to my rescue, but—"

"Didn't I just say that?" Lance asked, unable to meet Melissa's level gaze.

"Look, Lance," I said, surprising myself with my intrusion. "It's my fault, okay? I told her about Becky. About how she dumped you while you were overseas. I told her you were on the rebound. And like I told you back in Jersey to go easy, I also asked her to go easy on you, and that if she wasn't interested she shouldn't mislead you."

Lance looked from me to the person he wanted, nay, needed most to hear it from. "So you're really not interested?" he ventured with caution.

This time it was Melissa who was unable to return Lance's level gaze. It was the answer he feared most.

"I'm sorry, pal. I tried to tell you in the elevator."

"Yeah you did," Lance said, running the three words together as one. Nodding once, he finished in a single gulp what was left of his drink, which was nearly half. Then in a gesture I thought more than a little histrionic, he stood up and announced, "Suddenly I don't have much of an appetite. If you'll excuse me."

"Lance, please," Melissa called to his back, but it was too late. Lance was gone.

She turned back, visibly shaken, and I found myself taken by the authenticity of her mien.

"Well," I said after a long moment. "It seems we find ourselves alone once more."

Melissa withheld the smile I had hoped to elicit and I found myself far more disappointed than I would've imagined.

"I'm sorry," she said.

"Don't be. You did the right thing." I waited for her say something; when she didn't, I went on. "You don't have to worry, Miss MacIntyre, he'll be all right."

"But he looked so hurt."

I laughed and to a surprised Melissa explained, "Trust me, Miss MacIntyre. Lance was mighty disappointed by your disinterest, which should do wonders for your vanity. But the only thing that's bruised is his ego. He hates it when I'm right." Another, longer moment passed before I ventured to change the subject.

"You know, Melissa, I've heard it said that men have it easy because we get to do the asking, while women must sit by the phone, waiting for it to ring."

"Don't tell me you don't buy into that adage?"

"Of course I do. If I had been Lance just now, I'd have smiled graciously, thanked you for your honesty, and moved on to greener pastures."

"But you're not Lance."

"No, but I understand Lance. He's the type of man who needs to pursue a woman. In you he sees someone attractive. No doubt in his mind your phone is ringing off the hook. He sees you as the person with all the power, the freedom to mete out rejection. With so many potential suitors, you can afford to say no and still manage to have a date for Saturday night. There's truth to that, don't deny it."

"But the truth is my phone *isn't* ringing off the hook."

I ignored her statement. "You told him no, so he took it personally. Couple that with what Becky did to him and suddenly he views himself as undesired by every member of the fairer sex." Then, acknowledging her avowal, I added, "And if your phone *isn't* ringing, then that must be by choice. Face it, there are far more women in possession of far fewer desirable assets than yours who are *fated* to wait by the phone."

Having seen her in action these past two days, I already knew the answer to my next question, but I asked it anyway.

"Tell me, do you openly discourage potential swains or merely prefer not encouraging them? Which for a guy like Lance is the same as giving him a green light."

Melissa blushed.

"So you see, Miss MacIntyre, I *have* taken notice."

Melissa looked back across the table at me and said, "A moment ago you called me Melissa. And it wasn't a pretense as it was earlier. I like hearing you say my name."

I ignored her comment but couldn't ignore I was pleased she hadn't missed my intentional lapse in etiquette.

"It doesn't hurt either that you were a woman in distress," I said, making reference to her own admission to Lance that she was grateful for his offer to help. "That he was uncertain about your regard for him drove him to win your approval, or bust." Then, with a grin I added, "By the way, I wouldn't go so far as to say you're out of the woods just yet."

"You mean … after I …?"

"He's upstairs right now analyzing where he went wrong and amending his approach. He knows you're not my type and I've already told him I'm not interested. But it hasn't occurred to him yet that the reverse isn't true." I leaned back in my chair and downed what was left of my beer before adding cheerfully, "So you see, Miss MacIntyre, I'd say the chances are good he'll be back, but with a much more subtle strategy."

"Why do I get the impression you're enjoying this so much?"

"Because I am. I'm amused, astounded and left aghast by what people will do for love."

Melissa looked at me a moment, perhaps in silent admiration of my simple alliteration, before saying, "You like to think yourself above all that, don't you?"

"Not above it," I said with a simple shake of my head. "Let's just say my need for that sort of recognition—rooted in gaining approval from someone hell-bent on withholding it—is nonexistent. There are far too many women who are willing to accept what I offer, with no strings attached, to trouble myself fawning over someone who abstains from complying with my needs and will in the end abandon me."

"Why are you so convinced of that inevitability?"

"All relations come to an end, either through death, which is itself a form of abandonment, or by rejection of one party of the other."

"A moment ago," Melissa said, digressing, "you spoke of needs, yours, specifically. What might those needs be?"

"Too few to mention," I said. Then, after a moment I complied. "I love my work. It allows me to make right what is wrong in this small pocket of the world in which I live. I need to make a difference. And of course a warm body to lie with for an evening of pleasure."

"As long as it's transient." Melissa's tone was not one of condemnation, but rather of someone trying to come to some comprehension of a foreign tenet. "And what of your wants?" she asked, trying to understand if there might be some difference, to me, between the two.

"We've already had this dialogue."

"Yes, we have, and you were just as evasive then, too," she said, putting on a less serious guise in an effort to put me at ease. "I enjoy our discussions. They're so challenging, don't you think?"

"Hardly. A challenge is something to be overcome, and while I fully admit to being a challenge to you—that you hope to win me over to your way of thinking—I seek only to shed light on a lifestyle you evidently have yet to experience."

"To what end?"

"There is no end. Unless of course you view my intention to not mislead you as an end."

"Are you intent that I should stop pursuing you?"

"I cannot control how you act, only make you aware of the consequences of your actions."

"And if I was to ask you to come up to my room and make love to me—that I *needed* you, to use your terminology, to make love to me—what would you say?"

"A woman like you doesn't function on needs. To offer yourself in that manner would indicate you want something in return, and so I would question your motives."

"A well thought out answer, one which I wouldn't have thought someone who professes to acting only on a purely physical level to be capable of. It makes me wonder if you haven't already asked yourself that question."

When I didn't refute her statement, she continued. "So you would refuse me. Why, to save me from myself? Why am I any different than Lindy?"

I nearly blurted, *Because Lindy was a mistake and I learn from my mistakes,* but refrained from making that admission, knowing it to be the lie it would've been had I voiced it.

"Could it be," Melissa went on with her thesis, "that in Lindy you've discovered something you truly want?"

"My *wants,* Miss MacIntyre," I contested hotly, in defiance, as I waved my empty beer glass at a passing waitress, "are far fewer than my needs."

"Well, at least you don't deny you have one," she said, partly in jest, referring to my earlier assertion that my life was composed of but two needs.

"Listen, if Lance wants to torment himself by making a play for someone he can never have, that's his business. I tried to warn him."

"Perhaps he sees something of value."

"Something no doubt you would prefer *I* notice. Don't bet on it."

"Yes, how could I forget? You don't trust me, do you?"

"No, I don't."

The waiter was delivering another drink to the stranger

in the corner. I couldn't make out their exchange. Not that I thought it might be important; I couldn't have cared less what the stranger might've ordered for dinner, be it steak—rare, medium or well-done—frog legs, the pasta primavera, or anything else the menu offered. What was being said was unimportant. What *was* important was *how* it was being said: in a thick foreign accent that betrayed its German pedigree.

*The wienerwurst, then,* I thought, my suspicions verified.

"But there's got to be something more than just trust at stake," Melissa said, oblivious to where my attention had been drawn. "Something more than just me, else why would you be so angry?"

"I'm not angry," I said, suddenly aware that I'd let Melissa glimpse a part of myself I couldn't allow her, or anyone for that matter, to ever see. "I'm just passionate."

The stranger had risen and was heading toward the men's room.

"If you'll excuse me," I said, effectively cutting off further debate, and followed the stranger at a distance, leaving Melissa to puzzle over my sudden departure.

Outside the men's room I paused a long moment, reflecting on the procedure the German was going through as he stood in front of the porcelain urinal: unzipping his trousers and fishing inside for his stubby little wienerwurst. I waited a moment longer, imagining the German closing his eyes in anticipation of relief as the water rose from his bladder and passed through the plumbing that would ultimately lead it through the egress at the end of his pecker and into the cold white porcelain. The closing of the eyes was what I was banking on the stranger to do. It was a practice I'd noted over the years in which a lot of men indulged. I pushed on the door and stealthily made my way into the brightness beyond.

The German's back was to the door.

*Good.*

His head was tilted back at an angle that confirmed to me that his eyes were closed.

*Better still.*

The stranger's left hand was in his pocket, employing the right to take care of business.

*Too small to require the use of both hands,* I reasoned, while the familiar sound of water striking porcelain followed by a long audible sigh greeted my ears.

*Perfect.*

I stepped briskly over to where the German stood, grabbed his right arm and brought it up behind his back with a quick jerk while at the same time encircling his shoulders with my left arm, effectively pinning his left arm uselessly within my grasp. I watched urine arch up gracefully, striking the tile to the left of the urinal as I pulled back on my captive and was reminded of the Pulitzer Memorial Fountain just outside Central Park, marking one of the park's entrances along Central Park South. In the top basin stands the goddess Pomona.

"Oof," the German gasped, struggling to release himself from my firm grip.

I gave a quick upward twist on the right arm and the German abandoned his effort.

Maneuvering to my left, I faced my captive toward the mirror above and beyond the sinks, allowing him to espy his captor. I took note of the urine still trickling from the end of his limp pecker, striking the ceramic tile floor between his feet, and nearly laughed at the ludicrous image reflected back at us. Again I couldn't help but think of the goddess Pomona, who symbolizes abundance.

*No,* I concluded, *you're no goddess, nor are you particularly abundantly endowed. The superior race? I don't think so.*

The look on the German's face bore no hint of humor at his predicament.

"Hello, Herr Mac," I said flatly. "You here for the big race?" I asked, a cheap imitation of Hoosier hospitality, "or are you looking for someone in particular?"

"I haff no idea vat you are talking a-bout."

"Your pal in New York told me the same thing. Funny, I didn't believe him either." I gave another tug on the right arm.

"Ach!"

"Here in the States we practice a little something we call give and take. I imagine from where you come they have the same thing. Only where you come from I imagine you just take—usually from those too terrorized to say 'no.' But you're in my country now, Herr Mac, and over here it's done a little differently. Let me explain. Right now you're going to *take* a question from me and in return *give* me an answer. And if you don't give me what I want, I'll take it out on your arm, you follow me? So what do you say we try again?"

I held the German's gaze, as blue as his compatriot's, before phrasing my next question.

"Are you looking for someone in particular?"

"You vould be vell-advised to leaf here." The air of smug supremacy that accompanied the haughty statement nearly elicited a laugh from me.

"Well that's better," I said, satisfied that the German's answer at least betrayed no denial of his ambition, or of his alliance with our tail back east. "Now that we've broken the ice and you've managed to get your feet wet so to speak," I continued with an amused glance, through the mirror, at the German's shoes, dappled with droplets of urine, "let's try another question. Where's Professor MacIntyre?" I watched as surprise crossed the countenance of my captive; surprise that the opposition, me, lacked the knowledge of the professor's whereabouts. "I see you've heard of him," giving a tug on his right arm.

"Ja," the German grunted. "I haff heard der name you speak uff."

A hint of rascality now resided where before had been surprise, and I knew that here at my disposal was the brains of what I had correctly guessed to be a two-man operation, while back east I had encountered the brawn. Suddenly I regretted having mentioned MacIntyre by name. I'd been too eager to make the stranger talk. If the foreigner didn't know the professor by name, he did now, the result of my foolish blunder.

"He iss here, at dis hotel."

Just then the door swung inward and another patron of the dining room entered. I didn't have to say a word; one look at the blond man standing in a puddle of urine being held in check against his will, his genitals less than proudly on display, spoke volumes. Without a word, the newcomer spun around on his heel and departed.

"Where?" I demanded while forcing my prisoner's tightly gripped arm upward. I nearly added *room four-eleven?* but thought better of revealing that bit of information. Perhaps the German already knew; but if he didn't, I didn't want to inform him of anything his own ineptitude had failed to provide.

The German, on his toes now in an effort to ease the tension being exerted on his shoulder, laughed. It was a laugh, I noted, that bordered on hysteria. I relaxed my pressure and the German once more stood flat-footed.

"You do not ask der right question."

"And just what is the right question?" My mind was reeling. This interrogation was not going at all the way I'd envisioned.

"Iff I told you," the German said, "you vould not belief me, und my arm, I fear, vould bear der brunt uff your wrath."

"Listen, Herr Mac, if you don't tell me what I want to know, your arm will bear the least of my wrath."

The German laughed again. "You haff no idea vat you are letting yourself in for."

*As if I don't already know that,* I thought, recalling my distrust of Melissa and her iniquitous brother. Suddenly an alliance between the MacIntyre offspring—with or without their father's involvement—and the German tandem didn't seem all that farfetched.

Spinning the German around to face me, I grabbed him by the lapels and shook him violently several times.

"Then why don't you let me in on it?" I demanded.

The German's laughter rose, taking with it my fury.

"You know I do believe that losing the war has put you

over the edge," I said. My adversary ignored the derision.

"All in good time," he replied. "All in good *time.* Vat vonce vas, vill be vonce more."

No doubt his answer was meant to betray a hint of some secret knowledge that would be indecipherable to me, and I immediately picked up on it.

Not knowing in the least what that secret knowledge might be, I let my anger subside and opted for a feigned appearance of recognition. In turn, I watched the German's features contort with the realization that he had foolishly let slip knowledge he'd originally thought secure.

"Well," I said, fussing with the German's rumpled lapels. "It would seem that we have an understanding, you and me. We both want the same thing—to find Professor MacIntyre. And we both know *where* to find him. Now, as you say, it's just a matter of *time.* And when the time comes, Herr Mac, I'll be there and I'll be ready. Can you say the same?"

Just to prove I meant business, I reared back and caught the German with my fist, not on the jawbone, that was too hard, but on the cheek, just below his left eye, where I knew a shiner would result. The German stumbled backward and tried to catch himself on the waste vessel next to the sink; but his shoes, their soles slick with the urine he'd been standing in, slid out from under him and he landed hard on his coccyx with an audible crack. I couldn't help but wince.

"Remember to wash your hands," I said, striding toward the door. "Oh, and," I added with a glance back at the German, still sprawled on the floor with his genitals lolling against the inside of his left thigh, "don't forget to zip your fly, too."

"I was beginning to think I had been stood up twice in one evening," Melissa said as I sat down across from her. "Where did you disappear to?"

My brain was swimming with potential scenarios, all predicated upon the information I'd just learned. Melissa's question reminded me, along with the discomfort in my bladder, that I'd entered the men's room in search of relief from the puzzle of the missing MacIntyres and had come out with more apprehension still in need of relieving myself.

"Mr. January?"

"You may fancy yourself naïve, Miss MacIntyre," I said, "but surely you're not that naïve about what goes on behind the closed doors of men's rooms. I would've thought that with an older brother you'd know."

Melissa blushed and giggled, and I pictured her, age four, being coerced by her older brother to drop her pants so they could compare anatomy. I watched her image flee in terror—that she'd been born deformed, lacking the proper plumbing her big brother possessed—in search of her father. I then watched her father's image brush away the tears that streaked her cheeks as she conveyed to him her birth defect. Finally, I listened to that image—the one from the photograph I'd slipped into the envelope I'd had the desk clerk deposit into the mail slot for room four-eleven—as he consoled his daughter, telling her not to worry. That when she got older she could have as many of what her big brother had between his legs as she desired. I felt my face heat, ashamed of my vulgarity.

"You know you're very handsome when you blush," Melissa said.

The arrival of the waitress with our dinners saved me from further discomfiture.

"Will the other gentleman be rejoining you?" she asked.

"He wasn't feeling well," I said. "But if you'll have his taken up to room seven-o-seven, maybe he'll feel like eating later."

Melissa and I ate in silence, neither of us bothering to hide our disappointment: Melissa, that the informality of our pre-dinner discussion had come to an end; and me, that every answer to every question I asked did little to allay my many suspicions, and like my aching bladder, I saw no immediate relief in sight.

The German failed to return to his table in the corner. I reasoned he had opted to take dinner in his room, allowing him to nurse the black eye he had been issued. My aching right hand was proof that I'd caught him solidly.

# Chapter Fourteen

Thirty minutes later, as we crossed the lobby, nearly empty of patrons at this hour, I noted the envelope I had the desk clerk deposit in the four-eleven mail slot was gone. That didn't surprise me, considering my inability to learn anything of basis since agreeing to take on this case. But what did surprise me was the glimpse of a man I saw entering the elevator we were approaching. Somewhat disheveled and out of breath, the man had been watching the lobby as he waited for the elevator's arrival, as if searching for someone he didn't wish to meet. Then, not wishing to draw attention to himself, he entered the elevator with the nonchalance of someone not wishing to be noticed, which made him appear all the more conspicuous. I saw him for only a moment, but behind the beard I recognized the man from the photograph: Professor MacIntyre.

Moments later, as we waited for our own elevator, I hazarded a glance at Melissa. If she had seen her father enter the elevator, she certainly gave no sign of having recognized him. No doubt she still sought the man in the photograph, untouched by the intervening years; while my experience had taught me to look beyond the photograph for someone, a fugitive perhaps, who not only was six years older, but who might also wish to hide his appearance somehow. To me, the obvious choice for a disguise would be a beard. From across the lobby, I'd been unable to detect much passage of time; but having already imagined the image in the photograph disguised by facial hair, the beard had done little to conceal his identity.

That Professor MacIntyre might fail to recognize his daughter was understandable. He seemed on the lookout for someone menacing—perhaps the man whose acquaintance I'd made in the men's room. So his gaze, earnest in its search of that menace, would naturally travel past the non-threatening approach of the young woman alongside the tall stranger.

We rode the elevator in silence, my mind swimming with possibilities, while Melissa no doubt mistook my solitude for another of my moods.

Outside her room Melissa smiled awkwardly and thanked me for the evening, as if this were a failed blind date, then waited as if she expected me to ask if it would be all right to call on her again. When I said nothing, she opened the door, walked through, turned to look up at me and said, "Tell Lance I'm sorry, will you?"

"Sure," I muttered, oblivious to the reason why she wished me to pass along her apology. "Breakfast's at eight," I added, signaling the evening had come to an end.

A moment after Melissa closed the door, I turned and silently made my way back down the hall, toward the elevators.

I regretted not having put a finger on the German in the men's room. It would've been child's play to reach into his breast pocket for ID, proof of his legal status. With a name, I could've located the room in which he was staying. The German, had he been the mystery man behind the *Star* in the lobby when we'd checked in, could very easily have discovered which rooms we had been assigned. That was the primary reason I'd checked in under the name MacIntyre, a name I was hoping would draw attention. Now, most assuredly there was attention to be drawn, if the German's presence at dinner was any indication. Assuming this stooge was smart enough to check the hotel register, and I had my doubts about that, he now could learn in which rooms we were staying, while I remained ignorant of his whereabouts. He could be right across the hall from four-eleven, and I'd be wise to assume that was the case.

In the elevator I recalled the newspaper article I'd seen earlier regarding the murder that had taken place last week. From the cold and calculating blue eyes reflected at me through the mirror in the men's room, I felt certain the German was capable of murder.

I had told Lindy earlier, through the phone, that I didn't

expect much to occur on this outing. Why, because I didn't wish it to? That would amount to being obstinate, which was an extra vowel and one less consonant away from being abstinent, and I didn't like to associate myself with either of those words.

In truth, much *was* beginning to occur since we'd checked into The Severin. Not only in that Lance had gone down in flames, but also that I'd come to question my gut feeling regarding Melissa's trustworthiness, as well as my feelings where Lindy was concerned.

But those were mere subplots.

Start with our tail in New York; couple that with the second member of my suspected tandem here in Indianapolis; add in that I'd already managed to spot the good professor and like any recipe, all the ingredients were there for a tasty delicacy that was likely to result in a bad case of indigestion. The only missing element was Benjamin Junior, and I was fairly certain he'd turn up yet, probably when least expected, just to stir up the pot.

The elevator door parted and I stepped out onto the fourth floor. A young couple approached me; stepping into the elevator, they thanked me for holding the door for them.

I made my way down the hall to room four-eleven and gently rapped on the door to draw the attention of the room's occupant—if indeed there was one. I stood a moment, poised with my ear toward the door, listening for any sound within. There was none. It occurred to me that if the professor was in his room, the odds were in favor of him refusing to acknowledge his presence within. I could stand here all night knocking and succeed only in drawing unwanted attention to myself. If Professor MacIntyre *had* managed to slip back into his room unnoticed, I was loath to undo the professor's stealth by a show of knowledge.

Once again I was forced to wait, hoping that the message I'd left in the mail slot would coerce the professor into taking a chance; hoping also that the gentle knock on his door would alert him that the author of that message was aware of his whereabouts.

Across the hall, room four-twelve, its occupancy also unknown, beckoned forebodingly.

I stepped to the door and listened a moment. I heard running water from the bathroom and the clink of what I took to be ice. I pictured the German, his left eye swollen and already turning an ugly shade of purple, with a cold compress against his cheek. But it could just as easily be any guest dropping ice into a glass prior to pouring water over it.

I stood a moment longer in anticipation of voices, proof of double occupancy … Hearing none, I left.

Back in our room, Lance, his hair still damp from his shower, was putting the finishing touches on the dinner I'd sent up.

"Where have you been?" he asked between bites. "I heard you drop off Melissa a few minutes ago. Don't tell me you met someone at dinner and arranged to meet her for a quickie in her room."

"As a matter of fact I *did* meet someone, but it's not what you think," I said, not taking Lance's bait. I knew he was only letting off steam.

Lance swallowed and took a deep breath before continuing.

"You could've told me how she felt."

"I tried to warn you."

"Not about me, about you."

I took a deep breath of my own, unsure how to respond. I'd thought Lance incapable of the observation he'd just revealed.

"Lance," I said, sitting on the edge of the bed. "What I told you in Jersey was the truth. I'm no competition for you on this."

"But why not?"

The question surprised me, and because Lance was my friend I betrayed that surprise with a slight raising of my eyebrows. I thought a moment, and then laughed.

"You mean besides her being too skinny?"

I noted Lance failed to see the humor in my question.

Melissa was far too serious a subject for such a cavalier response.

"We've known each other for what, fifteen years?" Lance asked.

"Give or take. And I think I know where you're going. In all that time you and I have never competed with each other over the affections of a woman."

Lance nodded. "Why do you think that is?"

I pursed my lips as I thought about Lance's question; then, in order to set up my answer, I asked Lance the same question.

"Decorum?" Lance's answer was a stab in the dark.

"Well I suppose that might have something to do with it," I said and was reminded of Becky, a woman I'd often thought better suited for me than Lance; but Lance had seen her first and I'd thought too much of our friendship to let a woman come between us. "But don't you think that maybe you and I are attracted to two different types of women?"

From the look on Lance's face, I could tell the thought had never crossed his mind.

*Ah, Lance,* I thought. *It's true, you've a good heart and I love you like a brother, but why is it so hard for you to look at something from more than one angle?*

"Is it because you don't trust her?"

"That's part of it. But even if trust wasn't an issue I don't think I'd be attracted to her ... not in the way you are, and certainly not for the reasons she wants me to be."

"So you *are* attracted to her."

"I will admit when we first met—five-and-a-half years ago, not last night—I was attracted to her youthfulness. To tell you the truth, I found her inexperience rather arousing. But my tastes have changed. My attraction for her was not the same as hers was for me, even then, and so it wouldn't have worked between us. Not then and certainly not now."

"Why not?"

"You know the answer to that, Lance. Think about it. You know me. I prefer to keep my love life simple and Melissa is anything *but* simple. She's an intelligent woman.

Educated. That's not to say a woman has to be empty-headed to sleep with me, but *that* woman has an agenda. While I need lots of lovers, she has certain expectations. Expectations that I, on my best day, would almost certainly fail to meet. Which is why you might be well-suited for her, even if she doesn't know it. You'd be capable of loving her unconditionally, and in doing so you would undoubtedly meet her expectations."

"So why are your expectations so low?"

I laughed. "My expectations are anything *but* low, pal. They're just … well, let's just say they're much shallower, simpler to obtain, easier to satisfy, and a whole lot safer."

Lance could only shake his head.

"What?" I asked.

"I've seen you take more personal risk on some of the jobs you've taken without thinking twice, yet you talk about the risk of love as if it were potentially fatal."

I reflected a moment upon Lance's assessment before answering, my tone itself grave. "Perhaps in a sense it is."

"Come on, Joe, haven't you ever been in love?"

I chuckled. "You sound like Melissa." Then I added, "I've seen the type of devastation that results from the kind of trust love requires." It was the first time I'd revealed to anyone, including Lindy, that bit of information about my past.

Lance's eyes contained a hint of sympathy, lest I forget that he, too, had suffered at the hands of rejection. But with the sympathy resided curiosity. Lance was waiting for me to explain. I shook my head.

"Don't ask me to explain."

"Why not?"

"Because we haven't known each other long enough," I said with a grin. "But I will say that, contrary to popular belief, love does *not* conquer all. It *can,* however, become all consuming, especially if it goes unrequited."

I wondered for a moment if Lance would recognize what I was saying for what it was—a warning. Then I continued:

"There are women who find it easy to take what you

offer but difficult to reciprocate, other than with empty words offered to create for themselves a fervent, false illusion of what they want to feel while inspiring you to give even more of yourself. In the end, if you're fortunate, they'll return a portion of what you gave them, and that might make you feel at the very least that the gift you gave so freely and that they took so greedily held some value to them. More than likely they won't. They'll simply cast it away as something in which they held little value."

I'd been staring at a point on the wall to the left of my longtime friend. A long moment ensued before I again made eye contact.

"But hey," I finished, "you should know that, after what Becky did."

"That's just it, Joe. I *do* know. And despite the pain of her rejection, she did, for a time, comfort me. Maybe it was just as you say, all an illusion. That she told me the things she did to control me. But I know what she told me in the end was just a lie. You see, Joe, I *know* the value of what I gave to her. And nothing *she* says, or *anybody* says, can deter me from believing in its worth. Did she meet my expectations? I think she did, if only for awhile. While I was overseas, she gave me hope and something to look forward to coming home to. Or maybe I only deluded myself into believing she did. Either way it was a terrific feeling."

Lance chuckled before he went on.

"You might say I live in a world of make believe. Maybe I'm destined to suffer a dozen more broken hearts in my lifetime, but to me those feelings were real, and all I know is I want to feel that way again, even if it's only for a day, a week or a month. Go ahead and laugh, but illusion is all any of us has, you included. If you're honest with yourself, you'll admit you live in denial of the fact that your life is devoid of something. No, don't try to tell me your life is full because of your work and the many lovers you've had and those you've yet to have. I know different. I see it. I've always seen it. You're either running from something or searching for something. Either way, what's shared is the desperate way in which you go about it."

"Don't talk to me about desperate, Lance. All you needed tonight was a club and you could've knocked Melissa over the head and dragged her back to your cave. I'm not running *from* anything, and the *only* things I seek are a challenging case and the pleasure of a beautiful woman's body. I don't fool myself into pretending either is any more or less than what they are."

"That's delusory thinking."

"So what if it is? You've already admitted to as much yourself. Yet if our lives *are* composed of such, then mine can be no more delusory than someone else's. I'll gladly settle for the affections of a dozen women rather than the rejection of one. Beware of pedestals, Lance."

I ran my hand through my hair and added, "Haven't you ever wondered why it is a dame says she wants one thing in a man, yet her actions speak volumes to the contrary?"

"I don't follow you," Lance said.

"You're absolutely right, Lance. Everything you gave to Becky she at one time held in esteem. She must've, else why would she have accepted any of it? So why does a gal like her, who tells a guy like you you're everything she ever wanted in a man, dump you for a fella like me? Or better still, why does a girl like Melissa MacIntyre, who claims she's looking for a guy in possession of all the traits you possess, chase after a guy who has none of them?"

Lance could only stare at his empty dinner plate, where he found no answer forthcoming.

"Because she wants what she can't have," I finished. "Contrary to public opinion, women are into the chase just as much as men are. But where *we* get criticized for losing interest afterward, women are absolved of any misconduct."

"Why is that?" Lance asked.

"Because society is more than willing to accept that men behave in the manner we do—not that the behavior itself is acceptable, but that we behave in the manner we do is. While the notion that women can be just as ill-mannered—that they can be just as abusive, controlling and manipulative—is just a myth. A myth that women naturally find preferable to reality, and indeed one they help perpetuate, their desire to keep men ignorant of the truth because in ignorance is power."

"And what is the reality?"

"First, that for every man who is not very nice, a woman exists who is his equal. For every male beast a female bitch exists, just as capable of inflicting hurt. Second, that we are human beings foremost, with wants and needs. That we are created as man and woman is secondary; yet as man and woman, we are but two halves of a whole, neither complete without the other. In the womb we are one with our mothers and find comfort in that union. In birth we become segregated and discover loneliness, and for the rest of our lives we seek refuge from that loneliness in the company of others.

"As human beings we're born with needs and desires; but as men and women, how we achieve gratification is learned, passed down from generation to generation, mother to daughter, father to son. In each passing perhaps a little more is lost in translation. Trust me on this, Lance. Come the future volumes will be written on the many differences between men and women. Books intended to provide insight and a better understanding of those differences. But they'll serve only to confuse because they'll only succeed in turning something that should come naturally and easily—the treatment of others in a manner commiserate with what you expect in return—into something far too complex for understanding. Instead of accepting that we all seek the same from each other—acceptance and approval—men and women alike will accuse the opposite sex of being from another planet, perpetuating the belief that what the other desires is alien from what we seek. In that way it becomes easier to deny responsibility for our own shortcomings in providing for another's needs."

I thought Lance looked a little confused. Perhaps he was merely taking in all that I'd just said. Indeed, I'd always considered myself a man of few words, so it was understandable that my long diatribe would take him aback. Finally, he broke the silence.

"You're lonely?"

"Everyone suffers from that malady, Lance, at some level."

"You talked of approval and acceptance."

"For me that translates into approval of my lovemaking and my lovers' acceptance that they should expect nothing more."

"But if you treat them so shallowly, what can you expect in return?"

"The same. And what you term shallow I call simple. Why turn it into something complex? No pretenses, no conditions, no expectations. I put all my cards on the table. I'm honest in my requirements and even more honest in how I will reciprocate."

*I can honestly say there was a time, before Lindy came into my life, when I believed that credo. But in retrospect I can see that I freely chose to instill in my imagination the complexity of Lindy's pretenses, conditions and expectations, preferring to affirm in my own mind that I could never live up to what I only imagined she would demand of me.*

*Melissa professed, in some earlier chapter of this debacle I excuse as my life story, that perhaps Lindy saw in me what she, Melissa, saw. In truth, Lindy saw only the cards I allowed her to see, and I now confess that I was less than honest regarding my requirements and how I would reciprocate in providing for hers. Is the why so important? Perhaps it was at one time, to Lindy, when she was striving so diligently to understand me, to find a way past my veneer. Yet would it have mattered to me? Would I ever have questioned the why had this story not ended the way it did?*

*I sit writing these words, trying to make some sense of my life, a feeble attempt to give some meaning to the pathetic legacy I left behind so many decades ago. Powerless to change anything, despite a second chance, I curse the conceit of my youth, and further curse my unwillingness to act the first time, when I truly held the power to have made a difference.*

"And what if you can't reciprocate?" Lance asked.

"Then I don't get involved. I don't want to hurt anybody, Lance."

*Does anyone ever intend to hurt someone? I never wanted to hurt Lindy. There are some crimes, however, where intent carries little weight when it comes to passing sentence. Some people profess that their life is but punishment for sins committed in a previous life. Not so where my life is concerned. What good is reproach, what lesson is there to be learned from punishment of sins that cannot be recalled? I recall all too well the sins of this life, and I'm being punished accordingly.*

"Besides, there are far too many women willing to accept my arrangement for me to trouble myself over someone like Melissa MacIntyre."

Lance thought about that, and I wondered that we had known each other for so many years without ever having this discussion.

"But if it's as you say, that it should be as simple as treating someone as you expect in return, then it should be no trouble whatsoever. If you truly want—"

"*That's* the key," I said. "I don't *want* to become involved with Melissa, or any woman. Am I attracted to her, skinny as she is? Sure. But even if I trusted her implicitly with regard to her father and brother I wouldn't be interested, simply because she wants from me far more than I'm willing to give."

"But think of what she could give in return."

I laughed. "You sound as if you're lobbying for me." I paused a moment, and then said, "What about your interest? It's not like you to give up so easily."

"Who says I have?"

"That's the spirit!"

"Certainly our philosophies differ," Lance said, "but in wanting someone who wants me in return, we agree."

"There was a time when your pursuit would've been

blind, predicated on something else."

"I know, my need for approval ..." Lance trailed off, seemingly embarrassed by his admission.

"Is not unhealthy, unless taken to an extreme."

"I'm not the same person I was before I went overseas."

"None of us are, and it's not just the war, Lance. Time has a way of changing us all. Now, more than at any other time in history, we're a product of our ever-changing world. Some change is good. That's called growth."

"I feel I did more *growing* in the years I was abroad than I did in all the years prior. Yet I can't help but feel I'm less now than before I left."

"Not less, Lance, maybe just less certain. That's called wisdom."

"I thought wisdom was knowing all the answers."

"That's called youth," I said with a chuckle. "True wisdom comes with the realization that very few answers are yes or no, right or wrong, or true or false, and that for every answer uncovered several more questions will arise. There will always be more questions than answers."

Lance was resting with his back against the headboard of the bed, his feet crossed and his hands steepled across his chest. I'd never seen him look more pensive.

"Hang in there, pal," I said. "I've been finding reasons to reassess my distrust of Melissa. Just don't chase so hard. Be yourself, let her get to know you. Maybe in time she'll come to want what you want."

I hoped I wasn't building a false hope in Lance. While it was true that at times I felt myself wanting to trust Melissa, I had to remind myself that wanting something doesn't necessarily make it so. Besides, my gut feeling was still one of portentousness, and that gut feeling brought me back to the reality of why we were here in this hotel in rural Midwestern America.

Glancing at my watch, I noted it had been twenty minutes since I'd rapped on the door of what I hoped was Professor MacIntyre's room, and I questioned the wisdom of giving up the photograph in the manner I had—although in truth I could think of no ill that could come of it, other than incurring Melissa's wrath at having lost her treasured photograph.

*Well, it's late,* I thought. *There'll be plenty of time in the morning to consider my next move, which will probably be flying back to New York.*

While Lance brushed his teeth I unmade my bed and got my shaving kit and toothbrush from my overnight bag. When Lance vacated the bathroom I brushed my teeth and splashed some cool water on my face.

After toweling it dry, I stared at my reflection in the mirror and wondered a moment at what it was that both Lindy and Melissa saw and to which the likes of Ginger and Peggy were apparently blind. I dismissed the notion with a grunt that was more an exhalation, ran a hand through my hair, flipped off the bathroom light, and returned to my bedside.

By the time I got undressed and slipped under the covers, I could hear Lance's breathing, heavy with sleep.

As I waited for sleep, I thought of Lindy. Her naked breasts crushed against my own bare chest, her mouth on mine as my hands roamed freely across her back before sliding down to cup the soft pliancy of her buttocks. I imagined the flesh yielding amiably to my kneading hands, felt her breath, warm and moist in my ear, and vowed that the next time we made love I'd tell her how I felt about her.

# Chapter Fifteen

It was nearly eight o'clock; Lance and I had finished our showers, had shaved and dressed, when a knock sounded softly on our room's door.

I cracked the door and readied myself in the event the visitor was not Melissa, as I expected, and was instead the German from the men's room, a possibility I was loath to dismiss. I swung the door wide and stepped back to allow admittance to Professor MacIntyre. He was the last person I expected to see at this hour, having last night given up hope that he might respond to the message I'd scribbled on the back of the photograph.

*Perhaps,* I reasoned, *he thought he could more easily move with stealth in the morning than late at night.*

As he stepped past me, I strode forward to check the hallway. I closed the door and shot the bolt while wondering at the absence of Ben Junior. Maybe he had refused to join his father, but then how would he have known it was me who'd brought his sister to Indianapolis?

"Where's my daughter?" the professor asked anxiously, scanning the tiny room for evidence of his daughter, perhaps already regretting that he had so readily accepted at face value that which the photograph had promised. Other than the beard and the lines of distress around his eyes, I didn't think he looked all that much different than his photograph; certainly he looked no older.

"Relax, Professor," I said. "She's in the next room. I'm Joe January and this," I added indicating Lance, who was sitting on the edge of the bed looking somewhat perplexed, "is my pilot, Lance. Any chance you were followed?"

"I don't think so." He sounded like someone who had gotten mighty used to checking over his shoulder.

"Not that it matters," I muttered. "I'd be surprised if your pursuit isn't aware of our room numbers by now."

I again regretted having signed in under the MacIntyre name. Having no clues on which to go, my original intent was to draw attention to our presence, hoping someone would make contact with us. Now, feeling vulnerable, I wished I had instead opted for obscurity.

"What's going on?" Lance asked, dismayed that once again he'd been left out of the loop.

"Lance, this is Professor MacIntyre."

"I already surmised that," Lance said. "How did he know where to find us?"

"I'll fill you in later."

"Please, Mr. January. I'd like to see my daughter."

"Certainly."

I cracked the door once more and, after making certain the corridor was empty, stepped out and made my way to Melissa's room, where I gently rapped on the door. A moment later I heard her voice from within.

"Who is it?"

"January."

I heard the bolt slide and the door cracked open. Melissa, showered and her face made up, clutched at the robe she wore, just above her breasts, in an effort to conceal the treasure beneath. I imagined pale breasts, tipped with rose quartz nipples and couldn't say I was angry that she was not yet ready for breakfast.

"Why, Mr. January, what kind of girl do you think I am?" she asked with a smile designed to tease me to arousal, which under different circumstances would have succeeded.

"I think you'd better come with me."

Melissa sobered immediately.

"What is it? What's wrong?"

I glanced impatiently up one end of the corridor, then down the other.

Sensing our vulnerability, Melissa complied without further question.

Moments later she was facing the bearded man whom she recognized immediately as her father. In disbelief, as if by saying the word would make it true, she whispered, "Daddy?"

"Missy!" the professor said as he crossed the room to

take her in his arms.

I heard Melissa's choked sob and cursed myself for ever doubting her credibility. I could see the tears in her father's eyes. Not wishing to intrude upon their moment any more than Lance's and my presence couldn't help but be, I looked down at the floor.

"Let me look at you," Professor MacIntyre said, holding Melissa at arm's length. "My little girl, you're all grown up." And then, sotto voce, he added, "You look so much like your mother."

He gazed at her a moment longer before pulling her to him again, proof of her authenticity, lest his eyes deceive him.

I recoiled that I'd tried so hard to hear that which had been intended to be private. Yet ever the detective, I wondered whether Melissa had taken notice of her father's seemingly unaffected by time except for the beard appearance and decided, *No, she will see, for the moment, what she wishes to see—the final image of her father from six years ago. His appearance unchanged by the passage of time as she looks back, as we all are prone to do, to happier times, unwilling to admit that her vision might be blurred.*

Lance, I noted, still sat on the edge of the bed, not bothering to hide his sentiments as he shared in Melissa's joy at being reunited with her father.

"Ben Junior …" Melissa gasped, breaking the moment. "Is he with you?"

Confusion crossed Professor MacIntyre's face. His eyes met mine before he asked, "You mean he's not with you?"

I shook my head. "We assumed he was with you."

"But how did you know we were here?" Melissa asked. Her earlier emotions had begun to ebb. Now the questions would come, which pleased me. I surmised Professor MacIntyre would answer more openly questions put to him by his daughter than by a stranger.

"This gentleman," her father answered, handing the photo to Melissa, "got word to me that you were with him."

Melissa glanced at the note on the back of the photograph.

"Joe?" she said, dispensing with our agreed upon formality. She had believed more adamantly than I realized that I'd find her father for her; that I'd accomplished that task so easily and so soon after our arrival in Indianapolis, like my earlier appraisal of the favorite to win next week's big race, seemed to amaze her.

I blushed at the mention of my name, looked at Lance and was surprised to see no envy; yet I was puzzled to see something I was unable to identify. Looking back at Melissa, I felt the heat in my face warm further and wished, for Lance's sake, that she would instead bestow that look upon him. Finally, I glanced at Professor MacIntyre, who was drinking in the profile his daughter was presenting him, and wondered if he would recognize that which fueled his daughter's admiration.

"How did you know where to find my father?"

I quickly regained my composure. Shifting my weight to my right foot, I leaned my left shoulder against the wall and crossed my arms, my right hand cupping my left elbow, my left grasping my right biceps. Finally, I crossed my left foot in front of my right and stood it on its toe.

"Observation, Miss MacIntyre," I said. "It's what you paid me for, remember? Your daughter, Professor MacIntyre, hired me to find you."

"Mr. January is much too modest," Melissa remarked for her father's benefit, evoking a laugh from Lance.

"I've heard Joe called a lot of things," Lance said. "Modest has never been one of them."

"Maybe not," I said. "I guess I just take my powers of observation for granted. And if you hadn't been so antisocial at dinner last night, maybe you would've learned a thing or two of the art of observation."

Professor MacIntyre laughed—a rich, deep baritone, it rumbled with good humor, and I was surprised at the ease with which he, the suspected fugitive, offered it; but then, he might still be basking in the warmth the fortune his daughter's company provided.

"You two can only be friends," he said as he put his arm around Melissa's shoulders.

Melissa giggled.

"My father's own powers of observation are also fairly acute, don't you think, Mr. January?" she asked, unable to mask her pride.

Professor MacIntyre kissed her forehead, then tweaked her nose playfully.

"Daddy!" she cried in mock indignation.

I held up my hand for silence and made my way to the door where I thought I'd heard a noise. I listened for a moment, ear poised against the door, and then cracked it once more and took note of a young couple sauntering down the corridor. Satisfied, I came back into the room, my mood more somber.

"Well, Professor," I said, "it would seem you have a lot of explaining to do. Your daughter might think nothing of a six-year absence, but I'm a lot more skeptical. Obviously you're a man on the run—you've admitted to pursuit and I've already met two of your pursuers."

"Two?" Lance and Melissa piped in together.

"Yes, two," I said. To Lance, I explained, "While you were up here last night pouting, I was downstairs working an angle, making myself visible." To Melissa I said, "You may recall just before dinner was brought I excused myself."

"You mean someone was watching us from the men's room?" she asked with a laugh, and was joined by Lance and her father. I refrained.

"No," I said once their laughter began to ebb. "Someone was watching us from the corner table. When he left for the restroom, I followed. Turned out to be another German gent. Didn't learn much from him," I added, not wanting to divulge anything pertinent until it was to my advantage to do so, "except that he's hot to catch up with you, Professor. Any idea why that might be?"

Father looked to daughter for affirmation.

"It's okay, Daddy, you can trust him."

Professor MacIntyre looked at me for a moment,

measuring me, before conceding; that his daughter trusted me apparently was good enough for him. He sat down on the edge of my bed, a gesture that served to punctuate his concession. A moment later Melissa joined him.

"How much do they know?" he asked her.

"As much as she wishes us to know," I said, immediately regretting the harshness of my statement. To soften my accusation, I added, "She showed me the letter and the postcard."

"Joe thinks Melissa switched the two to make it look like the postcard had been written previous to the letter, making the authenticity of the postcard's reference to the letter in the past tense questionable."

I marveled that Lance had been able to offer that explanation, with everything in its right order.

"Mr. January is correct," the professor said quietly, staring ahead. "It's the only conclusion any *sane* man could reach." It was the statement of a man who at some point during some severe ordeal has questioned his own reasoning.

I felt the hair on the back of my neck prickle and asked, "Did you date the letter and the postcard, Professor MacIntyre?" I thought that a negative response, or even the least hesitation, would betray the hoax I desperately wanted to believe this to be.

"Yes, of course," he said without hesitation.

*Damn.*

"Proof, to myself at least, of the fact behind the audacity of what you will wish to believe fiction."

A moment passed before the professor asked Melissa, "Did you receive the package I sent you?"

"Yes, Daddy."

"And we brought it with us," I said, striding over to my travel bag to unzip it.

"You brought it with you?" the professor asked.

"Of course," I said, removing the cube. "I received a message yesterday morning, back at my office, that we were to bring it with us."

I pulled the page with the pasted letters from my breast

pocket and handed it to the professor.

"Are you going to tell us that that wasn't from you?"

Professor MacIntyre stared at the note with no comprehension.

"Mr. January, I had no idea you would bring my daughter to Indianapolis, and until just a few minutes ago, I didn't know who you were, so there is no way for me to have gotten this message to you, nor would I have wanted to. Having that object in this room poses a grave threat."

I nodded and said, "Maybe you'll be so kind as to tell us just what it is."

I handed the cube to the professor and watched his eyes widen at the sight of it.

"Don't blame your daughter, Professor; I'm the one who opened the package. I may be working for her, but I have a right to know what I'm in for. Not that that thing offered any clue."

The cube continued to randomly blink its lights while the professor considered my assertion.

"Yes, I suppose you do," he answered with a nod.

I could've asked any number of questions, but opted instead to let Professor MacIntyre tell his own story in his own way.

"Why don't you start at the beginning, Professor," I said as a prompt. "Six years ago—"

Professor MacIntyre laughed, the laugh of someone who has been locked away and insists, despite the drugs that have been given to him, that his story—that which his psychiatrists label as invention—is factual. The laugh faded to silence, and it was during that moment, the silence a sort of presage as three adolescents waited for their father to begin their favorite bedtime story, that he contemplated where or perhaps how to begin.

A small nod indicated a decision had been reached. Then he looked at each of us, Lance first, then me, before finally, his daughter. He took a breath.

"In 1941 ..." he began, and I sensed I was in the presence of someone who didn't think in terms of years gone by but instead of dates—or someone in denial of the passage of time. "… Dr. Dinsmoor, the head of my department at Columbia, foresaw the devastating effects the war would have on art and historical monuments in Europe. He also feared that it wouldn't be until after the U.S. entered the war, if it ever did, that our government would do anything about it."

"So this Dinsmoor had you organize a committee," Lance said.

MacIntyre shook his head. "My daughter must have told you my trips to Europe were somewhat routine."

I nodded.

"Well, I couldn't believe how much conditions had deteriorated during the weeks subsequent to my previous visit. This country, being on the other side of the world, is—was—so far removed from what was happening over there."

"I'm sure much was withheld."

"You're a very perceptive man, Mr. January," Professor MacIntyre said.

"He doesn't trust anyone," Lance said. "Not even the government."

"Trust in yourself only, and another shall never betray you."

"As true today as it was in Thomas Fuller's day," the professor agreed. "Perhaps more so."

"You'll find Mr. January to be very philosophical," Melissa told her father, her admiration evident once again, "and much more intelligent than he lets on."

"Really?" her father asked with raised eyebrows. "Then he'd best tread carefully around you hadn't he?" To me he said, "My daughter finds highly intelligent men irresistible."

"Daddy!" Melissa's embarrassment was masked beneath yesterday afternoon's sun. Mine was not.

I noted Professor MacIntyre's indifference to my presence as a potential suitor, so secure in his daughter's esteem that he wouldn't view me, or any man to which his daughter might be attracted, as a threat.

To regain control of the room, I said, "Professor

MacIntyre, your daughter and I have a business arrangement."

I resisted the urge to look at Melissa; to do so would be to show weakness. I knew that in her eyes I would see disappointment, and the control I was trying so hard to maintain would thereby come under assault.

To ensure Melissa could not peek at what was hidden behind my walls, I added, "She paid me to find you and now I'm charged with getting you to New York, if that's what you want."

Looking down at hands that cupped his knees, Professor MacIntyre let out a sigh.

"Just as I thought," I said. "It's not that simple is it?"

The professor met my scrutiny and held it a moment before conceding, "No, it's not that simple."

Professor MacIntyre glanced at Melissa, still seated beside him, and I glimpsed doubt in his mien. Doubt that despite being his own flesh and blood she wouldn't, or perhaps couldn't, believe the tale he was about to relate.

In that moment I knew my entire belief system—everything I held as true and irrefutably real—was about to be tested.

Then, turning back to me, resigned to whatever reaction his story was likely to engender, he took a deep breath and began his tale …

# Part Three

# Chapter Sixteen

*November 1941*

"Ben, it's good to see you!"

"Hello, Nigel," Professor MacIntyre said, giving Nigel's hand a brisk shake.

Nigel was a curator at the Victoria and Albert Museum, located in the Royal Borough of Kensington and Chelsea in London. Founded in the 1850s, by the 1940s it boasted the most diverse collection of decorative art and design in the world, spanning the seven continents and dating from 3,000 BC. Its collections encompassed diverse art forms such as photography, fashion, metalwork, sculpture, glass and ceramics. In the late 1920s, when the U.S. had been a far richer country, Nigel had been instrumental in helping MacIntyre acquire a number of literary first editions, as well as several elephant folios, miniature books, broadsides, early maps, and several framed pieces. Schermerhorn, home of the archeology department and fine arts library at Columbia, also owed to Nigel the existence of more than one ancient printing press. Nigel possessed the appearance and demeanor that one would typically associate with his position. He was obese, although he would good naturedly define his disorder as stalwartness.

"I've someone I'd like you to meet," Nigel said, indicating an oddly attired young man. His clothing was contemporary but looked, well, aged.

The young man's extreme good looks seemed, to Benjamin, rather manufactured. His complexion, flawlessly smooth, looked as if a razor had never touched it. The features, perfect in their symmetry and arrangement, seemed to have been selected from a catalogue. Blue eyes to go with the fine blond hair, and a nose specially crafted to fit with the high, broad cheekbones and squared chin; while the smile revealed teeth equally flawless in their brightness and evenness. The young man rose, rather elegantly, and offered, somewhat awkwardly Ben thought, his right hand.

MacIntyre took the hand, felt something unusual in its grasp, and failed to mask his shock when, upon looking down, he noticed the hand, as perfectly crafted and textured as the young man's face, was composed of six fingers.

"I'm—I'm sorry," he said, embarrassed yet reluctant to tear his eyes away from the anomaly that still gripped his hand.

Meeting the young man's eyes, MacIntyre saw no abashment, which further fueled his discomfiture. If anything the young man seemed rather amused by his loss of composure.

"Ben," Nigel interjected in his British cadence, and MacIntyre was grateful for the intrusion. "This is Regis Llewellyn. Regis, Benjamin MacIntyre, the Yank I was telling you about."

"Yank?" Regis asked, looking somewhat puzzled. Then, with dawning recognition, "The American."

MacIntyre wasn't at all surprised by the beautiful tone of the young man's voice—melodic, yet somehow nondescript, nearly genderless. Although he spoke perfect English, MacIntyre detected a faint German accent; not surprising considering his physical appearance. Still, he couldn't help but think there was something affected in its cadence.

"Yes, the American," Nigel replied with a laugh as he walked around to behind his desk. "Sit down, Regis. You, too, Ben."

After seating himself, he continued.

"This must seem awfully strange to you, Ben, and believe me it's going to get a lot stranger as we fill you in. All I ask is that you keep an open mind and trust that I—we," he amended with a glance at Regis—"have evidence that everything you are about to hear is true."

Nigel took a deep breath before continuing.

"You may have noticed that Regis is somewhat different than you and me."

MacIntyre said nothing; to him it was the polite thing to do: one did not point out the flaws in others, even though the flaw in this case was the obvious lack of any. A sixth finger, while certainly odd, was undoubtedly more beneficial than five and therefore would better be termed an oddity. MacIntyre merely returned Nigel's level stare, trying to guess what possible explanation was about to be offered in conjunction with the ominous preamble with which Nigel had opened.

MacIntyre's peripheral vision afforded him the sight of Regis, seated in a chair against the wall to Nigel's right; but he didn't need peripheral vision to know the young man was staring at him as well, for reasons of his own. He could feel the intensity of the young man's glare. Gauging him, perhaps judging him. But why?

"Regis is the product of genetic engineering," Nigel said. The words flowed easily, as if he were responding to a stranger's query for the time of day. "You don't look surprised, Ben."

MacIntyre shrugged and said, "I've heard the Germans have been experimenting in that area. That would explain his appearance," he finished with a nod toward Regis, careful not to make eye contact. "What I find surprising," he went on, surprising himself with his nonchalance, "is that they've managed to achieve this level of success. I—"

Regis laughed, but the laugh, MacIntyre noted, held no contempt. He was unable to stop himself from hazarding a glance at Regis and once again taking note of the features that, in their absolute perfection, seemed to draw attention to themselves as *im*perfections.

"They haven't," Nigel said. "Yet." When he was certain he again had MacIntyre's attention, he added, "But from where Regis comes … or perhaps it would be more accurate to say from *when* he comes, genetic engineering is quite common. Regis is from the future, Ben."

*"When?"* MacIntyre croaked. His utterance was not so much a question as an attempt to affirm the accuracy of what he'd just heard. He could see Nigel believed in the truth of the stranger's claim.

MacIntyre the scientist was intrigued if not yet convinced by the portentousness of what Nigel was alluding. Yet it was that same scientist who wanted to hold onto the belief that time flowed in one direction only; that the past was past and could never be revisited by those residing in the present. He couldn't argue that events occurring in the past go a long way toward shaping the future, nor that that future can always look back upon those events as part of its past. Yet he had never considered the possibility that the future could affect the present—the future's past. His notion that time is linear was something that had always seemed irrefutably logical. Now, if he were to believe what Nigel was telling him, through use of some device or technology, it was possible to travel upstream, *against* the flow of the water!

MacIntyre imagined himself traveling back in time one hundred years. The people of 1841 would consider themselves to be living in the present, with a past to which he also could lay claim. And he, while trying to convince them he is from their future, would be looked upon as a lunatic. To them in their present—yet still a past he would have just as much right to call his—the future of which he spoke, although shaped by events of 1841 as much as any other year in mankind's long history, does not and cannot possibly exist!

"When," he breathed again, as if the word now held, and forever would hold, an entirely different connotation.

"The Nazis in this time period are decades away from perfecting genetic engineering," Regis said. "Their methods are crude, their attempts clumsy, but they will succeed … in time."

"When?" A third time MacIntyre used the word, but this time with intent, a question directed.

"That is unimportant and, for you in this continuum, irrelevant," Regis said.

"Regis is from the year 2047," Nigel said, unable to keep the excitement from his voice.

MacIntyre thought about that for a moment before asking, "Who else knows he is here?"

"You believe then, all that we've told you thus far?"

Before MacIntyre could express otherwise, Nigel added, "I knew you would, Ben. You're a man of science, a man who understands that in science there are no boundaries, no limitations. Except those we impose upon ourselves."

"You spoke of evidence." While Ben the scientist wanted to believe, he also needed to see the proof behind the theory, to test the experiment, to taste its results.

"In good time, Ben," Nigel said, and laughed at his unintended pun. "In answer to your question, no one knows of his presence here, and it's important that you tell no one. He's here on an expedition and he needs our assistance."

"Why?" MacIntyre asked with all the innocence of a child. Inside, an alarm had just gone off. "Why would a man with technology at his disposal that we can't begin to fathom need the aid of two backwoodsmen?"

"Backwoodsmen?"

"A sort of euphemism," Nigel explained to Regis with a chuckle. "Ben means to say that to a man from your time period, with all the advancements you have available to you, we must appear somewhat primitive."

"You are," Regis said.

The simple honesty of his response made him seem all the more smug, if he were capable of smugness. Also, to MacIntyre, more dangerous.

"Nevertheless," Regis continued, "given my circumstances, my mission requires the aid of the locals."

"Locals," Nigel said, "are what Regis calls the people of any given timeframe he visits."

"So you make a habit of traveling to other time periods?" MacIntyre said. He felt his distrust begin to grow as he tried to imagine what obscure reason Regis might have for visiting 1941. He was beginning to dislike this manufactured being even more for his superior attitude toward the "locals." That was enough to color his judgment, despite his curiosity surrounding the how of his arrival.

On the other hand, it looked as if Nigel had been won over easily enough. Whatever his story, it must have been good since Nigel had never been one to suspend his disbelief without good reason—or evidence.

"No," Regis said. "This technology is new, and this is the first time it has been employed."

"Ben, I can see you're troubled by this, but please, give Regis a chance. I asked you to keep an open mind. I felt as you did initially—suspicious. But listen to his story. Then, if you're still not convinced he needs our assistance, you can walk away."

Ben the man wanted to walk away now. He sensed something was awry, that all was not as it should be. He sensed that Nigel had but scratched the surface with his explanation, that he'd been told just enough to pique his interest.

Yet Ben the scientist was too intrigued by the notion of genetic engineering and time travel to let Ben *the man* just walk away. MacIntyre couldn't deny he was curious as to why 1941 was such an important year in this man's past to which to travel. His first guess was the war. No doubt a World War—one of this magnitude—could have had a profound effect on this man's present.

So what could his agenda be? Was it simply historical research, as Nigel had intimated with his usage of the term *expedition?* Or was it something much more ominous, as Regis had implied with his reference to a mission?

MacIntyre looked over to Regis, the man of the hour, the product of a technology that didn't yet exist, and saw something cold and calculating in his eyes. He wondered whether, after he listened to his story and still decided not to get involved, Regis would let him just walk away.

"Ben?"

MacIntyre looked to Nigel, sitting behind his cluttered desk, his five-fingered hands flat upon its top.

"Just give him a chance. Please. Listen to what he has to say."

MacIntyre took a deep breath … and nodded.

Perchance MacIntyre was in possession of some small amount of prescience, for in that small gesture of accedence, he somehow knew his life would be forever changed.

*May 1947*

I took a long drag from my cigarette but betrayed no trace of what I was thinking; I knew there was more of the story still to come, much more.

Professor MacIntyre, a learned man, had given in easily to the temptation to believe this man Regis's story. Yet I wasn't ready to concede his truth with so much still left untold. Did that make me an ignorant man? No, a good investigator is certain he has all the facts before he decides on a course of action.

Like the professor, my curiosity, first aroused by the two mysterious letters and their conflicting dates, was now lifted to new heights by this new information even though, like the letters, there was no supporting evidence to back it—only the cube.

MacIntyre was on the lam, that much had been obvious from the start, and unable—or unwilling—to seek the aid of higher authorities. I was ready to yield to the evidence of the two nefarious Germans on the professor's trail as enough to at least validate the part of his story he had just related.

I recalled MacIntyre's description of Regis, the six fingers and perfect features, and thought of the German I'd questioned downstairs in the men's room, who'd had but ten fingers; but I refused to consider the implications.

*Evidence.*

Something told me that evidence supporting MacIntyre's story would be revealed to me, and because I knew it would be forthcoming, I was in no way anxious to have it revealed ahead of time. Not that kind of evidence. Potent enough to rip to shreds my own belief system of how the universe functioned, its governing laws.

Melissa sat staring at me, already convinced of the legitimacy of her father's claim, perhaps trying to appraise my stance on her father's story; while Lance looked at once both relieved as well as troubled that I hadn't jumped in with both feet to shoot holes in MacIntyre's tale.

As for the professor, he seemed to be looking within

himself, perchance seeking the best way to tie together the tattered remnants of his story to convince me, a potential ally, of what had, over what had been to him the past few months, become only too real.

Whether I ultimately believed the rest of the story was at this point extrinsic: there were those who *did* believe. The threat those believers posed was real, to Professor MacIntyre and to me, too, since I was now officially involved. Linked to a man who had in his possession something that someone would stop at nothing to possess.

So I wanted to know everything the professor knew, and whether or not our adversaries were privy to that knowledge as well, for the more knowledge I had at my disposal, the better my chances of getting us all out of this predicament.

I exhaled a ring of smoke, nodded once and grunted.

"I'm hungry," I said. "I don't think it's wise to have breakfast downstairs."

Once we ordered room service, I lit another cigarette.

"Go ahead, Professor. Let's hear more."

The professor nodded in conformance, steeling himself against the inevitable. Then, taking another breath, he began the second part of his strange tale …

# Chapter Seventeen

*November 1941*

“You must understand,” Regis said, “I am not here to educate you on the principles of time travel. They are much simpler than you can imagine, but with your limited means quite impossible to implement. Time is but a single moment, no past, no future. Merely the present. Yours here in 1941, mine in my own time one hundred years hence, and any moment throughout history, whether that history has already occurred or has yet to commence. Time is but a device created by man to mark the change of seasons, the passage of one day to the next, the old year to the new, and, of course, his own aging process. Time exists as a whole—past, present and future as one. Man, and all living things, animal and flora, are transient.”

“Time, then, is not fluid,” MacIntyre said.

“Not in the sense you suggest. It flows, for each of us in our own present, toward whatever destiny the creator has in mind for us. But …” Regis paused a moment. “You will find this difficult to comprehend, but the scholars of my time theorize that history has been foreordained.”

“Imagine a book, Ben,” Nigel said. “Every book is composed of a beginning, a middle, and an end.”

“With each of us,” Regis added, “playing whatever part we are written to play on whatever page we appear, as history moves inexorably toward its climax. Each chapter fits into the whole, each subsequent episode a result of what has occurred in its predecessor.” He paused, waiting for his explanation to sink in before continuing.

“So in a sense, time *does* flow, as indicated by the logical sequence of events of which history is composed. Had man, in the early chapters, not discovered fire and invented the rudimentary tools that ensured his success as a species, we three would not, in this much later chapter, be enjoying this discussion."

"Sort of shoots down the presumption that any of us has any freedom of choice, doesn't it?" Nigel said.

"If I understand Nigel," Regis said, "his comment is intended as jest. Put another way, it is the *circumstances* that have been predetermined—the text that is the plot of the book. You and I and Nigel, as well as all the players that grace the pages of this great cosmic novel, are free to react in impromptu fashion."

"How can I believe that when you tell me that future history has been predestined? How can I hope to be an influential force when the outcome has already been determined?"

"Because," Regis said, "the circumstances are unimportant. What is important is our reaction to those circumstances. How we respond to adversity is what is being tested."

MacIntyre considered Regis's assertion, and then said, "Then it isn't a fair test. While I confess that we cannot hope to understand why God allows his creation to suffer, I cannot fathom there is nothing I can do to influence the outcome of at least this small piece of history you call my present. I cannot believe that any man who has ever lived has failed to impact his present."

"I do not dispute," Regis said, "that many great men throughout history have left behind as their legacy something positive for those who followed. But understand this: God has nothing to do with the wretched place man has made of His creation. I reiterate *He* created the circumstances of our existence, but *we* are free to make of those circumstances what we wish, and so if there is suffering, it is because *we* allow it."

"You insinuate that God is to blame for the evil that torments mankind?"

"I do not blame Him. I simply point out that He gave man the freedom to *choose.* To choose means to select from two or more options. Without evil there can be no good, while the diametric is also true."

"But don't you see?" MacIntyre argued. "The conditions of the experiment have been fixed—the end result has already been determined!"

"And you assume the worst."

"Look at history!" MacIntyre said. "We keep making the same mistakes over and over again. World War I was supposed to be the war to end all wars, and yet a scant score of years later World War II commenced. When will World War III begin?"

"There will be no World War III."

"How can you be so—" MacIntyre stopped, suddenly aware of the folly of his query.

"Ben," Nigel said.

"No, Nigel, we *have* to assume the worst. Why else would he be here, if future history isn't disintegrating?"

"Which is precisely why he *is* here," Nigel said. "To amend the future. This is a critical point in their history, Ben. What happens in the next few months will have a profound effect on his present. Our future. Regis possesses the technology to rectify the mistakes that will be made between now and the end of the year. To make both our presents—his *and* ours—a better place."

"How do you know that?" MacIntyre said. "Has he shown you proof?"

"He hasn't actually shown me the future, if that's what you mean."

"Why not? What's he trying to hide?"

"I have nothing to hide," Regis replied.

"How do we know that what you propose will be beneficial to us?"

"Ben—"

"I don't even have to know what the future holds, Nigel. What do we know of him and who he represents? He's already admitted to viewing us as primitive. How are we to know to what end he'll manipulate our barbarous species in order to achieve his goals? Have you even asked either of these questions?"

"Ben," Nigel said again, appalled by the ferocity of

MacIntyre's attack on their guest, "you're forgetting one thing."

"What's that?"

"Regis is genetically engineered. He's incapable of lying."

"How do you know that? Based on what *he's* told you?" MacIntyre jerked a thumb in the direction of Regis. "I'm no geneticist, Nigel, but I'll wager that any being, whether manufactured or born, if he's capable of learning, he's capable of learning to lie, or at the very least to manipulate the truth to suit his ends."

"I have no time for this," Regis said.

"Finally! Impatience! Something that resembles a flaw in the perfect being!"

"The effects of time travel are temporary, Ben," Nigel said. "Regis has but three days to set his plan in motion before he must return to his own time, and one has been spent already. I beg you again, give Regis a chance. Please, hear him out."

But MacIntyre didn't want to hear Regis out. He was having difficulty understanding why he was trying so vehemently to disbelieve and sabotage everything that came out of his mouth. Was it simple fear of the unknown, or merely distrust of someone who purported to be superior? He pictured himself in his earlier vision, in which *he* was the stranger from the future visiting 1841. How would the "locals" view him? As benevolent, or as someone with dubious intent?

With the concepts of genetic engineering and time travel, MacIntyre now found himself forced to consider ethics and implications he could not see in simple terms. He was being asked to regard the moral undertones of a situation consisting solely of shades of gray. Not to mention to pass judgment on this stranger's claims and then take action—action that would affect the lives of countless people, many of whom wouldn't exist for decades. Suddenly he felt as if his values were being tested. Still, he couldn't argue against the curiosity that appealed to the part of him that was a scientist.

So it was against his better judgment, against an ominous feeling of foreboding, against a fear that by knowing too much he would be unable to turn his back on that knowledge, that Benjamin MacIntyre's curiosity won out.

He nodded to the blank features that in their perfection were so unreadable to him.

"Your friend, Nigel, is correct," Regis began. "The next few months of this war are critical. In my time, much knowledge of this period has been obliterated. That is because Germany won World War II. As a result, much of our history is predicated upon that which the ruling party wishes us to know."

"Sort of one-sided, you might say," Nigel offered.

"Much knowledge of your present is known to only a privileged few in my time. Authorities would disavow that knowledge if it were brought to light. Yet make no mistake, that knowledge exists, kept alive from one generation to the next by our elite group." Regis paused, trying to measure MacIntyre's reaction to his preamble.

"Imagine, Ben," Nigel said, impatient with the ensuing silence, "Hitler's dream of an empire that would last a thousand years is nearly a century old in 2047."

"And growing more powerful. Your country, Benjamin MacIntyre, does not exist in my time, and knowledge of its previous existence is obscure."

"The U.S. will fall to the Third Reich in a little more than three years from now, Ben."

"Authorities in my time would refuse to acknowledge that the United States was, at this point in our history, a world power, preferring instead to propagate the belief that it was just another weak country that fell prey to Hitler's supremacy. There are those, however, who believe the Allies lost the war because the United States remained neutral too long, failing to enter the war at a time when Hitler was still vulnerable."

"So you're here to lure the U.S. into the war, thereby ensuring Hitler will fail in his attempt at world conquest," MacIntyre said.

"Prime Minister Churchill will soon come across knowledge of a secret Japanese attack on Pearl Harbor," Nigel explained. "According to Regis, Churchill will inform Roosevelt of the attack ahead of time. Roosevelt will alert Hirohito of his awareness of their plan and they will abort their attack, thereby delaying U.S. involvement in the campaign. That delay will buy Hitler the time he needs to develop the atomic bomb first, before the U.S. He'll—"

"Stop, Nigel. I don't want to know how he'll use it or where he'll drop it, that's more than I care to know."

"Your friend is wise," Regis said, his tone sounding oddly compassionate in its dispassion. "Yet without knowledge, how can one make an educated decision?"

Before MacIntyre could refute his wisdom, Regis provided the fruit of knowledge.

"Germany exploded the first atomic bomb over New York City on October 16, 1944."

Then, with all the detached objectivity of a geology professor relating to his students how the earth's crust was formed, Regis went on to describe the catastrophic effects of his present's historic first use of atomic weaponry. Whether intended or not, his use of past tense lent even greater credence to his narrative.

"The Empire State Building was ground zero. The ten-kiloton bomb instantly vaporized it and everything within a six-block radius. The resultant firestorm lasted nearly six hours and burned out a two square mile area. The blast effect killed nearly half a million citizens. Hitler strategically maximized the effects of the bomb, exploding it during the height of the business day, when Midtown enjoyed its densest population. Thousands more died from radiation. Yet those numbers paled as the effects of that holocaust were felt for generations. Scientists would trace birth defects to radiation and its effects on the parents' genetic code." A note of sadness tinged Regis's voice, surprising MacIntyre, who had thought him incapable of pity.

Regis went on: "The United States surrendered unconditionally the following day under the threat that another more powerful bomb, its target a secret, would be dropped. President Roosevelt was executed along with both branches of government, assuring Hitler of seeing his dream of world domination come true. What was left of New York City was torn down and completely rebuilt. The Statue of Liberty was disassembled and used as scrap metal. Nothing of the city's former majesty was left, no memory of its previous existence remained. No memorial was ever constructed. To all in my present, save we few, it cannot be said that even those who suffered and died have been forgotten, for Hitler took great pains to eliminate all trace of their existence."

"But why?" MacIntyre asked. "I would think he would wish to promote that kind of tyranny so he could more easily maintain his iron fisted control."

"You are correct but only to a point. The United States was the last of the allied countries to fall and Hitler had much foresight. Once he had the world beneath his thumb, he realized a much more subtle form of despotism would be required to maintain his authority. He wished future generations to view him as a just martinet, and so he was careful to eliminate evidence to the contrary. In time, those who had lived the account firsthand would die. Such was Hitler's power, they feared passing their knowledge to their children lest they put them at risk. By the end of the millennium, almost no one from the original generation was alive. Successive generations were taught nothing of Hitler's private history, only what he wished them to know—that democracy had been the cancer and fascism the purge."

"Yet the existence of your movement indicates his failure to eradicate that evidence completely."

Regis smiled at MacIntyre's inability to see the obvious.

"His ego would not allow all validation of his ruthlessness to be destroyed. He reveled in the power he had wielded in bringing the United States to her knees. Yet he knew that public knowledge handed down from one generation to the next—in the form of any kind of memorial to those who had died in the blast and its resultant effects or text relative to your nation's former grandeur—would be a detriment to him."

"So Hitler created the movement himself." MacIntyre couldn't help but laugh at the irony.

Regis nodded, perplexed at MacIntyre's ability to find humor in his revelation.

"We were charged to maintain the historical accuracy of what actually happened."

"But why? To what end?" MacIntyre couldn't fathom the wisdom behind keeping that sort of damning evidence around.

Regis shrugged and said, "Who can say what goes on in the mind of a madman? Perhaps it was purely ego—like a great athlete who maintains a scrapbook despite that, years later, his records have fallen to a faster, stronger, perhaps more skilled athlete. Although he is but a name in the annals, he refuses to let go of his glory, his moment of victory. Or perhaps, like most sociopaths, it was a hidden desire to be found out."

MacIntyre thought about that for a moment before phrasing his next question.

"You think he was mad then?"

"That he would go to such extremes to achieve his end would seem proof of madness; that he cherished the memories of the atrocities he committed and kept them alive instead of denying them seems to substantiate that sickness."

"Surely after his death you could've gone public—"

"Impossible," Regis said. "First, the ruling party is much too strong. He chose his successor well. And no, he is not a manufactured being. Additionally, whether it was through wisdom or ignorance, he kept our persuasion small. Knowledge of its existence is obscure. Had we tried to reveal the truth, we at best would have been ridiculed, at worst, executed as traitors to the state."

"And?" MacIntyre asked to fill the void Regis had left with his reluctance to proceed.

"Third, *der fuehrer* is not yet deceased."

"What?" MacIntyre exclaimed. "But that would mean he'd be over a hundred-fifty years old!"

Regis held up a six-fingered hand. "Nor is he alive by your standards."

MacIntyre looked to Nigel for edification; when he found none forthcoming, he looked back at Regis, who nodded.

"In 1980, at the age of ninety-one, he was diagnosed with cancer. Inoperable, it did not respond to the treatment available, so he was placed in a cryogenic chamber."

"Frozen," Nigel interjected, unable to contain himself, "in suspended animation, his bodily functions kept at minimal levels. Kept barely alive, yet the aging process is negligible."

"Until a cure could be found," Regis finished. "Which it has. Yet they cannot resurrect him without this." Regis held up a small cube. Each facet of the cube was composed of nine squares, each a different color. The colors seemed to alternate in a random pattern.

"What is it?" MacIntyre asked.

"It contains the secret knowledge of where he lays frozen. He entrusted it to our faction, believing that in our perfection we could not be swayed."

MacIntyre's eyebrows rose at Regis's unspoken "however." Before he could pursue his line of questioning, Regis went on.

"There is another, as there must be for security's sake, who knows a portion of the ever-changing combination that will unlock its secret. His identity is secure from me, as mine is from him."

"Then it would seem that to complete total security, knowledge of that cube's whereabouts would have to be kept from both you and your counterpart." Regis affirmed MacIntyre's guess with a nod. "Then how have you come to possess it?"

"I have appropriated it," Regis said without inflection.

"He's *stolen* it!" Nigel cried with a loud guffaw.

MacIntyre watched the cube flash its lights as it sat in the palm of Regis's left hand. Somehow the lights seemed to indicate intelligence, as if it knew the value of the secret it had been charged to maintain.

"Why?" MacIntyre asked with childlike innocence.

"Because I do not wish him to come to power again."

In response to MacIntyre's shock, Regis continued. "*Der fuehrer* was correct in his assessment that a manufactured being cannot be swayed. Yet you, too, Benjamin MacIntyre, are correct in your assumption that we are capable of learning and of taking action upon acquired knowledge. Suffice it to say, Hitler will succeed in exterminating the Jewish people. Yet it will not end there. Afterward ..." he trailed off, weighing the wisdom of saying more before settling on, "he will systematically set about exterminating whole nations and races in an effort to purge the planet for the benefit of his perfect race."

"Of which you are a member," MacIntyre said.

"That I cannot deny. Still, there are those who see the flaw in extermination. There is no way of telling if we are in the majority since there are opponents who pursue power and would like nothing more than to see Hitler's goal attained."

"What is the flaw?" MacIntyre thought he knew but wished to see if Regis would affirm it.

"It is morally wrong to remove a people from existence. Like hunting the great whales to extinction, once they are gone they can never be replaced."

"What does that matter to you, a member of a perfect race?"

"I understand your skepticism, Benjamin MacIntyre. In your ignorance you view me with disdain. Perhaps you sense that as a manufactured being I am incapable of making moral distinctions. Because I am man-made you may think I possess no spirit, no soul. You may even think it blasphemous for man to seek to improve upon God's design. Whether that is so is for God alone to determine. He allowed the knowledge to exist. Man merely implemented that knowledge. I ask you to not harbor any ill will toward me for, like you, I had no choice in life. If I am guilty of living, then it is only through association with those who decided for me that

I should exist. Yet I, too, harbor a belief in a superior being. I believe in life after death, that death is but a part of life and not its cessation. All in Nature is predicated upon the cycle of life and death. Is not the setting sun akin to a dying day, only to give way to the birth of a new day? The seasons cycle from birth to maturation, to atrophy, and transmutation to new life. Why would a man's death differ? But since no one has ever returned from the hereafter, my belief, like yours, can be rooted only in faith.

"Your inferiority perhaps breeds a fear of me, and from that fear a need to maintain a sense of superiority in the face of the truth forces you to equate me with lower life forms—highly intelligent, able to learn, yet incapable of feeling emotion. But you are wrong, Benjamin MacIntyre. I feel emotion as acutely as you. I am capable of love and pity. I can feel outrage at moral indiscretions. In these you and I are akin. It is only in my superior intellect, sense of logic and much longer lifespan that we differ. My logic enables me to not allow my emotions to color my actions; therefore I am incapable of acting rashly.

"Furthermore, I confess to envy you and your type, procreated through the union of flesh. You, whose left ear is slightly more than a centimeter higher than your right, with your skewed smile, your nose that betrays your ethnic origins, and your eyes which are set too close together to be considered esthetically perfect by my present's standards. Yes, I see beauty in such imperfection and diversity. It was through such diversity that your country became great."

"The Melting Pot," Nigel said.

"Yes, the Melting Pot," Regis echoed. "The flaw in extermination is elimination of such diversity. Different thinking promotes challenge. Overcoming challenge results in growth."

"Eliminating growth results in stagnation," MacIntyre finished.

"Precisely," Regis said.

MacIntyre should have been angry with Regis and his point-by-point argument. Regis had countered each of his objections before he'd had a chance to even voice them. Once again Regis had maintained his superiority, and that should have infuriated MacIntyre; yet at precisely the right moment he had prostrated himself, leaving MacIntyre humbled. Now he found himself reevaluating his initial reaction to this manufactured being from the future.

"Still, you owe your existence to him," MacIntyre said.

In his confusion, Regis looked over to Nigel.

"Ben means to ask of your obligation to Hitler, of your ties to he who is responsible for your life."

Regis looked back to MacIntyre, weighing his response carefully.

"I do not pretend to understand why you feel indebtedness to those who procreated you."

"My parents," MacIntyre said.

"Your parents," Regis said. "In your not too distant future there will be far more effective methods of birth control available to you. Still, the majority of births will be, as they are now, unplanned, the result of passions termed love but more logically defined as the biological need to copulate."

"I may have been unplanned," MacIntyre said, "but once I came along my parents cared for me, nurtured me, and raised me to adulthood."

"Which perhaps explains your indebtedness to them. But you must understand I feel no such obligation to my father. I exist, no result of passions, whether real or imagined, of two betrothed professing a love for one another. My father, I have never met. He made no sacrifice for me, as perhaps yours did for you. I exist not because of his love, but simply because he wished that I exist to further his aim, the result of his dementia, to eliminate the flaws falsely represented by other races."

"By the end of this century," Nigel added, "he will have accomplished nearly thirty percent of his objective."

"You think his goal to weed out the differences among humanity is wrong?" MacIntyre said. He thought he had detected a hint of some passion in Regis's otherwise dispassionate voice.

"It is human nature to fear that which is different. It is morally wrong to judge those differences as objectionable, and ethically a sin to pass sentence upon them."

MacIntyre took a deep breath. He had been guilty of the first two offenses, and he couldn't help but wonder if he might be capable of the third.

Once again the magnitude of what he was being asked to consider, even though he had no idea what he would be asked to do, weighed heavily upon his shoulders. He sighed, resigned that his next question would only pull him deeper into the quagmire.

"Do you even know what effect your meddling will have on the future?"

"Only in theory."

MacIntyre looked at Nigel and saw that this was a line of questioning in which his friend had not indulged.

"Ah, another theory," he said.

"Yes, we believe history has been foreordained," Regis said, "but the tools are there. They have been placed for our discovery, and for us to use at our discretion. We have at our disposal the means to undo history."

"But at what cost?"

"Cost?" MacIntyre's question caught Regis off guard.

"Are you willing to sacrifice your future, or your existence in that future, in order to rectify the past?"

"I would gladly sacrifice my existence to stop the mass extermination of entire peoples."

"What if you're wrong?"

Regis seemed confused by MacIntyre's question.

"What if your theory about time existing as a singular present, with each of us living coincidentally in our own moment, is wrong?"

"Our scientists are seventy-eight-point-six percent certain of their postulation. We find that to be within acceptable parameters of failure."

"Seventy-eight-point-six percent?"

"Ben," Nigel said. "It's a risk we *have* to take."

"Is it? What about the other twenty-one-point-four percent?" Then, of Regis, MacIntyre asked, "Do your scientists have a theory about what might happen if they're wrong?"

Regis said nothing.

"Ben—"

"How do we know he's telling us the truth, Nigel? He expects us to make an educated decision based upon facts he *wishes* us to know. What about the facts he withholds? What if our involvement only ensures Hitler's victory?"

"You don't really believe that."

In truth, MacIntyre didn't. He had been a proponent of U.S. involvement in the war for months. He'd thought it morally wrong for his country to withhold its military might from supporting the Allies in the face of Hitler's tremendous tyranny. He also suspected the longer the U.S. avoided involvement, the more formidable Hitler would become. Yet in playing devil's advocate to Nigel's willingness to go along with Regis's claims, he found himself incapable of refraining from firing all available salvos.

"Nigel, who are *we* to change future history? If it's been foreordained that Hitler wins the war, we can't play God and undo His plan for humanity."

"Who says we can't? We've had these discussions for twenty years, Ben. If we could go back in time and prevent Christ's crucifixion, what effect would that have on our own present? Or if England had thwarted your colonist's efforts to win their independence—"

"That's different!" MacIntyre protested.

"How so?"

"Because it was just idle talk, an enjoyable way to pass an evening—only theories that could never be proven. Now we have at our disposal the means to actually *change* future history. I don't know about you, Nigel, but I find the moral implications to be immense."

"Each breath you take," Regis said, "every dilemma you choose to act upon, or fail to act upon, ameliorates in some small way all of your tomorrows."

"But the magnitude ..."

"As you say, is of epic proportions," Regis said, perhaps sensing MacIntyre's faltering resolve.

MacIntyre thought about that, and about all the points and counterpoints that had been made during this debate. With the knowledge of New York's imminent destruction, he could easily arrange to have himself and his family safely out of harm's way at the appropriate moment. But could he live out the remaining days of his life with the knowledge that he could have done something to prevent that end?

*May 1947*

"What about the other twenty-one-point-four percent?" Lance asked between bites of his scrambled eggs.

I glared at Lance. I'd wondered about that also, but was patient enough to let Professor MacIntyre finish his story with the hope he would make that information known at the appropriate moment.

"I was left with no other option but to trust Regis. His scientific theories amounted to mere guesswork, not the least of which was the complete and utter destruction of mankind."

"And that wasn't enough to deter you from taking part in his scheme?"

"I wanted to see Hitler's reign at an end, Mr. January, and I believed U.S. intervention would be the most expedient way to assure that end. And my choosing not to take part would not have prevented Regis and Nigel from putting the plan into motion."

I hefted the cube, weighing the implications of Professor MacIntyre's story to this point.

"So you concluded an inability to live with yourself had you held in your hand the instrument to prevent New York's destruction and the fall of the United States and done nothing."

"I'm glad you agree, Mr. January."

"I didn't say I agreed, I only meant I understand how you arrived at your decision. Whether or not I will agree remains to be seen, as I assume there is still much more to your story."

Professor MacIntyre nodded, and now, having been asked to believe the impossible, I found my resolve against being reeled in begin to crumble.

# Chapter Eighteen

*November 1941*

"It should not be difficult," Regis said, "to draw the United States into the war."

"In theory," MacIntyre said.

"That is unfortunately all we have to go on. Still, based on our knowledge of history and the events leading up to this point in the war, we were able to devise several plans. We then determined which of those plans held the most favorable odds of success."

"You make it sound like roulette."

"Roulette?" Regis asked.

"A game of chance," Nigel said. "Money is wagered on whether a spinning wheel will stop on a color—red or black—a number—odd or even—or a specific number. The greater the odds against, the greater the sum won."

"Or lost," MacIntyre said.

"I assure you both, this is no game of chance."

"At least we agree on something," MacIntyre said, unable to put out of his mind the twenty-one-point-four percent chance that Regis's plan to amend future history would result in something other than what was desired.

"Still, any plan employed must be predicated against its probability of failure."

"I know," MacIntyre said. "It's just that I've never been a risk taker. I've always heard it said, never wager more than you can afford to lose, and the stakes here are so great."

"Yet without risk," Regis said, "what is there to be gained?" Wisdom MacIntyre could not refute. "To refrain from this risk ensures a future of great loss—of life, diversity, humanity. Can you argue, Benjamin MacIntyre, that this chance to alter mankind's destiny has not been foreordained by your creator? A test that, by your failure to act, could weigh heavily against you?"

MacIntyre shook his head. "No, I can't argue against

that. I just hope I won't regret my involvement."

"There can be little regret in risking failure," Regis said. "While failing to risk at all would result in much greater regret afterward."

MacIntyre nodded; another truism against which he could not argue. "Tell me your plan."

"It is quite simple. President Roosevelt fears political repercussions should he commit American forces to the Allies' cause."

"Which he can't do without congressional approval."

"Still, history shows Roosevelt to be a great leader, and to quote Winston Churchill, 'It is in the President's power to make war without declaring it.'"

"Regis's historical records show the U.S. abandoned its negotiations with Japan," Nigel said.

"But …" MacIntyre began, and then he understood. Offering a modus vivendi to Japan was but a ploy to buy MacArthur time to furnish the Philippines with reinforcements. MacArthur's forces were thought to be a deterrent to Japanese southward movements into Indochina and Mainland China. To abandon those talks would be to risk disastrous consequences. Did Roosevelt believe the Japanese would sit idly by while the U.S. continued to build its forces in that arena?

"Snubbing Hirohito guarantees a Japanese first strike against the United States."

"Nigel is right," Regis said. "Much of the groundwork has been laid. Roosevelt denied the Japanese Prime Minister a summit unless Japan agreed to withdraw from China, as well as disavow the Tripartite Pact with Germany and Italy. Backed into a corner, with little in the way of diplomacy available, Hirohito's military advisers counseled that Japan be resolved to go to war with the United States, Great Britain and the Netherlands if they were to expand their empire. Yet Hirohito resisted, preferring Emperor Meiji's ideal of international peace. 'Since all the seas of the world are brothers,' he read from a poem written by his grandfather, 'why do the winds and waves of strife rage so violently?' Yet his military leaders insisted that the chances of achieving a pact with the United States were remote, and Japan's offer to guarantee neutrality of the Philippine Islands was gratuitous. History shows that Japan *will* attack the U.S., and under the right circumstances such an act would almost certainly outrage public opinion, while giving President Roosevelt the opportunity to declare war openly—without the support of Congress. The cries of his isolationist opponents would fall upon deaf ears."

"Not to mention providing future revisionists plenty of food for thought," Nigel said with a laugh.

"But to abandon negotiations before MacArthur's forces can be fortified invites disaster. Nigel, you said that Churchill will have warning of an attack on Pearl Harbor."

"There will be rumors of *Higashi No Kaze Ame,* or East Wind Rain," Regis explained. "These rumors will be interpreted as a Japanese intent to strike at the United States. The team at Bletchley Park will pinpoint precisely when and where the Japanese will strike. On December 8, a Japanese amphibious force will storm the north coast of Malaya. An hour later, to the east of the international date line, on December 7, the Japanese Fleet plans to raid Ford Island."

"That information will be passed to Roosevelt," Nigel added.

"Who without second thought will issue the appropriate warnings to his commanders," Regis said. "They in turn will warn the Japanese Fleet which, without the element of surprise, will withdraw before they can achieve their launch objective, two hundred miles north of Oahu. While MacArthur will be able to continue to build his forces in the Philippines. Hence, the United States will maintain neutrality until it becomes too late to help the Allies defeat Hitler."

"Intent is not enough to draw the U.S. into the war," Nigel said. "We *must* amend the circumstances which prevent Japan from achieving her purpose."

"So you're suggesting the U.S. *allow* a Japanese preemptive strike?"

"Our scholars," Regis said, "have deduced a plethora of

plausible results should the United States allow the Japanese to succeed with their planned objective."

"How have your scholars obtained such results?" MacIntyre asked, curious. He couldn't see how, by allowing the Japanese to destroy the fleet at Pearl Harbor, the U.S. could maintain a position of power in the Pacific arena.

"Computers, Ben," Nigel said. "Much faster and much more sophisticated than those used at Bletchley Park to break codes."

"Our scholars," Regis said, "programmed them with tangibles—precise facts from the annals of history. Certain intangibles were then introduced. The computer was then asked to surmise how history might have been written, the result of those intangibles."

"Sort of like our discussions, eh, Ben? 'What if Joan of Arc hadn't been burned at the stake?'"

"I can assure you our computer is much more certain in its conjecture," Regis said.

"How can that be?" MacIntyre asked.

"The human brain, in its limited capacity, cannot hope to conceive of the multitudinous repercussions, the result of a single change to a tangible, no matter how innocent."

"Like a chess master," Nigel said, "who can think a dozen moves ahead and be fully aware of the impact those moves will have—not only on his own tactics but on his opponent's as well—their computer has concluded the result of changing a single move on the chessboard that is the South Pacific, and with a far greater degree of accuracy than the human mind could ever hope to achieve."

"But a man doesn't always think rationally or logically," MacIntyre said. "How can a computer account for a man's actions when those actions themselves might be considered intangibles—irrational, predicated upon fear or heated passions of a particular moment?"

Regis: "Computers function on logic, but human personality traits are unique; they can be charted. From these charts, patterns can be noted and incorporated into a computer's logic, thereby allowing for the human condition.

Therefore, our computers have been programmed, within an acceptable range of probability, to account for those intangibles."

Looking down at his own five-fingered hands lying flat against his thighs, MacIntyre fell into silent contemplation. He found unsettling the notion of a computer programmed to think like a human being. He glanced at Regis, as if to fend off the stranger's scrutiny, before looking at Nigel.

"Roosevelt *must* allow the Japanese to strike," Nigel said.

"Allowing Japan to kick the sleeping dog," Regis explained, his analogy sounding odd to Ben, "will assure that the United States will declare war on Japan."

"Hitler has already vowed that any such U.S. action against the Tripartite would result in Germany's formal declaration of war on the U.S. Roosevelt would have no choice but to join with the Allies in defeating the Axis."

MacIntyre ignored Nigel's assessment of Hitler's reaction; he was skeptical of Regis's assertion.

"How can you be so certain?" he asked.

"Your country is proud. Attacking the Hawaiian Islands, despite it not being a state, would be viewed as an invasion of American soil. In the face of such bold action, Roosevelt would have no alternative but to declare war. Anything less would anger the American public."

"But *allowing* them to attack Pearl Harbor? Wouldn't that only serve to weaken our military might?"

"Only for a time," Regis said. "Admiral Yamamoto hopes to inflict enough damage to the American Pacific Fleet to prevent its interference for six months or more—the estimated time needed for Japan to secure defenses of its newly acquired Pacific empire. However, our computers show that despite its tactical brilliance, a successful raid on Pearl Harbor would prove to be a strategic disaster."

"How can you be so certain?" MacIntyre asked yet again. He needed more than just a computer analysis of a probable outcome predicated upon an intangible.

"Because of the cautious nature of the strike force commander, Vice-admiral Nagumo. Our forecasts suggest he will withdraw from the contested region after the initial raid rather than launch additional strikes in an effort to destroy fuel oil tanks and dock installations."

"That's it," MacIntyre said. "That's all you have to go on?" He'd expected something a lot more convincing. "How can a computer, programmed with a few personality patterns of this Nagumo, arrive at such a conclusion?"

"A total surprise attack can hope to accomplish no more than eighty percent of its objective during its first wave," Regis explained, ignoring MacIntyre's cynicism.

"So why wouldn't they go in for the kill?" MacIntyre asked, taking the bait.

"History shows Nagumo was opposed to Yamamoto's Hawaiian Operation. He believed it put the Japanese Fleet at far too great a risk. Achieving total surprise would, of course, result in minimal losses to his attacking force. However, our computers indicate that Nagumo will reason that, with his enemy now alerted by their first strike, subsequent raids would risk greater losses of his own resources. Rather than destroy the oil tanks, thereby forcing the U.S. Fleet to withdraw to the west coast of America, our scholars have determined Nagumo will deduce that his initial attack will have inflicted enough damage to prevent the American Fleet from interfering with Japan's Southern Operation. Also, our historical records—and I stress this as one of the tangibles—indicate the Japanese had no plan for any type of submersible blockade around Ford Island. This would seem basic and essential if they hoped to deny the Pacific Fleet its forward base. Finally, historical records also show two carriers were on maneuvers the morning the U.S. learned of the Japanese presence north of Oahu. It is perceived that should the Japanese attack be allowed to proceed, they also will not be at their moorings on the morning of December 7. In all probability, after the raid on Ford Island, Nagumo will not pursue them. In short, the strike against Pearl Harbor will amount to nothing more than a raid, one which in all probability would only succeed in antagonizing the might of a world power."

"More probabilities!" MacIntyre could see the roulette wheel wildly spinning.

"We conclude," Regis continued, "that such a strike, while on the surface viewed by the Japanese as successful, will only provide the United States the impetus to join the war effort on behalf of the Allies. Our forecasts anticipate that as a result of Japan's failure to deliver the crushing blow for which they had hoped, American carriers will begin raiding Japanese bases in the Marshall Islands within six weeks."

"So your mission is to undermine British efforts to provide Roosevelt with information pertinent to Japanese fleet movements in the Pacific."

"That is the primary focus of my mission, yes."

"Sounds simple enough," MacIntyre said. "It also reeks of treason."

"A small price to pay, wouldn't you agree," Nigel said, "to prevent the destruction of New York City as well as the downfall of the greatest democracy the world has ever known?"

MacIntyre couldn't remember ever having heard Nigel sound so serious; but then, he couldn't remember ever having been confronted with anything quite as serious as saving the entire free world from the threat of Hitler's Tripartite.

MacIntyre took a deep breath and asked the question he had been dreading: "I assume you've seen his proof?"

Nigel let out a sigh—perhaps he viewed MacIntyre's question as acceptance of the role he would be asked to play in Regis's plan—and pushed across his desk a closed folder.

MacIntyre took the folder and held it a moment, fearing not what lay concealed within, but instead that, once revealed, its contents would prevent him from sitting out this hand. He nearly snorted aloud at the realization that he'd already made up his mind.

This entire discussion had been designed to pull him in, little by little. He'd been intrigued, as any scientist would be, by theories of time travel and changing history. Nigel was right; they'd had many similar discussions. But that's just what they were—"what if?" discussions; theories, with no way to prove or disprove their relevancy to the present. But now he held in his hands proof of a possible relevancy that just such a theory might have on an anything but unsuspecting future.

MacIntyre opened the folder.

A series of newspaper clippings or, more accurately, reproductions of newspaper clippings as might be seen in a textbook. MacIntyre ran his hand over the first one to confirm what his eyes suggested: it was made of a fabric unknown to him. As thin as paper, the shiny fabric was nearly transparent, except where the image resided. The article was from a German newspaper dated October 18, 1944—two days after Germany, in Regis's version of history, dropped the atomic bomb over New York City. MacIntyre didn't need to be able to read German to understand the gist of the article, the photograph told him everything he needed to know: an aerial view of New York City, a huge mushroom cloud over the approximate vicinity of Midtown.

"That photograph was taken shortly after detonation, by a German spotter plane that had accompanied the bomber," Regis explained. "They took off from a German landing field in Labrador. Two days later the photograph appeared in newspapers all over Europe as proof of German supremacy."

Other newspaper clippings in the folder were dated anywhere from a few days after the detonation to several weeks later. Photographs of a New York City turned unrecognizable by the destructive power of the first ever use of an atomic bomb over a populated region. At ground zero, where the mighty Empire State Building once reigned as the world's tallest structure, nothing remained. For blocks around where it once stood, proud symbol of what Leon Trotsky once described as the fullest expression of our modern age, there was nothing but rubble. Further out from the blast area, a few skeletal remains of buildings stood. They reminded MacIntyre of some of the old barns which still stood on many of the farms upstate; frail structures leaning dangerously out of kilter, waiting for even a weak gust of frigid winter wind to send them collapsing into a heap of firewood.

Other photographs depicted the charred remains of the victims of the blast; hundreds, perhaps thousands, piled high, and MacIntyre tried to imagine how many more similar heaps of remains might exist throughout what once was Midtown.

*Are my remains among that carnage?* he thought, *or Melissa's and Ben Junior's?*

MacIntyre shuddered and felt his stomach tighten as he glanced through the last series of articles and their accompanying photographs—the unlucky survivors, some horribly burned; others showing the effects of radiation exposure. Their living nightmare was only beginning, and he could only hope that, through death, he and his children would be spared this post-apocalyptic trauma.

*I'll probably be at Columbia—certainly far enough away to survive the blast, but what of the radiation? And what about my babies?* Their home in Gramercy Park was just a few short blocks from the Empire State Building, and if Melissa and Ben Junior were to be home on October 16, 1944, then MacIntyre could only hope that their deaths would be quick and painless.

MacIntyre thought about asking Regis if there was a list of survivors but quickly decided against asking; somehow, not knowing seemed preferable.

One last photograph remained, and if MacIntyre hadn't already been convinced of the validity of what lay in wait for the near future, he was now. Nazi storm troopers stood before the nation's capitol building. Huge banners bearing the Nazi swastika, symbol of success, hung between the massive pillars at its entrance. Germany's flag had been run up the flagpole on the roof above the pillars. Prisoners of the state, bound and blindfolded, stood before a firing squad. To the left was a pile of corpses—no doubt those traitors who had already been executed.

MacIntyre closed the folder, but its density could do

little to conceal the images it had previously masked from his eyes—images forever burned into his mind's eye: the destruction, the death, and worst of all, the suffering. Suffering that would continue for generations.

Sighing deeply, MacIntyre closed his eyes and thought of Regis and his mission, of his claim that he had come to prevent all this. He felt sudden shame that he had ever doubted the legitimacy of this strange being's claim, while at the same time he was filled with self-loathing for even considering refusing to render whatever aid he could.

MacIntyre opened his eyes to find Regis studying him, perhaps trying to gauge what thought processes he might be going through in his effort to come to some conclusion, and suddenly he understood his fear of this manufactured being.

Genetically altered to be free from flaws, Regis, in view of his desire to right the wrong of his ancestors, was perhaps more human than those who had created him. That realization laid MacIntyre open for self-inspection, a look to within that left him with uneasy feelings of a prejudice he had never before suspected existed.

# Chapter Nineteen

*May 1947*

"Nigel," Professor MacIntyre explained to Lance, Melissa and me, "had a personal connection with Brigadier Stewart Menzies, the Director of the Foreign Office's Secret Intelligence Service. They grew up together but went their separate ways in their adult years. Nigel was the least likely candidate for involvement in the Secret Service. To look at him, you wouldn't think him a hero."

"Heroes are created by popular demand," I said, "sometimes out of the scantiest materials."

"Such as the apple William Tell never shot, the ride Paul Revere never finished, the flag Barbara Frietchie never waved," MacIntyre finished.

"Mr. January is much more learned than he lets on," Melissa explained for her father's benefit. "He has a quote for nearly every occasion."

"Quote?" I said. "I thought I'd made that up."

Melissa laughed and I felt my face warm.

"How Regis had been able to discover their relationship after a century is beyond me," the professor went on. "At any rate, to maintain anonymity, Menzies was assigned an alphabetic listing, 'C.' 'C' not only directed Britain's global espionage operations, but he was also responsible for the Foreign Office's secret code breaking enterprise. Churchill received all intercepts of enemy communications through 'C', as well as various translations of diplomatic messages from friendly nations, the U.S. notwithstanding."

"That's impossible," Lance said.

"Why, because we gave the Brits the decoders?" I asked. "What makes you think Churchill wouldn't find it useful to monitor high-level U.S. communications?"

"I can't believe our security could be so lax."

"I remember reading," I said, "that sometime after Pearl Harbor, Churchill admitted to Washington that his code breakers had stumbled upon our cipher system and advised them of the Axis achieving similar success. What makes you think they weren't eavesdropping prior to our joining the Allies?"

"Mr. January is right," MacIntyre said. "And according to Regis, they continued to monitor our transmissions long after they assured us they had stopped."

Setting down his cup of coffee, Lance only shook his head.

"Churchill received decrypts several times a day, via special courier. He loved second-guessing his chiefs of staff, sometimes involving himself with military operations. There were several exchanges between London and Washington regarding Japanese decrypts a few months before Pearl Harbor. But since the U.S. had provided London the key to Japanese codes, London seemed content to assume Washington was privy to any transmission they had accessed, despite knowing they were well ahead of Washington in the art of intelligence gathering. That several transmissions to Washington were met with arrogance—an attitude of 'Thanks, but our decoders have already provided us that information'—only made London less anxious to share their intercepts. That a taskforce had set sail from northern Japan in late November 1941, and that one of its targets was likely to be Pearl Harbor, was but one of those intercepts. Originally, Churchill passed that intercept on to Washington."

"Originally?" Lance said.

Professor MacIntyre nodded. "That vital information was passed, via the secure channel the Secret Intelligence Service maintained with its Rockefeller headquarters in New York, through a British Typex cipher machine. Thus alerted, Roosevelt advised his commanders accordingly. The rest, as they say, is history."

"But that's not how it happened," Lance said, struggling with the potency of what MacIntyre had intimated.

"Suffice it to say that armed with that knowledge, Roosevelt was able to stay the Japanese raid on Pearl

Harbor, thereby delaying our entry into the war long enough to allow Germany to grow too strong to defeat."

I hazarded a guess: "So this friend of yours, Nigel, who had the ear of Menzies, was able to convince him to withhold from Churchill that particular decrypt."

"No, the decision was Churchill's alone—but make no mistake, he was greatly influenced by Menzies, who convinced the Prime Minister of the importance of luring America into the war—at any cost."

"You have proof of this?"

I was pleased to hear Lance question the professor's claim—that he wasn't buying it on face value alone. At the same time I feared the reality of its validity.

"I suspect his proof," I said, "is conspicuous by its very absence. After the war, most decrypts were declassified, with the exception of one entire section of Churchill's secret file relating to Japan. That section was marked closed for seventy-five years."

I looked from Lance to Professor MacIntyre, waiting for my statement's impact to take effect, before concluding, "Can you think of any information that could be so sensitive, so vital to national interest, that the British government forbid its release?"

Lance only sighed.

"If what you're telling us is true, Professor, why didn't your friend Nigel approach Menzies on his own? Why did he need to be convinced by Regis?"

"Nigel never concerned himself with political matters. It never occurred to him to approach Menzies because he had no opinion on U.S. involvement in the war; he was too wrapped up in his work. He never believed he could influence someone that high up in the Secret Intelligence Service."

I couldn't dispute that. Although I'd never met Nigel, I had encountered many of his type—bookworms. Neither leaders nor followers, they were loners, rarely involving themselves in the affairs of others, preferring isolationism to societal contact.

"You haven't told us your role in this plot, Professor," I said.

Professor MacIntyre let out his breath. "My role was largely back-up. Regis's plan originally allowed only for Nigel's involvement. Nigel convinced Regis that a contingency plan should be devised and recommended me. He later told me that Regis had been skeptical about making me privy to his plan, and in retrospect I think I understand why."

"Why, Daddy?"

It was the first question Melissa had asked, and I was glad she had asked it since I felt her question stood a much better chance of being answered than if I had. Professor MacIntyre looked at his daughter, weighing how he should word his reply.

"My best years at Columbia are yet to come." His preface seemed to harbor some secret knowledge of the future. "Those years were obliterated with the destruction of New York. Previously my work at Columbia went largely unnoticed, and so a hundred years from now Regis had no knowledge of my existence, nothing against which he could predicate his odds. Ultimately, since he trusted Nigel, he accepted me as trustworthy."

"Still, his hopes lay predominately with Nigel," I said.

MacIntyre nodded. "If Nigel failed to convince 'C' to advise Churchill to withhold the critical decrypt, or if Churchill decided to release that information to Washington despite 'C's' recommendation, then I was to use my influence at Columbia to spur their efforts in splitting the atom and ultimately construct the atom bomb before Germany did. Remember Regis said that by foiling Japan's attack on Pearl Harbor, U.S. involvement in the war was delayed by six months—long enough for Germany to become too strong to defeat in a land war. The Allies' hope would then hinge on the power of the atom."

"Obviously Nigel succeeded," I said, "and you were never called upon to implement Plan B."

"Correct," Professor MacIntyre said, "but all did not go according to plan."

"Oh?" I said, feigning intrigue. I knew there was more to MacIntyre's story still to come. Such plans rarely come off without a hitch. In fact, I suspected all the professor had related thus far was but the tip of the iceberg, a prelude to what had gone awry and been the cause of his mysterious disappearance, not to mention the reason for the two Germans hot to find him.

"There were two things we hadn't counted on. One was that Regis would be found out, that the opposition faction from the future would send its own agents to prevent us from carrying out Regis's plan. Regis suspected such an attempt could be made, and he also knew that once he returned to his own time, the possibility existed that our success might still fall short of accomplishing his aim. So he took certain steps."

*Here it comes,* I thought, *the real meat of the story.*

After a moment of silent deliberation, Professor MacIntyre said quietly, "He entrusted the cube to me."

"Why?" I asked. I suspected I already knew, but I wanted to hear it from the professor. "Returning to his present, the effects of a successful implementation of his plan should have been apparent."

"I can't be certain what he expected; certainly there was much he withheld from Nigel and me. In truth, I surmised he didn't discount the possibility he wouldn't survive the return trip. Think about it … if the Allies won the war, there was no telling what effect it would have on the sciences, despite his scholar's best efforts to determine the effects of an intangible upon a tangible. At best, genetic engineering might be put off for decades; at worst, it would be a science deemed immoral by a society Regis hoped would be far more moral than the one that had created him."

"Talk about your unsung heroes," Lance said. And then, "So he could only hope to return to a more utopian society?"

"Or he wouldn't return at all," I said, "since how can a manufactured being exist if the means of its creation has been erased? But then again …" I muttered, my analytical mind taking my summation a step further.

"You begin to see the paradox," MacIntyre said, his tone oddly akin to his daughter's.

"What?" Lance asked.

"Cause and effect," the professor said.

"Huh?"

"The effects on a future that already exists, the result of tampering with, or altering, its causes," he explained.

"I *still* don't follow you," Lance said. "I thought the aim of his mission *was* to affect the future."

"You said this Regis character withheld certain information," I said. "A third theory on effects?"

"Regis would tell me later that his scholars had deduced this as an extremely low probability theory, which was why he initially withheld it from Nigel and me."

"Go on," I urged when MacIntyre did not.

"Regis returned to his own present three days after his appearance in 1941, as expected. Nigel carried out his part of the mission. He found it easy to convince Menzies, who in turn advised Churchill of the necessity of withholding the pertinent decrypt from Roosevelt. Churchill complied, the Japanese raid on Pearl Harbor was successful, and the U.S. joined the war."

"I can't believe Churchill would do that to us," Lance said.

"We hadn't yet joined the war effort, remember?" I said.

"Nor can I believe that our own intelligence in the South Pacific didn't access that Japanese transmission."

"Who said they didn't?" My question caused a veil of incomprehension to fall across Lance's face.

"Go on, Mr. January," MacIntyre said, intrigued.

"It seems to me the key to the success of this mission lay not so much in convincing Churchill to withhold the decrypt since, as you've already told us, our own intelligence was enjoying similar success in reading Jap transmissions. In short, there were too many other parties monitoring the airwaves to think that Churchill would be foolish enough to think he held the only trump card. The odds against would be too high. The best way to ensure the success of the mission would be for Churchill to convince Roosevelt of the necessity of allowing the Japs to strike first."

"Very good, Mr. January. I'm impressed."

"Already at the congressional hearings there have been testimonies concerning how much was known about the Jap fleet's presence—those who claim to have known when the fleet set sail, its destination, and tracked its movements. If Churchill knew and said nothing, there were too many others who could've blown the whistle. I'd say Menzies convinced Churchill, and Churchill in turn convinced Roosevelt that the only way to get the U.S. to throw in was by allowing a preemptive strike."

"But that would mean a conspiracy," Lance said.

"I've believed that all along," I said. "How else can you explain Admiral Kimmel's disgrace at Pearl, while MacArthur goes on to be hailed as the American Caesar, despite his negligence in the Philippines."

"General MacArthur is an icon—a symbol of the embattled American hero!"

"Which is why he'll never be called to testify at the hearings. And if we're to believe Professor MacIntyre, the only truly damning piece of evidence is locked up in a box for seventy-five years. By the time the truth is known, you and I won't be alive, and those who will be won't give a damn."

"You're right," the professor said. "I *was* keeping it simple, and I apologize, Mr. January. I had no way of knowing you were so adept at reading between the lines."

My perception of what Professor MacIntyre had left unsaid was, to me, child's play. More important was the bomb I suspected he was about to drop on this unsuspecting group assembled in this tiny hotel room located as far from the familiar environs of New York City as the professor's story seemed to be fact from fiction. And still I couldn't find the fault. Still I couldn't expose the flaw that would relegate the professor's professed facts to mere fiction more akin to a H. G. Welles story about time machines.

"So the mission was a success," I prompted.

"The mission succeeded," the professor said, his eyes on his daughter. "Of course Nigel couldn't reveal his knowledge of the attack on Pearl Harbor; to reveal his source would only invite Menzies' scorn. His task was to convince Menzies to convince Churchill to open discussions with Roosevelt on how he might be able to support the Allied cause openly and actively, without the support of Congress and without risking the political repercussions of the public. It was only when the British stumbled upon the Japanese decrypt specifying the date and time of their planned raid on Pearl Harbor that the conspiracy in the Pacific was hatched. Yet the effects of the plan's success in the future proved futile."

"But how can that be?" Lance argued. "Any change in the past *must* have affected the future. If Hitler lost the war, how could he possibly still be in power in a hundred years?"

"In theory you are right—provided your theory is rooted in yet another theory: that time is linear. That it flows in a straight line from point 'A' to point 'B.' But time is *not* linear." The professor paused. "While it most assuredly flows inexorably toward whatever its destination might be, Regis discovered, upon return to his own time, that an occurrence in the past, if undone, cannot undo that which proceeds from that moment on."

I was listening intently to every word the professor was saying as I studied first Lance and then Melissa for their reaction to his discourse. Neither seemed as if they fathomed what the elder MacIntyre was intimating. Yet I'd already sped ahead to draw a hastily construed conclusion, one that I dreaded hearing confirmed.

If I was to believe MacIntyre's story—and I had to admit that I was powerless to disbelieve it, at least until such time as I could find the proof to disprove its authenticity—that he and Nigel had managed to alter the course of history, in short, helping to bring about the downfall of the Third Reich, and the effects of their amendment had gone unfelt in the future, then—

I felt the hair on the back of my neck stand up, and saw

the confirmation I dreaded as Professor MacIntyre recognized in my expression the conclusion I had reached.

"If I'm to believe your story, Professor," I said. "If you caused an effect that altered the outcome of the war, and this revised outcome had no affect on the future, then that can only mean you succeeded in creating …" No linguist, I was unable to bring my summation to a satisfactory conclusion.

"An alternate timeline," MacIntyre finished for me.

"Alternate timeline?" Lance asked.

"Future history," Professor MacIntyre explained patiently, "what is yet to come, as Regis believed and hoped, cannot be changed by altering that which has preceded it. However, it *can* be rewritten. That is to say, by affecting events at this point in time, another timeline can be created."

I saw Lance struggling with the concept.

"A fork in the road, Lance," I said. "If time runs in a straight line and somebody at the far end came back toward the center to affect a change in the course of events, that change would have no effect upon the course of history that had already transpired subsequent to the change."

"However," Professor MacIntyre said, "an intersection is created."

"From which this alternate timeline sprouts."

"A parallel timeline," the professor said. "Parallel in that it exists, side-by-side with its counterpart, free to write its own future, never again to merge with its predecessor."

"And we are living that alternate timeline," I finished.

"Mr. January," Melissa put in, "you believe my father's story?"

I could see her relief mingled with disbelief: I had teased her once before—last night at The Famous Door—gaining her trust before pulling the rug out from beneath her, ridiculing her, implying that she was a liar.

"I can't say that, Miss MacIntyre." I saw disappointment arrange itself among her delicate features. "But I can't *disprove* his story either. He's on the lam, that's for sure, and our opposition certainly believes in some aspect of his story, so I'd be a fool not to acknowledge its potential authenticity at this point."

"But how come we have no recollection of this previous timeline?" Lance asked, proof that he was at least looking for the loophole in the professor's story.

"Because you never lived it," MacIntyre said.

"At the fork in the road we veered left, while history, as it had originally been written, continued straight ahead."

"Quite right, Mr. January."

"But do we four exist in the other timeline, too?" Lance asked.

"I can't deny that we don't—or did, up until the apocalypse."

"But how can that be?"

"That, Mr. Cantrell, is for greater minds than mine to explain."

"So it *was* you who dated those two letters, and they *were* meant to be a clue."

Melissa's question seemed out of place and I had to stifle a laugh. At that moment she reminded me of Lance, who would fixate on some event or comment, turning it over in his mind as he sought resolution while everyone else forged ahead; and then at some later point, when least expected, he would proclaim his discovery in a most magniloquent manner, his enthusiasm proof of his naïveté.

"My little girl," the professor said with a smile. "I knew you'd see it as a clue, although I couldn't hope that you might discover its meaning."

"I didn't. Mr. January did, although he discounted its credibility," Melissa said, a note of triumph in her voice.

"Given the circumstances, you can hardly fault me for belying their legitimacy, and now that you've brought them up, I'm sure there is still more to your father's story, and I'm equally sure those letters play no small part."

"There is and they do," MacIntyre said. Then, as a sort of preamble, he said, "I would see Regis twice more—the first time a scant day after his return to the future, the very evening after Nigel had met with Menzies. My third encounter with him would be four days after my second.

"Regis returned to his future to find it unchanged. Worse, he'd discovered our plan had been discovered and that agents from the opposition had been dispatched to prevent us from carrying it out."

"But your friend Nigel had already spoken with Menzies," Lance said.

I recalled our earlier discussion of alternate timelines and said, "They could've gone back several days before your meeting with Regis and Nigel and killed Nigel, preventing the meeting from ever taking place, in short creating another timeline."

"You're right," MacIntyre said. "But since we were about to encounter the opposition, I think it's safe to say that didn't happen. But I'm getting ahead of my story."

"Go on," I said.

"When Regis discovered he'd been found out, he returned to the past to ensure the safety of the cube. Entrusting it to me, he sent me forward in time, to May 12, 1947—nearly six years after our initial meeting. He felt that the cube would be much safer in the future of the newly created timeline."

"But how did you get here, Daddy?"

"This time travel device," MacIntyre said pulling out a tiny object that looked very much like what, decades later, would pass as a pocket calculator. "Not only can it transport its carrier across years, it can also transport that person to other locations. He was able to set coordinates for a location just outside this hotel."

"But why Indianapolis?" I asked.

"He wished to keep me away from London to decrease my chances of being located by the opposition. New York was out of the question. He feared I'd be too easy to track should they learn my name, and he feared I might be tempted to contact my future family. He chose Indianapolis because it holds a certain sentimental value for him. In the original timeline, after the fall of the United States, the Indianapolis 500 was discontinued. It was also a test to see if our plan succeeded—he wished to see if the seed we'd sown had taken root, if the United States still existed. Since his own present was unchanged, he wished proof of the alternate timeline theory.

"The time travel device would return me to London three days later. By then he hoped the opposition would have returned to the future. Regis had just finished showing me how the device functioned when we heard the front door forced open. Instinctively I glanced to the window as an escape route as Regis gave me a push, ensuring that he would be free from the effects of time travel, as the doors to Nigel's study crashed in.

"I activated the time travel device and immediately felt the onset of vertigo. My vision blurred as I watched three men advance into the room seemingly in slow motion. The first held a gun trained on Regis, his mouth working soundlessly; the second held a gun on Nigel, while the third moved towards me."

# Chapter Twenty

"Of course," Professor MacIntyre explained, "when I arrived in Indianapolis I believed I had made the jump alone, that the third man had been too far away to have been affected by the influence of the device."

"But you were mistaken," I said.

The professor nodded. "He had been caught, too, but a moment after I made my jump, so his arrival in 1947 post-dated mine. The refraction of the space-time continuum apparently widens at the point of destination. Like a mathematical equation, a mistake of one or two decimals can mean missing your solution by whole numbers. I have no idea when he arrived, only that it wasn't until my third day in 1947 that we made contact."

"The man I roughed up earlier in the men's room ..." I said, not wanting MacIntyre's affirmation.

"We must assume is the man who followed me from 1941. He must be staying in this hotel, but how, without currency—"

I recalled the front-page follow-up article to last week's murder I briefly scanned the previous day and said, "You read the local paper, Professor? Last week a murder took place a block or so from here."

"My God, you're right," he said. "I never put the two together."

I again questioned the wisdom of having gotten involved in a missing person case. It was just as I'd told Lance the other night—often the missing person is in more trouble than I care to get involved with. Time travel notwithstanding, the duo in pursuit of Professor MacIntyre apparently wouldn't stop at murder in order to achieve their ambition. I said nothing of my conjecture that the nameless murdered man in the paper might be Benjamin Junior.

"Go on," I said.

Professor MacIntyre nodded. "Regis warned me against

contacting my family. Perhaps it was prescience on my part, but sitting in my hotel room I couldn't help but think that to Melissa and Ben Junior, nearly six years had elapsed since they'd last seen or heard from me."

"So you wrote the first letter," Lance prompted.

"Obviously the mission had succeeded—America was still a free nation. But since I had not yet been a part of that revised history, I surmised I must surely be missing. I wanted to let them know I was all right. I thought a note from me would be harmless. Certainly it wasn't the same as first person contact."

"Hardly what I'd call keeping a low profile."

"Mr. January, can you honestly say that if you were me you would've refrained from letting your family know you were safe?"

"If I were you, no, I probably wouldn't have played it any differently than you did. But if it had been *me,* I wouldn't have taken the risk. You were acting on a supposition that you were still missing from your family's refurbished future. Obviously many of Regis's theories had already fallen by the wayside. What if you had been wrong?"

"You're right, of course. I had no way of knowing what effect I might have caused on the space-time continuum. It seemed logical to assume that, since I had played a part in creating this alternate timeline, an alternate Benjamin MacIntyre couldn't possibly exist. My assumption on that aspect, as you will learn, was correct."

"What if your action had succeeded in creating a third parallel timeline?"

"I can't be certain that my mere appearance here didn't do just that, but in comparison to the rest of the mission and what we had hoped to change as a result of its success, I could only hope the impact would be minimal. My theory was that since my letter would only influence the lives of but two people—my children—its impact would not be nearly as monumental as altering the outcome of a World War, and so another timeline would not result."

"I don't see that it's hurt anything," Melissa said to me.

"We haven't heard the rest of your father's story."

"He's right, Missie. If I'd been more careful—maintained a low profile, as Regis had warned I should—I would have returned to 1941 in three days, after the effects of the time travel wore off. But that didn't happen, perhaps the result of my foolishness. Even so, there's no way to tell whether that foolishness resulted in good or bad. All I can say is that since we're both here together, and although we're not yet out of the woods, it seems I made the right decision."

"You're right about not being out of the woods, but go on with your story," I said.

Professor MacIntyre nodded.

"I was in the lobby. It was Thursday morning, my third day, and just a matter of hours before I was to be recalled to 1941 London. I'd just dropped off the note at the front desk and had started toward the elevators when I saw him, the man from Nigel's library. Although my vision had been blurred then and it was only for a moment, it seemed much longer since he seemed to be moving in slow motion. There was no mistaking those features, set in a murderous glare." After a pause, he continued. "Before I could lose myself in the crowded lobby, he spotted me, and if there had been any doubt before, there was none now, as he immediately started toward me."

Without waiting for her father to continue, Melissa asked, "What did you do, Daddy?"

"There was nothing I could do. I knew I'd never make the elevator before he caught up with me, and I could see he was reaching into his breast pocket. I had the time travel device with me. I took out the device and pushed the key that enables it. It still contained the original date in its memory, the date Regis had programmed into it. I had no time to contemplate *when* I wished to travel let alone input a new date field, he was nearly upon me, and I could see what had been concealed in his pocket. So …" he trailed off.

"You pushed the key and traveled back to Monday, the twelfth," I finished for him. "The day of your arrival in

1947."

"Little did I know then, but perhaps Regis had no idea what effect another leap would have on my previous jump."

"I take it that it negated your return to 1941."

"Correct again, Mr. January."

I thought a moment and suggested that an alternate timeline had indeed been created, since MacIntyre's name had disappeared from the guestbook.

"I hadn't realized that."

"Your return must've created another timeline—one in which you never registered at the front desk. Yet I wonder why you didn't lose your German nemesis."

"A mystery to be sure," MacIntyre said. "Perhaps we are linked somehow, through the time travel device."

"You're fortunate that your room hadn't been assigned to another guest," Lance said.

"But how did you know I was staying in room four-eleven?"

"I called the hotel last week," Melissa said, glancing at the front of the photo she still held. "They gave me your room number."

"That was obviously before I employed the time travel device," the professor said.

"It also explains why you seemingly haven't aged since that photograph was taken," I said. "For you it was taken only last summer, but for us six years have elapsed."

Melissa looked confused; she was still seeing her father through the eyes of a much younger woman. Or perhaps the beard had been enough to at least provide her with the illusion that he had aged since she'd last seen him.

MacIntyre nodded. "You're very observant."

"It's my job."

"Needless to say I kept to my room. I assumed my pursuit couldn't possibly identify me by name, so my only risk was in being seen. I had room service bring me my meals and the daily paper. I soon realized that my use of the time travel device to escape my pursuit had negated my return to London. It seemed that the device hadn't recalled me to the moment of my original departure.

"Then I knew: the only way back to 1941 would be to set the device for the date and time of my original departure and make another jump. I assumed my pursuer, without a time travel device, was stranded in this time period with no way to return to London and 1941. However, his two colleagues might yet learn of my identity and whereabouts through Regis or poor Nigel. If that were true, it was possible they'd send someone in search of me."

"Staying in your room was no longer your safest option," I supplied.

"Nor was returning to New York."

"Daddy! You went back to London?"

"I had to, Missie. I had to find out what happened to Nigel and Regis. Even if it meant walking back into the lion's den, it made better sense than trying to get on with my life here in 1947, forever wondering when someone from the future might show up at Columbia or at home looking for me."

"You still had the cube," Lance said.

"A burden, to be sure," I added.

"I couldn't hope that Regis would know what had become of me—that I had been forced to make a second jump, and perhaps even his scholars hadn't theorized what effect a second jump might have on the first one."

"Did it ever occur to you," I asked, "that you could've learned what had become of them from here and now?"

"Yes it did, Mr. January," MacIntyre said, almost defiantly, "but that seemed to me to be the coward's choice. Besides, without the time travel device, Regis would find himself stranded in 1941, never able to return to his own present in the future, assuming of course that he'd managed to rescue himself and Nigel from the predicament they were in when I'd left them. Finally, although it had been only a matter of days for me, I couldn't risk the lengthy wait it would be for them. It seemed cruel to make Nigel wait five-and-a-half years to learn of my fate."

I said nothing; it had been the right response to my

question.

"And I took certain precautions."

"Such as?" I suspected I already knew, but I was anxious to learn something more of this man's thought process.

"I packaged the cube and addressed it to Melissa at my home in Gramercy Park, along with the postcard with instructions to lock it away in my office at Columbia. That was Tuesday—two days before I'd sent my first note. I dropped the package, with the postcard attached to it, in the hotel's postal bag for pick-up just before I jumped. If I never returned to Indianapolis, I knew it would be safe, and where to find it, until Regis came up with another plan."

"Good thinking," Lance said. "I never would've thought of that."

Melissa smiled, proud that Lance approved of her father's ingenuity, and then looked to me, anticipating my confirmation.

"You took a big risk," I said.

"How's that, Mr. January?"

"You had no way of knowing whether, by making another jump, you'd be creating another timeline, one in which the package would no longer exist."

"The thought never occurred to me. Regis feared the same result when I told him of what I'd done. It would seem however, that luck was on our side."

I nodded, silently wondering how long the professor's good fortune might yet hold up, while Professor MacIntyre gathered his thoughts in preparation for what I reasoned would be the final chapter of his fantastic story …

I selected the date of my original departure from London for my arrival. I then picked London from the list of pre-set coordinates, and when the red light flashed on, I engaged the device. As the nausea set in and my vision blurred, I wondered where in London I would appear.

When my vision cleared I found myself standing at Nigel's front door, at once amazed at the technology that could allow a man to travel to any year in history with such precision. No doubt if he'd wanted to, Regis could have appeared at Nigel's bedside. I concluded that he'd opted to arrive in a more customary fashion—via a knock on the front door. Yet despite that precision, the traveler is unable to select a precise time of day. Whether I traveled six years or a hundred, I would arrive at my destination at the same time of day relative to my departure. I left Indianapolis at ten in the evening, so when I arrived in London six years earlier, allowing for the time differential between the eastern and western hemispheres, I found it was three the next morning—just before my original departure. My intent was to warn Regis of the opposition's arrival ahead of time.

I knocked on the door wondering whether Regis had already arrived, or if I'd gotten there before he'd traveled back from his own present. Imagine my surprise when the force of my knuckles against the door affected no sound. I knocked harder and although I could feel the unyielding barrier that was the door against my knuckles, I failed to elicit any sound whatsoever. My surprise turned to dismay as I tried to reason out my dilemma; my dismay mounted towards panic as I hastily construed numerous theories, all centered on my illicit use of the time travel device.

Regis had assumed I would wait for the device to recall me to my point of origin, as he had instructed I do. But he had not thought to expound on the effects of using the device as I had been forced to—making a second and subsequently a third jaunt before the effects of the first had worn off. Had he deliberately withheld the information from me, more knowledge he had deemed as on a need to know basis? Or perhaps he had no idea what effect such use of the device would have, since he himself had waited to be recalled to his own time.

I tried the doorknob, but to no avail. Although I could feel its solidity within my grasp, my efforts to turn it resulted in failure. My panic began to mount.

I left the porch and hurried around the corner of the house, toward the window of Nigel's library. Like my fist upon the door, my steps made no sound as I traipsed over autumn's dried leaves; nor did my feet leave impressions upon the soft earth. I wondered if this is what it must be like to be dead, since I certainly felt like a wraith.

The light in Nigel's library was on; the curtains were sheer enough to allow me to peer in. Regis was seated as he had been the night of my departure, and Nigel, too, was seated behind his desk as he had been then. What I hadn't been prepared for was the sight of me, seated, casually conversing with the two of them. The closed window muted the sound of our voices."

I listened to our exchange, silently mouthing the words I easily recalled as if they had been spoken just days ago instead of six years before realizing that, despite what the calendar claimed, to me it had been just a matter of days since this exchange had taken place.

I stumbled backward, unable to draw breath, as if I had been dealt a physical blow to my midsection. I held my hand up in front of myself to verify my own validity. My worst fears began to take shape. I had traveled to a time in which I already existed, and apparently the two of us could not coexist within the same timeframe. I was unable to make my presence known in this continuum, and so I wondered if I had caused my own existence to cease, inducing my own death, and further wondered what would become of me in three days, when I would be recalled to 1947—if I would be recalled at all.

I had been so intent on arriving in time to warn Regis, I had foolishly not given any thought whatsoever to the repercussions of my actions—about what would happen if two images of myself were to come face-to-face. Now I knew. Yet there was comfort in that knowledge, since my folly had not seemingly caused any harm to the very fabric of the space-time continuum. It seemed I had merely erased myself from existence. A small price to pay for my foolishness when I began to think of the far greater consequences I could have initiated.

The sound of hushed voices from around the corner intruded upon my reverie. I realized I was about to learn the fate of my comrades. I crept closer to the window. Whether it was the result of some prescience on my part or merely instinct I cannot say, but this time I took much greater care to remain hidden from the view of the room's occupants than I had earlier, which worked to my advantage.

A moment later, the door to the library burst inward. I watched my twin glance at the window as I had done when I had been in his place—the same window that now framed me. Instinctively I shrank back, but my twin saw nothing beyond the veil that was the window's curtains, just as I recalled having seen nothing when I had been him. Regis pushed me away in one fluid motion and my other self's image began to glimmer and fade as the third intruder advanced into the room, but this time, as I watched from the relative safety of my hiding place, he moved at real time speed. I watched myself disappear from the library, and a moment later my stalker faded. I shuddered at my other self's ignorance of that fact; that his foolish assumption of his safety six years into the future would nearly prove to be his—my—undoing.

At that precise instant I heard a twig snap underfoot. After my inability to affect any sound whatsoever despite my exertions to do so, it sounded frightfully loud, and so I froze, at once fearful that any movement would draw attention to my presence, yet grateful that I had taken more care in positioning myself to one side of the window.

I shifted my weight and slid my right foot an inch or two. Relief washed through me as the muffled rasp of the sole of my shoe against the flowerbed greeted my ears, and another piece of the puzzle fell into place. At the precise moment my past self left this time period for the future, my presence had at once become palpably real. I hadn't erased myself from existence, as I had feared.

I couldn't hope to understand the physics behind what had just occurred, but I concluded that the laws of physics must have prohibited my two selves from cohabitation in one time period. Yet upon further reflection it struck me that perhaps, since my past self had yet to leave Nigel's library and traveled into the future, my present self couldn't possibly exist but as a specter until my arrival in Indianapolis six years later enabled my presence here and now to become real.

My concealment enabled me to take in the details my previous hasty departure had precluded. I guessed the being who had followed me to Indianapolis was like Regis, manufactured; his perfect features seemed proof. But the third member of their party had a scar that began just beneath his jawbone and ran up his face in a diagonal line from right to left. The angry purple line crossed his lips, hideously displacing their natural juxtaposition; the angle of its slope increased slightly, disappeared behind a black eye patch, and reappeared to sever his eyebrow and continued on up his forehead where it disappeared beneath his hairline. The severing of the muscle tissue caused the right side of his face to droop; the whole effect was that of a Picasso painting, the scar serving to divide the reality of living tissue from a painter's demented impressionistic interpretation of his subject. I surmised he was no product of genetic engineering.

I listened to the scarred man bark a directive in German at Regis, who said nothing. The scarred man struck Regis twice across the face and blood trickled from the corner of his mouth. Still, Regis remained mute. The scarred man turned and said something to his compatriot, who in turn trained his weapon on Regis. I tried frantically to think of something I could do to stay the inevitable, but at the last moment the man with the weapon turned and, without hesitation, fired once at the scarred man, his weapon discharging soundlessly. The scarred man fell, soundless, a gaping wound in his chest.

The man with the weapon said something to Regis, who nodded and replied. Then he stood, wiped the blood from his mouth, and I heard him say to Nigel, "It is all right, he is one of us."

I felt relief wash through me, and I shuddered to think how this scenario might have played out if the man who had followed me to Indianapolis had instead been left behind. I was convinced, by the memory of his murderous glare moments before I had left London as well as from the intent I couldn't help but read on his features later, from across the lobby of The Severin, that he was an advocate of Regis's opposition.

Regis and his associate were conversing in German, and I rapped on the window of Nigel's library. The sharp sound, startling the room's occupants, was a greater comfort to me than I would have imagined. Regis's associate aimed his weapon at the window and I withdrew a step, realizing my foolishness at announcing my presence as I had. Regis stayed the man's arm and Nigel came to the window to draw wide the curtains. When he saw that it was me a look of confusion crossed his face, but the confusion was short-lived, replaced by a look of joy as he realized that no ill had befallen me.

*November 1941*

"Ben!" Nigel cried as he threw open the window. "What's happened? You just left."

"I know," MacIntyre said, stepping through the window. "I watched the whole thing."

MacIntyre quickly explained everything that had transpired while he had been away, Regis acting as translator for his associate, who had no facility for languages. Regis betrayed no surprise when he learned that MacIntyre's forced use of the time travel device had prohibited him from returning to London automatically, and that his subsequent appearance here was the result of his improvisation.

"You have proven what our scholars have only theorized," he said. "Each time you employ the device, that moment then becomes your new point of origin, and you will subsequently be recalled to that moment."

"You'll be returning to 1947?" Nigel exclaimed.

"You were unable to exist here prior to your other self's departure for the future," Regis continued, "since your existence in the future was necessary in order for you to make your presence known here."

MacIntyre thought about that for a moment, pleased that he had been able to deduce that himself before muttering, "The egg then." Regis and Nigel looked at MacIntyre, prompting him for enlightenment. "A conundrum," he explained more for Regis's sake, "that has plagued scientists and philosophers alike for ages. Which came first, the chicken or the egg? My presence here was 'hatched,' when my origin in the future became real."

"But," Nigel said with a chuckle, "you could also view your past self—the Ben that just left here—as the chicken without which the egg could not have been hatched."

"A paradox to be sure," MacIntyre said with a nod.

"An interesting similitude," Regis offered, "and your adage is one with which I am not, not surprisingly, familiar. Yet not being a philosopher, I can only respond as a scientist that your presence in 1947 was necessary before you could appear here now. That your present self could not possibly exist in a time previous to your past self's departure from this time period. Tell me about 1947."

"Tell you about ..." MacIntyre said, startled by the sudden change in discussion, and then it struck him. In the 1947 he had visited, America had been a free nation. Yet it seemed that 2041, the year of Regis's origin, remained under the oppression of fascism. The agents that had been sent to stop Regis from carrying out his mission were proof.

"The race," Regis prompted, "were they planning the race?"

"Yes, it was all over the newspapers. I thought that was why you sent me."

"Yes, the Indianapolis 500 was, in my present, last held in 1941. By then, America had joined the war and the race was suspended. After the U.S. fell, the race was never revived."

"But that's not right," MacIntyre said. "The local paper listed all former winners since the inaugural race in 1911, and the last person to win, prior to the war, was Floyd Davis in 1941, and George Robson won in 1946—the first race since the war ended."

"History has been changed," Nigel whispered.

"It would seem the mission has indeed succeeded," Regis said, a moment later adding, "While at the same time it has failed."

# Chapter Twenty-One

*May 1947*

"The alternate timeline theory," I said.

Professor MacIntyre nodded. "The mission succeeded. Churchill convinced Roosevelt of the necessity of allowing a successful Japanese attack on Pearl Harbor. You were correct, Mr. January, in your assessment of a conspiracy. It was necessary in order to ensure that anyone in the Pacific monitoring Japanese transmissions who might notify those in a command position would be ignored."

"No doubt the congressional hearing will amount to an exercise in futility," I said.

Professor MacIntyre nodded.

"So the mission managed to amend our future while doing nothing to change this Regis character's present."

"I'm afraid so, Mr. January."

"Hardly seems fair."

"Fair?" Melissa said.

"That we, in our ignorance of what's happened," I said, "should be the beneficiary of such a gift, while the gift bearer should come away empty-handed."

"Oh, but you're wrong," she said.

"How so?"

"You once told me that you needed to make a difference in the world, and that your work is in itself its own reward."

I said nothing.

"Don't you see?" she said. "Regis may have failed to change anything in his own time, but he succeeded in giving us a chance at something better, and that's something from which he should take great satisfaction."

"She's right," her father said, a note of pride in his voice. "I've confessed to you my fears of my involvement, how I cringed each time Regis spoke of theories and odds. I can't say that if I had been in his place I would've had the fortitude to act as he did. Yet in science there comes a time when in order to prove a theory you must test it outside the laboratory."

"I won't argue against that," I said, "but I suspect even his limited success puts us at great risk. Since his timeline remains unaffected, what's to prevent those who oppose him from coming back to try to undo his success?"

"Or to prevent it?" Lance asked. "What if another team from the future succeeds in stopping your friend Nigel from carrying out his objective?"

"Because preventing it would only succeed in creating another timeline, as the original mission did," MacIntyre said. "They're also uncertain what effect such tampering would have on the space-time continuum, and even they're not foolish enough to risk destroying it.

Lance nodded, but I wasn't certain he understood the professor's explanation.

"Their mission now is to retrieve the cube so they'll be able to resuscitate Hitler," the professor said. "They'll now revert to a much more subtle strategy in order to obtain their objective, recruiting locals to do their dirty work for them. Yet make no mistake, should they ever learn how to spread their future brand of fascism in our timeframe, they would not hesitate to act. Imagine the tyranny if they manage to take control of both timelines."

"I suspect they've already managed to recruit at least one local bumpkin," I said.

The ensuing silence gave me a moment to consider. Whether I believed MacIntyre's story completely was immaterial; there was nothing I could do about Regis's future. Yet there was no denying the validity of our present predicament and immediate future.

"They'll stop at nothing to possess the cube," the professor said. "It is the one thing common to each of our timeframes. Without it they cannot revive Hitler."

"Do they really need him?" Lance said.

"Perhaps not," MacIntyre said, "but they are obsessed with him. He is, after all, a legend."

I sighed. I realized that many of the questions I'd asked,

as well as most of the comments I'd made, had served to betray my belief of MacIntyre's story. I couldn't deny that a certain party was indeed after the professor, no doubt for the cube he possessed, and so I couldn't in good conscience dismiss the whole of it; indeed, the oddity of the cube itself seemed to portend some measure of proof of his tale. I felt my resolve weaken further.

"Since Regis was unable to alter his own timeframe by changing its history," MacIntyre went on, "he can only hope to succeed in preventing the opposition from returning Hitler to power. Only then can his faction endeavor to be a positive influence on their own timeframe, preventing the annihilation of whole races and nationalities of people. He will return for the cube when a new plan can be devised—one that will either assure its destruction, or prevent its use to return Hitler to power. Unfortunately, since it no longer exists in the original timeline, it will be impossible for him to travel back directly to retrieve it."

"It would seem," I said, "that logic dictates that you keep both the cube and the time travel device. That way, if there is some way Regis can get a message to you ..."

Professor MacIntyre smiled. "You're one step ahead of me, Mr. January."

"Nigel?"

"Very incisive."

"What?" Melissa and Lance both asked as one.

"It's quite simple, really," the professor said. "While I was in 1941 we devised a plan. Nigel's the focal point. Like me, he's common to both timelines. Regis will get a message to Nigel in 1941, and Nigel in turn will pass that message along to me. All I have to do—all I've been trying to do since I returned to 1947—is keep the cube from the opposition until I hear from Nigel."

"For you it's been a matter of days," I said. "Yet for Nigel ..."

"Regis has had to keep him alive for nearly six years," MacIntyre said, nodding.

"No easy task, to be sure."

"Precautions were taken to ensure Nigel's safety. He will not be easy for the opposition to trace; yet there are no assurances he will have succeeded. I can only wait and hope, and try to keep one step ahead of the opposition."

"Still," I mused. "Of the three goons who tried to prevent Nigel from carrying out his mission, one—the scarred man—was killed, one was secretly in allegiance with Regis. The third—the one who followed you to 1947—"

"Is trapped here without a time travel device."

"So he has more than one reason to find you." I said. After a moment, I added, "The opposition continues its efforts to locate you; no doubt spearheaded by someone in 2041. Obviously the clown who traveled with you from 1941 knows where you are and *when* you are, and I imagine the chump we met yesterday in New York was probably recruited by someone from the future who came back from the old timeline so that they'd have a contact."

"Which is my assumption also."

At that point, the door to Lance's and my room burst in and I turned to see the German I'd roughed up in the men's room last night, his left eye an angry purple and swollen nearly shut, and I froze—I was staring down the barrel of the strangest looking pistol I'd ever seen, and I felt my stomach sink. My holster and gun still hung on the back of the bathroom door; not that having it on me would've done much good—any move to draw it would only have rewarded me with a bullet.

I watched the German survey the room at a glance, and when his eyes alit on the cube the professor still held, I saw a sinister smile creep onto his perfectly formed mouth, and if my stomach could sink any further, it did: we now held no bargaining chip whatsoever. I'd succeeded in finding Professor MacIntyre, but by delaying our departure for the sake of breakfast and hearing his story, I would fail to bring him back to New York safe, as I'd been hired to do. Worse, it looked as if none of us, not Melissa, Lance or me, would live to see another day.

The German transferred to his left hand the gun he held

trained on me, stepped quickly to where I stood, and launched his right fist to catch me under my left eye, as I'd caught him last night. I'd been expecting it—his revenge for spilling him so incommodiously in the restroom—and I had the satisfaction of steadfastly maintaining my balance and holding onto my feet. I saw the German's disappointment.

Lance launched himself from his sitting position on the edge of the bed, but the German was quick to turn and fire his gun at Lance. It discharged without a sound and Lance fell back onto the bed, a gaping wound in the middle of his chest. So quick had his death come about, there wasn't even a moment for him to register surprise.

Before Melissa had even a chance to unleash a scream at Lance's untimely demise, the German turned and discharged his weapon, in rapid succession, at her and then Professor MacIntyre.

Startled, I launched myself at the German and managed to grab his wrist before he could point his pistol at me. We grappled a moment; he sidestepped and I countered, like a dancer following my partner's lead. I struck him on the left side of his head with my right fist, but in such close quarters my blow had little force. He surprised me with a head butt that stunned me and I stumbled backward. He pointed his pistol at me and I made no move.

The German arrogantly stepped over to the second bed and confidently picked up the cube which, silently, in its own confidence, flashed its lights. Bending over Professor MacIntyre's body, prone on the floor with his chest still smoldering, he rifled through his pockets until he found the time travel device.

"Now," the German said, "it iss your turn."

With that, he fired his pistol a fourth time and my last thought, before my head vaporized, was of Lindy.

# Epilogue

*September 2083*

*I hear your collective dissatisfaction and disbelief: how can I sit, alive and well one-hundred-thirty-seven years hence from the events depicted and conclude with my own demise?*

*You may recall reading, in a much earlier chapter, of my having been given a second chance to rectify the mistakes I made the first time, and of my failure to have made a positive impact on the outcome. In short, my story, in its entirety, ends here. But how I arrive at this conclusion remains untold.*

*A lengthier explanation: I created another timeline, the result of my own foolishness in thinking I could give my past self another chance to find the happiness he so desperately sought while ignorant of the fact that he had it, had held it, but all along chose to deny.*

*The strange letter composed of cutout letters pasted into semblance of a note that arrived at my office the morning of our departure for Indianapolis was my own device, a bold attempt to change the original events that resulted in my being thrust one hundred years into my own future. I couldn't hope that a letter written in my own clumsy and cramped script could persuade my past self, who had yet to be convinced of the reality of time travel, to return the contents of the package to Professor MacIntyre. I hoped that the critical nature of the cube left in Professor MacIntyre's possession, were it returned to Indianapolis instead of being left behind in Melissa's cabinet in her office at Columbia, would result in sufficient change to create another timeline in which I might avoid the events that led to my being torn from my own tormented present and deposited into a future that I would and should never know; or at worst, my past self could make right with Lindy what I'd managed to leave in such an untidy state, and that one of us at least would live happily ever after. I failed on both counts, and my past self paid the ultimate price.*

*How I ended up in the twenty-first century and how I came to decide, many years later, to act upon the opportunity to give my past self a new lease on life—that's my next story.*

*But it's late and I'm tired, and so I lay down my pen with little more to look forward to than closing my eyes and, in sleep, waiting for the long night's end. Perhaps tomorrow, with a pot of hot, strong coffee brewing and a cigar clenched between my teeth—two of the simpler pleasures left to me—I'll take up my pen once more and begin the next chapter of my memoir.*

*—JCG/December 2002/December 2010*

# Author's bio

In 1992 a man approached me to tell his story. His name was Joe January. A private investigator from the South Bronx, circa 1940, January can best be described as an indignant Humphrey Bogart. That encounter resulted in *January's Paradigm. Current Entertainment Monthly* in Ann Arbor, Michigan, wrote of *January's Paradigm*, "Personal identity—the slipperiness and the malleability of it—makes up the major theme of the story ... (readers) will not be able to put it down." I've since completed the second and third books in January's saga. *One Hot January* and *January's Thaw* (forthcoming from *Second Wind Publishing*), are companion novels to *January's Paradigm*, although they need not be read sequentially. Combined, they paint a profile of a man out of place out of time.

J. Conrad Guest is the author of *Backstop: A Baseball Love Story in Nine Innings*, published by *Second Wind Publishing*. For a peek into J. Conrad's literary world, visit him at www.jconradguest.com.

Special sneak preview of

January's Thaw, the exciting

sequel to

One Hot January

For the next several miles, leaving downtown behind, we played cat and mouse; I managed to gain some distance at what seemed alternating intersections only to lose it at the others, always maintaining a lead of between a half-block and a block. I was relieved that traffic in this small suburb of Indianapolis was but a fraction of what it would've been had I been playing this high-speed game back in Manhattan.

The track suddenly sprang up on our right—I caught sight of the walkway Melissa and I had used yesterday to cross over the backstretch too late to negotiate the necessary right turn to access it.

*Improvise,* I thought, and kept going.

The next right turn would take us into the infield, where the Stinson T was parked, by crossing the racetrack. I was getting us closer to our getaway vehicle, but unfortunately I was no closer to losing our tenacious pursuer.

I stood on the brake pedal and turned the wheel hard to the right; the cab's tires screamed their protest as we slid around, fishtailing wildly several times while I fought to keep the car under control; I stepped on the gas and the cab straightened out. The German would have more time to slow for the right turn I'd taken, and I knew I'd lost precious distance. But that seemed secondary in the face of the wooden barricade that suddenly appeared in front of us, designed to regulate the flow of cars entering the infield. Beyond the moveable barricade, the wooden swinging gate that spanned the gap in the concrete retaining wall of the track during the race was, thankfully, open.

"Oh, no!" I heard Melissa whisper.

"Joe!" Lance said, bracing his hands against the dashboard.

"Hold on," I said, slowing to give the barricade's attendant the illusion we were coming to a stop. As soon as he neared the cab's window I stood on the gas again—through the open window I heard the attendant call, "Hey!" his voice fading out with distance even before it finished its single syllable exclamation—and I drove through the barricade in a shower of splintering wood.

The German was right behind us. While I'd slowed to nearly a stop, he'd been able to keep his momentum, and I felt his bump from behind just as I drove onto the track. He caught me on the left corner hard enough to cause our cab to spin in that direction. I heard Melissa stifle a scream.

*Improvise.*

I steered into the spin to keep us from doing a complete one-eighty, and at ninety degrees I hit the gas again and headed off down the brick racetrack toward a broad sweeping turn to the left. Glancing in the mirror I could see the German bringing his cab around to continue pursuit. I'd bought us some time but now I heard and felt something amiss—our cab had sustained enough damage in the collision to cause a fender rub.

As we picked up speed the sound of the tire rub grew louder. The sweeping turn emptied us out onto the backstretch. I saw the walkway that spanned over the track and beyond that, better than half a mile distant, the brick surface of the track seemed to dwindle to a tiny dot on the horizon. On our right, lying up against the outside retaining wall, I caught a glimpse of a rabbit. I surmised it had been struck by a practicing racecar, and an image of the racecar as a dog in pursuit of the rabbit in front of a bloodthirsty cheering crowd came to my mind's eye. No blood, the rabbit hadn't been run over and crushed but instead struck and sent flying into the wall, at the base of which it now lay in a fetal position; yet it didn't really matter, dead was still dead, despite its appearance of mere peaceful repose.

*Hell of a place to take a nap,* I thought, checking the rearview mirror. The German was gaining on us at a rapid pace. I could see his murderous glare above the steering wheel of the cab, and I wondered if the swollen black eye I'd given him last night might affect his depth perception.

As we picked up speed the sound of the tire rub seemed to lessen: its pitch had either reached a higher decibel, or the fender was fast removing rubber, alleviating the pressure of the tire against its surface. The cab wanted to veer left; I fought the wheel to keep it going in a straight line.

The walkway flashed over us as we continued to pick up speed; I saw the end of the long straightaway begin to curl to the left as a new sound came to my ears. I glanced up into the mirror to see the German still gaining on us, but bearing down on him was a blue and white racecar. I inched the cab over closer to the inside of the track, away from the wall, to allow the racecar to pass us on the right. A moment later it thundered past us, a rocket on wheels, its shiny body dotted with colorful decals, its big narrow fenderless tires gliding over the bricks while its driver, in the open cockpit, clutched at the big steering wheel and looked over at us from behind goggles, leaving us behind in a wake of high octane exhaust as if we were standing still, despite our speedometer's claim that we were traveling at nearly ninety miles per hour.

"Joe ..." I heard Melissa squeal, nearly hysterical.

I hazarded a glance at Lance, his hands braced against the dashboard, eyes big as portabella mushrooms, and I wondered if the poor rabbit we'd passed had seen the speeding car at the last moment (I saw the oncoming car reflected in its eyes), and whether they, too, had grown to such overwhelming proportions.

We were fast approaching the next turn and I guided the cab out toward the middle of the track. I wanted to take the turn at the highest speed possible, and I reasoned that to do that I'd have to take the longest possible arc through the turn; not the shortest route, but the fastest. I glanced up into the mirror to see the German had slowed noticeably, perhaps in deference to the approaching turn or unsure of my intention, and I noted also, with satisfaction, that he was still close to the apron of the track.

We had reached the end of the long straightaway. Without lifting my foot from the gas, I gently aimed the car back down toward the inside of the track. I heard both Lance and Melissa call out "Joe" at the same time I heard the professor's more formal "Mr. January ..." all three tones rising slightly at the end, as if we were on a rollercoaster anticipating our stomachs dropping as our car topped the next crest. I reminded myself that this was no thrill ride.

The tires squealed as they fought against the cab's desire to slide back up toward the wall. Halfway through the turn I remembered to exhale and felt the cab drift back up toward the outside wall. I risked a glance into the mirror to see we'd put considerable distance between ourselves and the German, but I also noted that he'd moved over to take a similar line through the next turn, hoping to make up the distance he'd lost.

We were halfway down the short straight to the next sweeping turn that would lead us onto the long front straightaway and toward the south end of the track—away from where Lance had parked the Stinson T. Still with my foot to the floor on the gas pedal, I pointed the cab toward the apex of the turn; a moment later the tires again voiced their displeasure at being treated with so little regard.

Halfway through the turn we began to drift toward the concrete retaining wall I was certain had claimed the life of many a racecar driver. The sound of the tire rub had further diminished and, grateful that it was a left side tire and not one on the right side—the side that had borne most of the stress as we raced through the long left turns—I wondered how much tread might yet remain.

We came out of the turn in the middle of the track with another five-eighths' mile of straightaway in front of us. In the rearview mirror I saw the other cab fishtail wildly. The German steered into the slide, which took him to within inches of the wall; still he was gaining on us rapidly. In front of me, to our left, was the entrance to the pit area, where during the race the cars received their service—fuel, tires and whatever maintenance might be required during a 500-mile marathon.

*Improvise.*

I eased my foot off the accelerator and pointed the cab toward the pits. The other cab was beside us now, on our right, and I felt its nudge as the German bumped us, hoping to scare me into bringing us to a stop. I heard Melissa squeal and I braked, not to placate her but to allow the other cab to pass us; when he was clear of us he veered left and, now directly in front of us, began to slow. I hit the gas and steered right. Before the German could react, I managed to come abreast of his right rear quarter panel with my left front; at that point I veered left, hitting and causing the German to start to spin. The German turned left, realizing too late that he was heading for a large holding tank, used during the race to put gas into a racecar. I heard the squeal of tires—thankfully not our own—and wondered how much gas might be in the tank. I glanced up into the rearview mirror to see the German throw up his hands as his cab hit the holding tank at nearly forty miles per hour and explode in a mushroom cloud.

I kept up our speed, driving down the pit lane looking for an opening in the wall through which we could find our way into the infield. On the wall to our left, as we passed individual pit boxes, colorfully painted car sponsors flashed by—*Preston Tucker, Federal Engineering, Bowes Seal Fast.* We sped past the blue and white car that had passed us on the backstretch—*Blue Crown Spark Plug* the letters painted on its engine cowl identified. Its driver, still strapped in the cockpit, its mechanics huddled around the car, watched us go by. Seconds later we passed half a dozen men on foot racing toward the burning cab we'd left a quarter mile behind.

Eventually I saw an opening in the pit wall; I slowed and wheeled our cab to the left and drove under a sign that proclaimed *Gasoline Alley.* A cab driving through the garage area drew many curious glances, but no one approached us. Perhaps they were too startled; they couldn't know that the rising smoke beyond the grandstand hadn't been caused by a racecar that had crashed.

A few minutes later, while Lance fired up the Stinson T, I loaded our bags in silence; a few minutes later still we were airborne. As my adrenaline ebbed, my fear of flying caught up with me as we cleared the trees at the south end of the track.

10918044R0

Made in the USA
Lexington, KY
28 August 2011